Summer Serendipity at the Twist and Turn Bakery

Helen J Rolfe writes contemporary women's fiction and enjoys weaving stories about family, friendship, love, secrets, and community. Characters often face challenges and must fight to overcome them, but above all, Helen's stories always have a happy ending.

You can visit Helen online at www.helenjrolfe.com, on Facebook @helenjrolfewriter, on Instagram helen_j_rolfe and on Twitter @HjRolfe

Titles by Helen J Rolfe

The Friendship Tree
Handle Me with Care
In a Manhattan Minute
The Summer of New Beginnings
You, Me, and Everything In Between
Christmas at Snowdrop Cottage

Magnolia Creek series:
What Rosie Found Next (book 1)
The Chocolatier's Secret (book 2)
The Magnolia Girls (book 3)

New York Ever After series:
Christmas at the Little Knitting Box (book 1)
Snowflakes and Mistletoe at the Inglenook Inn (book 2)
Wedding Bells on Madison Avenue (book 3)
Christmas Miracles at the Little Log Cabin (book 4)
Christmas Promises at the Garland Street Markets (book 5)
Moonlight and Mistletoe at the Christmas Wedding (book 6)

Heritage Cove series:
Coming Home to Heritage Cove (book 1)
Christmas at the Little Waffle Shack (book 2)
Summer Serendipity at the Twist and Turn Bakery (book 3)

Orion Publishing - Books written as Helen Rolfe:

The Little Café at the End of the Pier
The Little Cottage in Lantern Square
The Little Village Library
The Kindness Club on Mapleberry Lane

For my wonderful readers

xxx

Summer Serendipity at the Twist and Turn Bakery

Helen J Rolfe

Chapter One

Jade's thumping headache matched the thunder outside the cottage and the way she felt this morning mirrored the dreariness she imagined lay beyond the dormer window. Rain continued to lash against the glass and she wondered if the weather had decided to rob summer from the entire country or if it had saved its worst to batter just Heritage Cove, the picturesque village where she lived on the east coast of England.

She groaned, put the pillow over her head and tried to block out the rumbles. Running a bakery, she was used to getting up and about early and, normally, once awake, she'd open the blind to let in the light, fling open the window to allow the smell of summer to filter in and around the top floor of the cottage. What had once been a dingy loft had gone through a conversion to give Jade and her sister Celeste two bedrooms and a beautiful bathroom upstairs at the home that was mere metres from their bakery business. They often laughed about their terrible commute, the thirty-odd steps you had to take from the back door of the cottage to the bakery and its rear entrance.

Today was supposed to be the first lie-in, the first chance to recharge. The girls had finally given the go-ahead to renovate the bakery and its kitchen space; they'd be closed for three weeks, so their workload would be reduced somewhat. They had a few summer-function orders from businesses in the area, some locals had put in their regular orders with the girls, unable to fathom going to the supermarket for their bread or their rolls or their cinnamon rounds, and Jade had cake orders to fulfil.

She couldn't blame anyone other than herself for how rough she was feeling right now. Last night she'd made the most of the lack of early starts at the bakery and hadn't held back in celebrating with the locals at the village pub, The Copper Plough, old and young alike raising their glasses to the upcoming wedding of everyone's favourite septuagenarian, Barney. His fiancée, Lois, had officially sold her house in Ireland and moved to the Cove, and with every day that crept closer to the wedding, excitement was mounting, because at last they'd found their happy ending after decades apart.

Jade had willingly leapt in and agreed to do the wedding cake last night, but it wasn't talk of flavours and styles that had been the problem at the pub. The real issue had been Celeste and the other girls all seeming to be determined to zone in on Jade's love life. With the entire village consumed with wedding fever – what with Barney and Lois's nuptials and the village's annual fundraising event, the Wedding Dress Ball, taking place on the same day – it appeared everyone was focused on happy endings. And Jade could understand why. The dress code for the ball requested previously worn wedding gowns and suits – or, at the very least, attire smart enough that it could be worn for the occasion. Some went for debutante dresses, others had their own garments adjusted as the years went on and kept up the true tradition for the event, and that in itself sparked a lot of interest. With all the buzz in the village, yesterday

Jade had overheard Zara who ran the ice-creamery telling a friend she'd met the man of her dreams, the day before she'd been in the convenience store and Lottie who ran the local shop had been pondering over who would be the next to be lucky in love in the Cove, and even Benjamin, the chef at the pub, had picked himself up again and was a bundle of positivity despite a recent messy breakup with his long-term girlfriend.

Now, as Jade tried and failed to find a comfortable position in bed, she shuddered, remembering exactly why she'd become the focus last night. She'd had one too many glasses of prosecco and had made the open admission to Melissa – and anyone else in earshot – that she'd fallen in love with a man not so long ago and she'd never got over him. As soon as the words were out she'd wished she could stuff them all back in again, because she had been doing her very best to move forwards over the last eighteen months.

Melissa, who was engaged to be married, had then floated the idea of honeymooning in Italy. She'd been telling the girls that she and Harvey couldn't make up their minds where to go – they could go to New York in the winter months and experience Christmas there, they could go on a safari, or they could go and do Sardinia with its architecture and breathtaking turquoise waters. Melissa went on to talk about how romantic a honeymoon in Italy would be, all the places they could see, and Jade only managed to finally steer the girls away from the topic of all things Italian by talking about the wedding cake for Barney and Lois. Celeste was always happy to talk shop so it wasn't a problem getting her to talk about something else and Melissa, being a lover of the bakery, fell in line soon after to Jade's relief, because a mere mention of the country and the man she'd left behind had already left her feeling once again the pain of what she'd found there and lost.

Jade turned over in bed to see if covering her other ear might work better to drown out the noise of the storm but it didn't make an ounce of difference. She reached over and picked up her clock: 6 a.m. Wide-eyed, with no hope of drifting off again, she threw back the covers and lay there on her back staring at the ceiling.

Her thoughts briefly drifted to Italy until she registered that it wasn't thunder that had woken her up and continued to disturb her but something else – a relentless thump-thumping that was starting to make her head hurt. She padded over to the window and lifted the blackout blind, not squinting as she usually would when the sunlight streamed in. It was still raining but it wasn't half as gloomy out there as she'd imagined. And as she peered out, her eyes fell to the kitchen at the back of the bakery and the light coming from inside.

'Seriously,' she muttered. Harvey was in charge of renovating the bakery for them and had told her he'd hired someone called David to make a start today while he was busy with his main job as a loft fitter, but he'd also agreed they wouldn't start at an uncivilised hour for the first week, giving the sisters some time out. Obviously whoever it was making the racket wasn't used to listening to a boss's instructions. And that was a red flag to Jade.

Huffing and puffing, she reached for the cream cardigan hanging on the rounded handle of her wardrobe that, small in height, slotted in nicely below the eaves. The space might have been converted but it was still quirky and characterful and, being close to five-foot-ten, she had to watch her head in certain areas, including around the wardrobe. She didn't always manage it when

4

she was this sleepy and irritated and so cursed now when she banged the top of her head just as another almighty clatter made her jump.

She tugged the cardigan around herself to cover the camisole top of her pyjamas and stepped out onto the landing. A bathroom and the staircase leading down separated her bedroom from her sister's and she crept towards the half-open door and peeked in on Celeste. But Celeste was fast asleep. Growing up, Jade had never ceased to be amazed at how she could do that. She'd slept through a fire engine roaring up the road for their next-door neighbour in the early hours one bright spring morning, she'd slept through the tent blowing down in a gale on a family camping trip, their parents successfully transferring her to the car from the air bed she'd been on without her stirring until they pulled into the driveway at home; Jade on the other hand had been wide awake and soaking wet as she'd helped gather everything up to shove in the car. And then when they flew to New York for an adventure in their early twenties, Jade had spent the flight getting irritated by the passenger behind who kept kicking her seat whilst Celeste had shut her eyes the minute they'd boarded the flight and not woken until it was time to disembark.

Jade closed her sister's bedroom door quietly so at least one of them could get the rest they both needed, and as yet another thump-thump threatened to disturb the entire village's peace, she went back to her own room, where she looked out of the window again to see the back door to the bakery kitchen wide open and what looked like a huge length of wood flying out. Good job it wasn't Harvey. She liked him – but a lackey she could handle, and she had no qualms about setting down some ground rules. Harvey obviously hadn't made it clear enough. But she would.

Or maybe it was a bad idea to confront whoever it was, especially while wearing only flimsy pyjamas. She downed the glass of water by her bed and instead hunted for her phone. Perhaps it would be better to get hold of Harvey and have him lay down the law instead. But after looking in all the usual places – the bedside table, the chest of drawers, on the floor by the bed – she still couldn't find her phone.

'Where is it?' she groaned, unable to find the device or even her bag. Admittedly there were clothes strewn everywhere – she'd neatly piled fresh washing on her bed ready to put away, but chucked it all to the floor when she flopped into bed last night. She looked under the detritus on the floor, beneath the bed, in the wardrobe just in case she'd put it there. And before she could go downstairs to call her phone using the landline she had to stop and sit on the edge of her bed as her hangover reminded her she'd planned to spend most of today sleeping it off. She didn't stay there long, however, because regardless of the noise levels and her distaste at being woken so early, she had more pressing issues. Where was her bag, her phone and her purse?

She tugged on a pair of jeans and a pink cotton shirt that tied at her midriff. She now had no choice but to go outside and confront whoever was in her bakery, and after she'd done that she'd have to hunt down her bag and belongings. She ran her fingers through her hair to tug it into something semi-presentable. Her graduated bob was easy maintenance and the ebony strands that fell against her face didn't take long to tame. She rinsed her mouth with mouthwash in the bathroom because even though she'd had all that water, it still felt so dry she

6

wasn't sure she'd be able to make conversation – and laying down the law didn't sound half as effective if your voice cracked and broke when you were midway through trying to make your point.

Out the back of the cottage Jade made a run for it in her flip-flops, neatly jumping from one paving slab to another in the hope of not getting entirely soaked. She'd almost made it to the back door when, next thing she knew, something came flying right at her.

She cursed as a piece of wood whacked her on her temple. She stumbled against the open back door and didn't register someone grabbing hold of her to stop her falling completely.

'Get inside out of the rain,' the voice encouraged.

She was so discombobulated after the wooden missile that she didn't think to question going inside with a man who was a stranger.

'Can I take a look?' he asked, brow furrowed in concern as he inspected her head.

She gingerly took her hand away as he stepped closer.

'There's a bit of blood.' He washed his hands at the sink and then opened up the first-aid kit that sat on the shelf by the door. He looked at her as he fished through for what he needed. 'I'll clean it up for you. I'm so sorry.'

'I can go back to the house and sort it myself,' she said, beginning to move, but he was back beside her already.

'It won't take a minute. And I'd hate for the blood to drip onto your shirt.' Instead of waiting for her to make a choice, he reached up and gently dabbed her temple with a piece of damp, warm cotton wool.

It was more soothing than she expected and she forgot for a moment that she'd come in here to give him a piece of her mind.

'I'm really sorry I threw the wood at you.'

'I'm kind of hoping it wasn't *at* me,' she smiled, because despite the early wake-up call and the knock to the head, this man seemed kind and she wasn't so affected by the noise or the morning-after feeling that she failed to notice the way his slightly-too-long-on-top hair curled in places, his tentative smile had a hint of cheekiness, and glossy ocean-blue eyes kept bringing his attention back to her.

'You're right, it wasn't *at* you. I wasn't exactly expecting anyone to walk in at this time of the morning.'

'I'm Jade, I own the bakery with my sister.'

He stopped dabbing and looked down at her and smiled. 'I kind of realised that. And although I did expect to meet you today, I didn't think it would be before mid-morning because Harvey told me you and your sister were both making the most of your lie-ins.' He threw the spent piece of cotton wool into a bag for rubbish plonked in the corner of the kitchen before he grimaced. 'Don't tell me, you *were* enjoying your lie-in right up until I woke you.'

'Got it in one.'

He peeled the backings off a plaster.

'Do you always disobey a direct order?'

'Direct order?' He stepped forwards to place the plaster in the right spot on her temple, his fingers brushing her skin and sending a little tingle all the way through her, a welcome relief from the feeling of a growing hangover. Perhaps the whack with the piece of wood might've hurt all the more if it wasn't dulled by all

8

the drinks still lingering in her system from last night. 'That sounds dramatic, I'm not in the military.'

'I told Harvey to tell you not to start early. He said he'd cleared it with you and that you were more than happy to start late for the first week.'

'Never got the message.' He zipped up the first-aid kit.

'Harvey wouldn't lie,' she protested, a little taken aback this man would suggest it. He wasn't proving himself to be much of an employee. 'He said he'd told you a couple of weeks ago.'

He put the first-aid kit back where it came from. 'Then I think I see where the problem might be. You think I'm David.'

'You're not?' David was the man Harvey had put on his payroll for this job.

'No, I'm not. David chose to have his own lie-ins for the next four weeks, on holiday in America. Last-minute summons from his mates, apparently, so he let Harvey down.'

'Seriously?'

He seemed amused by her dramatic summation and repeated it. 'Seriously. Between you and me, I don't think Harvey will be putting any work David's way again.'

'I wouldn't either,' she agreed.

'Harvey found me to step in at the eleventh hour, but in all the organising, I guess he forgot to mention not to start early. I couldn't sleep so I came to make a start.'

'Right.' She supposed she should be grateful someone else had been available to step in. Harvey and the firm he worked for had done such a stellar job on the cottage converting the loft space, a job Harvey had been in charge of coordinating, that Jade and Celeste had been

9

more than happy to employ his services for their workspace as he begun to get going with his renovations business with a view to becoming his own boss eventually.

'I'm Linc.' The man held out his hand to introduce himself formally. 'Good to meet you, apologies again about the early start and the knock on the head. I assure you it's not always so dramatic when I meet someone new.'

She shook hands with him and, aware of his attention and the fact she'd only just fallen out of bed, asked when Harvey would be joining him. She wished she'd had the foresight to put some deodorant on or check how bad the dark circles were beneath her eyes. The problem with porcelain skin from the family's Irish descent was that it didn't hide much at all, especially after a big night out.

'I'm not sure what time Harvey will be around,' said Linc. 'All I know is that I'm fine to go ahead and rip stuff out – supposedly the easy part.'

He got back to what he'd been doing, either because he had a job to do or because he sensed her discomfort, she wasn't sure which. He threw another piece of wood from a kitchen cabinet out of the door and onto the pile in the garden that stretched between home and workplace. 'Do you want me to stop so you can go back to sleep?'

'I'm awake now,' she grumbled, suddenly remembering her mood when she'd come down here.

He was already on to unscrewing another pine cupboard door from what had at one time housed dry ingredients in a tall pantry lined with shelves that would likely be the next casualty. And while Jade would have loved to go back to sleep, she needed to fulfil the second part of her mission, to find her bag and purse.

10

She looked on the kitchen surfaces that had so far survived the cull. She lifted up a few pieces of stray wood, but no luck there. She could vaguely remember coming in here last night with Celeste as they talked business and recounted their plans to transform the bakery. They weren't doing away with the village feel but nevertheless they did want to spruce up the interior and put their own stamp on the business. The frontage would remain the same – a beautiful Tudor-style exterior. They'd have the whitewashed stone façade repainted now that it was summer, the deep timber panels could be restained and the criss-cross glass windows that had lasted well only needed replacing in a few of the weaker or cracked sections to bring them up to scratch.

Another bang reminded Jade of each glass of prosecco last night as Linc slung an old shelf out of the back door and it clattered to the ground with the rest of the pieces. 'Are you looking for something?' He watched her carry out her fruitless search, even peering down the side of the cabinet that was half-in, half-out as he progressed through the demolition. 'I put it beneath the counter in the bakery. Your bag,' he added when she regarded him suspiciously. 'I thought it was better there than in full view. I found it sitting on the front counter. You're lucky someone didn't break in and grab it.'

She cringed. She'd left it in full view? Now that was the behaviour of someone who rarely let loose at the pub. 'Luckily people around here are fairly honest.'

'Hey, there are thieves everywhere, you can't be too careful.'

His voice followed her as she went to retrieve her bag. Phone and purse were both inside, thankfully. She picked up the notepad beside it though and wondered if

Linc had read what was on it. She had a patchy recollection of her and Celeste standing in here talking about the renovations and debating a name for the bakery, something they'd left rather late. They still had to inform the company making the new sign, and time was running out as they'd need a bit of notice for it to be ready for their grand reopening, but so far nothing had come close to being right. And the list on the notepad had some downright silly ideas, some of them suggestive, others embarrassingly rude. They'd started the list with Melissa and Tilly's help at the pub. Tilly owned Tilly's Bits 'n' Pieces, a shop a few doors down from the bakery that sold beautiful items for the home, and most of her recommendations involved the amalgamation of Jade and Celeste's names, none of which sounded right. She'd then suggested All You Knead but Melissa thought it sounded like a massage parlour, and not a respectable one. Melissa had come up with Queens of the Cove but they'd rejected that outright as Celeste said people would think it was run by a couple of drag queens. Another few names were already taken, according to their Google searches, and the suggestion of Upper Crust not only was met with someone saying it's already in use but also had Tilly in stitches having misheard and thought the suggestion was Up Her Crust. They'd left it there but Celeste and Jade had come back to the bakery and written down as many ideas as they could think of. But they were still no closer.

With her bag on her shoulder, Jade walked back past Linc with plans to return to her bedroom for at least another hour of lying in a horizontal position regardless of the banging. 'Thanks for putting it somewhere safe,' she smiled, and because she couldn't not mention it and was pretty sure he'd seen it, she added, 'Excuse the list, we're not quite there yet.'

He briefly paused as he lifted the large door away from the corner storage cupboard where they kept the enormous bags of flour when they were delivered from the supplier and moved to lean it against the wall. Jade supposed the door might be wanted intact and that was why he hadn't lobbed it out along with everything else. Good job that hadn't come hurtling at her or she'd have had more than a little graze on her temple.

'Did you get the photo too?' He'd moved on to the shelving inside what had been the cupboard. His wrist rotated with the screwdriver in his hand as he released one of the fixed pieces of wood. 'I found it on the floor, although I guess it might not be yours…I put it next to the bag.'

His voice trailed off and she went back into the front of the bakery and from beneath the counter where her bag had been, she pulled out the black-and-white picture that was most definitely hers. Usually tucked in her bag, it must've fallen out when she tugged the notepad out last night in their enthusiasm to carry on dreaming up names for the renovated bakery. Sometimes it was like there were two sides to her – the woman who was together and owned and ran a business, and then the sap who couldn't get over the man she'd once fallen in love with.

Jade went back through the kitchen. 'I'll leave you to it then.'

'Boyfriend?' Linc asked, his gaze not shifting from the shelf that was taking quite a bit of strength to release from its position. The tendons in his arms twitched while he moved it this way and that and once he'd got it, he turned and slung it out of the back door onto the pile.

'Sorry, what?'

'The photo,' he said, screwdriver in his hand once again, multitasking as they talked. 'Boyfriend, right?'

'Oh. Er, no. Not anymore.'

'Dumped?'

Was he taking the mickey out of her? Or was that usually the sort of information he demanded of someone he barely knew? Whichever it was, she didn't appreciate it, especially not this early and especially not with a headache that lingered insistently. 'I don't see that that's any of your business.'

He looked at her then. 'I apologise, that was rude.' She was about to at least smile politely back when he continued with, 'I'm right though, aren't I?'

'Again, none of –'

'My business,' he shrugged. 'I get it. But if you ask me, carrying a photo of your ex around with you is hardly a recipe for being happy.'

'Yeah, well, I didn't ask you, did I?' It riled her that he'd seen the photo and he'd got it in one – carrying it around with her wasn't helping her to move on. But having that pointed out only made her feel a whole lot worse. 'Just keep the noise down, it's very early. And not only for us but for the rest of the village too.'

He gave her a salute, which didn't go down well and sent her marching off back to the house hardly caring that the rain was coming down relentlessly; her hair was so wet when she got in that she had to give it a good rub with a towel.

She stomped into her bedroom, pulled down the roman blind again, climbed into bed and snuggled beneath the duvet. The side of her head was sore from the collision with the piece of wood and her hangover was here to remind her that it was the last hurrah for her

14

for a while – because last night had not only been a celebration, it also marked the path of the way ahead for Jade. She hadn't shared it with anyone else but she had a plan way beyond the business and dreams of what might have been. She had a way to move forwards that not everyone might approve of, but one that she'd come to terms with some time ago, and now she was ready for it.

She only hoped her sister would support her in this as much as they had each other's backs with the business.

Chapter Two

Why did he have to wind up the first woman he came across in the Cove? He was supposed to be coming here to help, not cause trouble.

Linc's auntie Etna had called him early evening yesterday, which wasn't all that unusual as they talked regularly, but this time she'd got hold of him to ask if he wanted to come and stay with her in Heritage Cove, where she owned and ran the local tea rooms. She'd told him there was an urgent situation – a friend of hers needed help with a job renovating a bakery; a second pair of hands was the way she'd described it. As it was, Linc had been in laid-back mode given he'd wrapped up supply teaching a few weeks before the end of term and, with not much else on the horizon, he'd agreed. And it was a bit of extra cash between jobs, which was always a good thing. He'd been to the village a handful of times over the years, though never hung around for long, but Etna had still insisted on selling it to him, rambling on about how beautiful it was, how she longed to see more of him, how staying with her would be a change of scene and the perfect antidote to his problems. 'It'll give you a new perspective,' she'd told him. 'It'll help you to de-stress, doing something entirely different.'

Linc had never held a long conversation with Etna, or anyone for that matter, about his problems, or misgivings, or whatever it was you wanted to call them.

Because there was nothing concrete. Nothing had happened to which he could attribute his being in a rut, being all over the place, not really happy – whatever description you wanted to label it with. It wasn't that a singular thing had occurred, it was a lot of things that had built up gradually along the way and he'd never really found his place again. This was one of the reasons he'd never taken another permanent teaching position. He didn't want the same faces, people getting to know him on a deeper level and asking him questions. He wanted to sort his head out a bit and know what direction he was going in before anyone else asked him that question. And he wasn't quite there yet.

Etna's last proclamation had been that by coming to the Cove Linc could find the person he was deep down inside. He'd laughed at that part and told her he'd have to dig really deep to have much of an epiphany. She'd merely brushed off his sarcasm and told him she'd happily find him a very big spade to do so. And while he didn't believe this sea change would do much at all, Etna had always been able to read him better than anyone else could. And so he'd taken her up on the offer and he'd arrived in Heritage Cove late last night.

'I hope I didn't annoy any other locals,' Linc told Harvey when he came into the bakery kitchen just before midday. 'It was early, but I was eager to get started and I kind of forget the time when it gets light so early. I've never been one to laze in bed, even when it is pouring with rain.'

'Hey, my last guy let me down big time so don't apologise for anything,' said Harvey. 'I had visions of not getting this done in time, and it's the girls' livelihood. I don't want to mess with that. So, you might

17

have ruffled a few feathers,' he added with a grin, 'but there's no real harm done.'

Linc didn't want to mess with the bakery business either. He got the impression Jade wouldn't let them get away with much. They'd only met briefly but already he sensed she was strong, decisive and, he suspected, used to having the last word.

'Jade will recover,' Harvey assured him. 'I'll smooth things over. The girls were all out last night, she's likely nursing a hangover – much like Melissa. I had to take her a cuppa in bed this morning and she told me not to open the curtains.'

'Not a morning person?'

'Never was. And she's particularly bad after a late night.'

Harvey had brought along a heavy-duty trolley and Linc helped him manoeuvre the largest of the two commercial ovens onto it and shift it a good few feet away from the wall, alongside the smaller one he'd already managed to move himself, so they could clean around the back. Both ovens would be removed for flooring and slotted back into position at a later date.

'Another smaller oven will be delivered soon enough,' Harvey told him, pointing to where it would go. 'Over there, in what will be Jade's baking corner.'

Most of the fixtures and fittings were to be stripped out, creating one enormous space and blank canvas. But as well as the ovens, the industrial fridge would become part of the new tapestry too. Harvey positioned himself one side of it, Linc took the other and, using the same trolley, they shifted it out of its comfy position. Linc got on with the cleaning – the tangle of cobwebs, plenty of dust, a good few marks on the walls to add to the many others left behind once cabinetry was torn from its position. Any holes or dents would need to be filled, walls would need to be smooth and clean, all in preparation for a spanking new kitchen.

There was a certain therapy in physical labour that Linc wasn't used to and it stopped his mind brewing any issues that lingered, it helped him forget he'd ever had anything to worry about. As they worked, they talked too, about how Harvey hoped to build up a portfolio of renovation projects and therefore his reputation as well as those all-important contacts necessary for when you had your own business.

Linc added the final pieces of old wood from the set of drawers by the door to the pile outside that he'd at last covered in tarp. He'd been so into the job that he hadn't thought to do that earlier when it was teeming down with rain but after watching Jade head back to her cottage, he'd dragged the sturdy covering from the outside shed Harvey had commandeered for their time renovating. The girls didn't use it apparently and it was conveniently situated at the side of the garden for them to house whatever they needed.

Linc had Harvey help him with the countertop that had been next to the second of the commercial ovens. The edge didn't want to come loose and it took both of them to prise it off with the use of a chisel and a bit of strength, the wood disintegrating part-way through and leaving behind the section of it that was much harder to remove. No wonder the bakery was in need of a renovation. It was only up close you could see that although the kitchen might be operational, it was old and battered. The floor had taken some abuse along the way too, with stains and areas that were damaged and likely a tripping hazard.

Once they'd slung the last of the countertops outside, Harvey asked Linc how he was settling in.

'I only got here yesterday and I've visited before, but it's nice to be staying with Etna.'

'I imagine she's a good host.'

'She looks after her guests, for sure. And it'll be good to have a change from the norm, spend a bit of time so close to the sea.' Despite the cooler temperature after the humidity of late June, Linc had worked up a sweat in the kitchen no matter that the door and the windows had been flung open the entire time and he refilled his water bottle at the tap as Harvey took a call.

'The window man is coming later this afternoon,' Harvey said once he ended the call. 'He'll give us a quote for replacing a couple of panels in the latticed glass at the front of the shop.'

'I'll keep an ear out for him and let him in. Do you have to go?'

'Was it me checking my watch that gave the game away?' Harvey smiled. 'I've only got an hour for lunch and I need to get back to a property to take a delivery of floor joists. But don't worry, I've got plenty of scheduled time here over the next few weeks and I'll be around evenings and weekends to get the job done. Just not today.'

'Your boss doesn't mind this working on the side?'

He shook his head. 'I've always been very honest about it and he knows I'm trying to get my own business off the ground eventually. He's a great guy, understanding, but I think he also knows if work was quiet for me on the renovation front then I'd always jump back in on any jobs he has, so maybe it'll work both ways.'

Linc wished he was as settled in a career. He'd been a teacher for a long time and while he liked the variety of supply teaching, moving here and there depending on where he was needed, he knew the avoidance of a permanent role was part of his problem. He'd wanted to let loose, but in a controlled way – he was a grown-up, after all, and couldn't throw everything away just because his head had been a bit all over the place for a time after his mum's illness, his failed relationship and his dad's health scare. Mind you, sometimes it had been tempting, especially when some of his mates erred more on the side of irresponsibility and didn't seem ever to think long-term. Perhaps that was what innocence gave you, but when life delivered a few hard knocks it forced you into being a little more realistic, recognising that the future was a vast open space and you could be pulled in any direction.

Harvey picked up his keys to make a move. 'It looks pretty grim in here without the cabinets and with nothing on the walls.'

'Blank canvas, remember.'

'Would you mind continuing with the cleaning up?'

'I'm working for you, of course I don't mind. And don't worry, I'm not about to do a runner – I've got it too good at Etna's place for a start.'

'You read my mind. And thank you, it'd be great if you didn't.' He whistled as he took in some of the grime on the walls. 'I suppose it's only to be expected in a food joint. All that baking over the years…any more stuff you might need for serious cleaning is in the shed,' said Harvey. 'And before I go, I'll see Jade.'

Linc realised he'd been hoping his new boss might say that. 'I'd appreciate it.'

Harvey checked his watch again. 'I'd say it's safe given it's officially the afternoon. She'll be fine. And I'll explain that while it's nice to give her a lie-in, I need to have you working as many hours as possible at this stage. The last thing I want is to get behind.'

'I get the impression you'll be talking her language. And suits me too, I hate leaving things until the last minute, too much pressure.'

'I think we're going to get along just fine.' And with that he waved a cheery goodbye.

When Harvey left, Linc went out to the shed to get a big bucket and a mop that was clearly brand new and wouldn't have its fresh cream strands of thick cotton on the head for long. He found a box of cleaning solution, sponges and cloths as well as a scrubbing brush that looked strong enough for the more brutal stains. But after he'd taken it all into the kitchen he realised the whole place needed a damn good sweep first and went back for the broom.

Linc had been tackling the floor – sweeping, scooping up dirt and throwing it out, then sweeping some more – for a good hour before Etna swung in through the back door armed with an afternoon tea fit for a team of ten workers rather than just him, but he was more than ready for it.

'You're spoiling me,' he told her after washing his hands at the sink that was to stay in place in the kitchen, the metal sturdy and undamaged and perfectly fit to fight another decade or so he suspected.

'I'm allowed. It's lovely to have you here.'

Etna was more than ten years older than his dad but to Linc she'd always seemed so much younger than her seventy-two years. She still had the same cropped grey hair he'd seen her with in photographs over the last couple of decades and it suited her now that it was growing a bit longer around the sides, it made her seem younger. Perhaps her secrets to staying youthful were being her own boss, eating good food like this bacon roll with all the trimmings she'd brought him and not having a family to race around after. Maybe this was the winning formula, and he wondered if he'd ever find his.

'Good?' she asked him as he bit into a soft roll filled with bacon, eggs, mushrooms and lashings of HP Sauce.

He nodded to show his appreciation and gestured to the other supplies Etna had brought with her, lined up on the window sill. There was a see-through plastic container filled with colourful fruit salad, a jumbo sausage roll wrapped in a serviette and a tub of yogurt sitting alongside an extra-tall latte. 'Exactly how much do you think I need feeding?' he laughed when his mouth wasn't full, although he soon bit into another piece of the bacon roll, the salty taste too moreish to neglect.

'My memories of you growing up involved your dad saying you ate him out of house and home,' she laughed, thoroughly enjoying the moment. 'He used to tell me how he'd go to the supermarket and no sooner had he unpacked than you'd fill up on whatever was there and he'd be adding things to his list for the week after.'

'I've grown up a lot since those days,' Linc smiled.

'It didn't stop me stocking up my own fridge and pantry in preparation.'

'Ah, that explains all the food shoved in the cupboards with the mugs, more beneath the sink where you keep the detergent, even more in the Welsh dresser in the lounge. It's like you're stashing in case the supermarkets suddenly close for a month.' He'd given her money for his keep – she'd not wanted it, said he was a guest, but he knew his appetite and she wasn't responsible for him. He didn't want to be living off her, no matter that it was only for a few weeks over the summer. He might have made a mess of a lot of things but not his finances.

'I get very few visitors so when I do, I like to spoil them.'

'I suppose I can't argue with that.'

This opportunity had come at the right time, before he'd even realised he needed it. He'd been happily going about his days as though there was no alternative, living close enough to his dad that if he needed him, Linc could be there in less than fifteen minutes. But lately he'd got the impression his dad was beginning to feel smothered, or at least responsible for Linc not quite being the together man he'd once been. His dad had suggested he go on holiday for the six weeks that schools weren't in session, tried to convince him to go somewhere hot and have a real break, but Linc had known he'd worry too much if he did. And so he hadn't booked anything.

Seven months ago Linc's dad had had what they termed a mild heart attack. But there'd been nothing mild about it in Linc's opinion and since then he'd watched his dad like a hawk. He'd already lost one parent; he wasn't ready to lose another. But rather than easing things for his dad, Linc knew he'd become a bit too attentive, he'd been fussing, and despite being aware he was doing it, he couldn't stop. Linc knew too that sometimes he wasn't pleasant to be around. He was miserable, angry on occasion, and even *he* was starting to not want to spend time with himself. He was carrying a frustration, a sense of loss and lack of direction that he knew he took out on the people around him. And he didn't know how to move on from it. Linc had wondered briefly whether his dad had begged his sister to do something. Who knew, perhaps they'd even paid off this David to do a runner and let Linc come to the Cove for work instead.

'No more,' he groaned after demolishing the bacon roll, a bit of fruit and Etna tried to push the yogurt towards him. 'I won't be able to bend down to rip out any more of the cabinets if I put anything else in my stomach. The coffee will do though,' he winked.

Etna definitely enjoyed being the one to look after everyone else; it was why she was suited to a business that saw her running around serving others and bringing joy to their day with snacks and beverages and the art of conversation. He'd often thought she'd missed out by never being a mum. She would've been a good one too – ruled with an iron fist but with the perfect balance between discipline and love. But it wasn't something she'd ever talked about, and why would she with her nephew? It was every woman's – and every man's, for that matter – right to choose whether they wanted to be a parent or not. Etna had never found anyone else after Linc's uncle Wyatt died over twenty-five years ago either. She must've been in her mid-forties when she became a widow but to Linc's knowledge there'd been nobody since. She had the business and it seemed that had always been more than enough.

Etna, unprompted, gave him another rundown of who lived in the Cove. Not Heritage Cove – it seemed locals dropped the Heritage part, and he was fast getting used to doing the same. He now knew who all the business owners were, the frequent visitors to the tea rooms, and all about the upcoming wedding plans for local man Barney and his fiancée Lois.

'Jade will do the wedding cake,' Etna told him, 'and the catering team is Tracy, who runs the Heritage Inn – the guesthouse on the corner as you came into the village – Celeste from this bakery, and me. Barney loves nothing more than to keep things local where we can. You should get amongst it while you're here.' Being bossy was another quality she had down to a tee, but he didn't mind a bit.

'What are you suggesting? I offer to be an usher at the wedding?'

'Not quite, but make sure you don't hide yourself away in here – get out and about, take in the fresh air and the scenery. Get to know the locals. That's why I keep telling you about them.'

'I've already been doing that by upsetting Jade.' He explained about the early start this morning. He didn't tell her he'd found the photograph and teased her about an ex-boyfriend she was clearly still hung up on.

'I find an apology usually works, Lincoln.'

'No need to full-name me. But you're probably right.' And he expected it was a better approach than winding her up. He knew he'd been an idiot. But being wronged by a woman did that to a man sometimes; it was difficult to separate the good ones from the ones who might be out to take you for a ride. 'Harvey said he'd have a word and when I next see her, I will apologise, I promise.'

'Glad to hear it.' She patted him on the knee as though he were ten years old. 'You should walk down to the cove one day too, walk on the sand, see the water. It's magnificent. It's almost a local hideaway, accessed via a track beside the chapel. Or there's the pub quiz,' she added, barely pausing for breath. 'There'll be plenty taking part – all ages too. And Harvey is a frequent flyer as well as a frequent winner.'

'I'm not a released prisoner, you know.' He knocked back the rest of his coffee, a welcome bitterness after the tangy roll. 'You don't have to integrate me back into society. What has Dad been telling you exactly?'

'He doesn't tell tales; I know you, remember. I want you to have a good summer, sort your head out. Because any fool can tell you're not quite right and haven't been for some time.' She patted his knee once again. 'Nobody, including me, will push you if you don't want to know, but at the same time it wouldn't harm you to make an effort and find some friends. Whatever you've got going on – and I don't need to know the details if you don't want to talk about it – you need to make the most of your time here.'

'Are you trying to get me out from under your feet?' Her place wasn't exactly big and he was aware how easy it would be to get in the way.

'Don't be daft, there's only one of me and I work all the hours I can anyway.'

'You're never going to retire, are you?'

'Not if I can help it.' She pushed her hands against her thighs and stood up. For someone in her seventies she moved well – she had to with a job like hers. Perhaps that was another secret. Move it or lose it. 'Quiz night is tonight, get yourself to the pub.'

'I'll think about it,' he told her as she made her getaway through the back door with a reminder not to let the rest of the fruit salad or the yogurt spoil now the rain had stopped and the sun was gracing the garden behind the bakery and creeping its way towards the window sill.

After Etna left Linc scrubbed at the walls of the bakery, their marks stubborn and set in after years of neglect. He dealt with the window man, who would email a quote through to Harvey, but he didn't get

27

anywhere near the mopping-the-floor stage. That would have to wait. And by the time he'd worked off all that physical energy come dinnertime, he decided maybe he was ready to be a bit more sociable and brave the pub.

It couldn't hurt, could it?

Chapter Three

The Copper Plough was heaving by the time Linc arrived at the four-hundred-year-old pub with its decent beer garden at the rear. The inside had classically low beams and a bar with a brass rail running around the outside part of the wood. Soft lighting illuminated the faces of customers and was needed even in the summer months with the traditional pub's low ceilings, small windows and cosy corners. An open fireplace had an arrangement of deep-red flowers placed in front of the grate. Linc expected come autumn and winter a roaring fire would be there instead and punters would be able to sink into the maroon leather chairs positioned at angles in front of the hearth to enjoy the warmth.

Melissa was in the pub too and according to Harvey his fiancée was his better half when it came to pub quizzes.

'He's having you on,' Melissa told Linc above the din as excited punters made their way from the bar to the tables ready to listen for questions and scribble down answers. She swished her auburn hair up into a ponytail as though she meant business. 'He's in this as much as me, we both like to win.'

'You sure you don't want anything stronger?' Linc asked her, feeling guilty it was his round and she'd opted for the free tap water.

'Definitely not. I was in here last night – one too many with the girls, remember.'

'Ah, yes. How can I forget? Jade really wasn't happy with me this morning but Harvey said he'd apologise on my behalf. I'll do it again myself too.'

'Jade's lovely,' Melissa assured him, 'just not a morning person after a night out. I get it, I'm not either, although when she's at work she doesn't seem to have a problem getting to the bakery on time.'

'I suspect that's different.'

'You'd think so, but when she told me she was going to have a bit of a break over the next three weeks, I did laugh. The girl doesn't know the meaning of down time. She's always busy, even when she's not supposed to be. She's still fulfilling cake orders, running a bit of the business from right there in the cottage. She needs a proper rest, if you ask me.'

'I'll apologise when I next see her,' he reiterated as they squeezed past punters to join Harvey, now at the back of the pub ready for the quiz. Linc didn't know Jade well enough to start talking about why she wasn't taking a proper break or whether she truly needed one.

Harvey had found a corner for them to sit in, pretty much the only remaining space, and Linc thought again about the guy in the photograph he'd found after it had fallen out of Jade's bag, Mediterranean-looking with thick dark hair, tanned skin and an expression that said he was a heartbreaker, and he wondered what the story was. Etna's summary of everyone who lived in the Cove had included marriages, divorces and relationships but there'd been no hint of anyone lurking in the background for Jade. Perhaps it would be better if there was, though, because as much as he'd teased Jade this morning, her company hadn't been completely unappreciated – and

Linc wasn't sure he wanted another woman in his life, at least not for a while.

Linc's best mate, Toby, thought Linc's ex-girlfriend had 'done a number on him', but then Toby was all about the love-them-and-leave-them approach. That was another reason Linc didn't want to be available this summer – so Toby couldn't rope him into going on the lads' Ibiza trip he'd organised with a load of his work buddies from the building site he was managing. Although Linc had been hurt and he'd lost his trust in pretty much all females other than Etna, part of him had begun to see why his ex, Orla, had behaved the way she did. As far as Toby was concerned, everything was black and white when it came to women, but Linc knew there were plenty of shades of grey in there too. And Orla wasn't a bad person for what she'd tried to do, just mixed up. Then again, he wasn't a bad person for walking away either.

Linc was about to sit down but managed to whack his head on one of the overhead beams and stifled a swear word the best he could.

'Did that hurt?' he heard a voice mock from behind him.

When he turned, he was face-to-face with Jade. And she looked quite pleased. 'Happy?' he asked, taking his hand away from his still-throbbing head where he'd been rubbing the skin beneath his hair. 'I guess that'll teach me to look where I'm going.' Only modern pub ceilings were built for anyone on the tall side.

'Yes, I suppose it will,' she grinned. 'Let's call it payback for waking me this morning.'

With the quiz about to start and Harvey and Melissa looking as though they were in this for the win, Linc whispered to Jade, 'They take this seriously.'

31

'Those two are known around here as the ones to beat. It's a legacy from their teenage years.'

'Their teenage years?' He had a vague recollection of Etna talking about Melissa and Harvey but he couldn't recall all the details, she'd fired so many at him at once. 'Wow, that's a long time to have been doing this. What kind of village have I come to?' He didn't mind at all how close they had to be to stop anyone overhearing their conversation. He could pick up a light scent of something either from her hair or worn as a perfume and he wouldn't have minded talking to Jade all night rather than feign an interest in a local quiz he didn't have a hope with. He might want to avoid getting hurt again in any way and not get involved in a relationship, but it was hard to resist a woman who was intriguing, never mind attractive.

'One where people look out for each other,' Jade answered and it took him a minute to remember he'd asked about this village.

'Sounds like a good place,' he said.

Despite the daggers she'd given him this morning, her green eyes danced now as though assessing him. She had on cropped white jeans and a midnight-blue shirt that tied at her midriff much like the pink shirt she'd been in that morning. She wasn't wearing a lot of make-up but she'd done something around her eyes that complemented their shape and shade, her hair looked a slightly neater version of its earlier style and her skin was just as delicate but not quite as drawn as it had been after her rude awakening at the crack of dawn.

'Truce?' he suggested hopefully as they squeezed in, her next to Melissa and him the other side of Harvey. Perhaps he should try to shake off the temptation to think of Jade as someone he might get to know better.

Etna was thought of highly around here and the last thing she needed was him having a fling with one of the locals.

'Truce,' Jade agreed.

For the duration of the quiz, which contained many themes other than local knowledge – he could answer some of the music questions when the others couldn't, earning him brownie points – he found himself relaxing enough to enjoy it. Once again, Etna was right, the best thing he could've done tonight was integrate himself into a bit of village life and be around people his own age. He'd spent a long time caring for his mum when she got sick, then the worry and care of his dad had forced him to grow up that little bit more. His dad said he'd missed out on much-needed carefree years but Linc hadn't seen it that way. It was the hand he'd been dealt and nothing meant more to him than family. He'd like his own one day too – one day, when he decided the time was right.

With round one over Harvey and Melissa went to get the drinks in, both girls on fruit juices and water rather than anything alcoholic. 'I'm assuming Linc is short for Lincoln,' Jade asked him the moment they were alone.

'You'd assume correctly.'

'Ever use your full name?'

'Nope.'

'Your family don't either?'

'Etna did earlier, she forgets sometimes, but apart from that, nobody. For some reason I hated anyone shortening it when I was younger, but once I got into my teens I became a Linc and never went back.'

'I saw Etna earlier, she's glad to have you here. She's a strong woman with a big heart, for sure.'

'You get on well with her?'

'Of course, and I wouldn't want to get on the wrong side of her. 'Harvey's brother, Daniel, was once – he never did it again though.'

He thought hard, most of the locals' names gradually seeping in. 'And Daniel owns a waffle shack, right?'

'That's right. Just across the village green.'

'I've seen it. Not tried it yet, but Harvey told me there's some work there for me once we're done with the bakery.'

'So, you're hanging around?'

'Might be.' He enjoyed the flirt and she clearly didn't mind it either. Yes, coming to the pub tonight had been exactly the right idea. And, his guard down, he was enjoying Jade's company.

'I've been in Etna's bad books too, you know.' She didn't hold his gaze long, as though the situation made her a little uncomfortable and she wanted to change the subject.

'Really? Can't imagine that.'

'I was. And all over a posh coffee machine.'

He laughed, glad the pub was crowded and the others were taking their time with the drinks. 'So, you're one of the girls who went travelling and came back with some fancy notions of Italian coffees.'

She looked shocked. 'She told you?'

'She ranted about it, more like.' He loved the way she grimaced, slightly embarrassed that the tale had made its way down the family tree. 'You'd thought about putting in your own machine and she was livid. But she also told me you and your sister did the right thing by her in the end. I always remembered that.' And he had. He'd heard Etna's worry when she feared she'd lose too many customers, then her absolute relief after she and the bakery's owners came to an agreement and it was she who would put in the new coffee machine. He could remember thinking at the time how lucky she was to be living in a village where modernisation hadn't taken over the high street, where people still cared and looked out for one another.

'Of course we did,' said Jade. 'This isn't the sort of place where strange businesses land and do whatever they like. My sister and I took over the bakery and it was always important to us that we fitted in. We wanted to make a home here in Heritage Cove as well as a living.'

'Etna has always said she'd never go anywhere else, and now I'm beginning to see why.' He loved the way she flushed under the hint of praise.

'I'm glad she's the business next door – and not only because it's so close for me to get a coffee. It would be awful if none of us got on, especially with the renovations happening for the next few weeks. I wondered whether she'd get irritated by the noise, particularly with it being summer, the busiest season.'

'Why did you do it in summer rather than at a quieter time?' Where they were sitting, they had a nice breeze coming in from the side window. Lucky, as most faces around them were being wafted by makeshift fans – the odd menu, and in one case a credit card – given how much it was heating up inside.

She shrugged. 'The timing was right, that's all. I didn't want to wait for another season to go by.'

He got the impression there was a reason to speed it along, but he could also tell she wasn't going to say much more. 'Well, no need to worry about Etna being bothered by the bakery renovations. She's already talking about the grand opening and she can't wait for the name to be unveiled.'

'I suppose we'd better think of one then.'

'You're running out of time,' he laughed before their drinks arrived, chatter amongst the group resumed and round two of the quiz got under way.

Linc didn't get to talk to Jade on her own again until the papers for the quiz were handed in, the marks totted up, and he'd got another round in for the table. 'Etna told me you got the idea for the coffee machine from your travels,' he probed.

'We're back to the coffee-machine talk?' Her smile suggested she didn't really mind.

'It was more the travel I was interested in. I never did much of it myself. Sometimes I wish I had, but, you know…'

'Life got in the way?'

'Something like that. Anyway, tell me more about it – I can live vicariously through you.'

'Another time maybe,' she smiled, as Nola, the landlady, got everyone's attention and her husband, landlord Terry, announced the marks and the winners of the quiz. Harvey's team had come in first place by one mark.

'Couldn't have done it without you, Linc.' Harvey shook his hand. 'I'm not great on music questions and you pulled us up there. They're really making the quiz broader; I think our winning days are almost over.' He pulled Melissa in for a kiss. 'Maybe it's time we moved on from our teenage years.'

'Probably not a bad idea,' Melissa told them all. 'I'm getting too old for bottomless-pint-glass prizes – which is what it was last time. Thankfully, tonight it's a voucher for a meal and Benjamin's cooking is well worth it.'

'It's not about the prize, not really,' said Harvey. 'I just love coming here and being a part of it all. And it's time spent with friends when we're all so busy.'

Melissa kissed him on the cheek. 'You're lovely, you know that.'

'You big sap,' Benjamin laughed as he walked past to collect a pile of plates and bowls and discarded napkins from the next table.

Harvey took the teasing in his stride and the crowds thinned out pretty quickly after the quiz and Jade waved across to someone she knew. 'Come on,' she said to Linc, 'let me introduce you to Barney.' She was already heading towards the bar before he had a chance to answer.

Linc lived in a village too but it was much smaller than Heritage Cove – a single street almost, with a local pub and nothing much else apart from surrounding fields and woodland walks. The pub had recently been bought by a big chain too and in the short time they'd owned it it had already been depersonalised, from the different fixtures and fittings to the menu and the general vibe of the place. It felt good to be in here, a proper village pub that didn't seem to have lost any of its community feel. It was inclusive in a way that suggested Heritage Cove residents were holding on to something unique.

'Barney is the one getting married, right?' he clarified before they reached the bar.

She turned back, almost so close they were touching. 'That's right and he's a local favourite. If he hadn't been here tonight, I don't think it would've been long before he came and introduced himself to you at the bakery.'

Jade wasn't wrong about Barney. He was popular and seemed to know everyone in here tonight and he welcomed Linc as though he'd come home rather than arrived as a stranger to most of them.

'Etna is enjoying having you here,' said Barney. 'She couldn't stop talking about you before you arrived, let alone now you're sharing her flat. She's a happy woman but you've made her even happier. I had my teacake in the tea rooms this afternoon and she told me all about you. I left her talking away with Lois at a pace even I couldn't keep up with. They're at my place tonight too, putting the world to rights.'

'Lois is your fiancée?'

'She certainly is. Oh, I know, I look too old to be getting married, but let me tell you, it's never too late for love.'

Barney wanted to know everything about him and Linc found, with pint in hand, he was happy to chat. They were in the middle of discussing the pluses and minuses of supply teaching when Jade came back from the bathrooms and Barney said he'd better get off home and see how many gin and tonics Etna and Lois had got through. 'Hopefully only two – any more and Lois will suffer in the morning.'

'Etna will keep her in order,' Jade assured him. Linc nodded because Etna rarely drank more than a tipple and would most likely have had Lois hydrated with water or tea all evening long.

'She's usually with him,' Jade explained when Barney set off for home having regaled Linc with back stories of other locals, adding to what Etna had already told him. 'And take no notice of him when he says he can't face all the talking amongst the women. He's way more of a talker than anyone else and I suspect Lois needed a bit of down time this evening.'

Jade set her empty glass on the bar and Linc was on the cusp of offering to buy her another, stay a while longer, but she was already waving goodbye to Terry and Nola and by mutual agreement they made their way towards the back door of the pub. It seemed easier than trying to get through the large group of remaining customers gathered at the front.

Jade briefly recapped on Barney and Lois's story as they walked across the paved area out back by the beer garden filled with people enjoying what was now the perfect summer's evening. A trellis filled with purple and yellow flowers lined the wall and carried the heady scent as they turned down the side of the pub to the gravelled path that led towards the front. And by the time they reached The Street he'd heard all about Barney and Lois, their emotional history, the tragedy and loss they'd endured.

'They're lucky to have found one another again,' Jade told him. 'But it shows how sometimes love can be mended even if it's broken.'

Linc wondered whether that was what she was looking for with the man in the photograph.

'I'm glad we cleared the air after this morning,' he said as they began to make their way from the pub towards the bakery and tea rooms.

'Yeah, I'm sorry about biting your head off.'

'Hey, it's me who should apologise. I was banging away like I was in the middle of nowhere.' He thought she'd done well not to yell at him more, but he sensed she was apologising for the way she reacted after his teasing about the man in the photograph. She didn't need to, he'd been an idiot to do it.

'Please tell me it's not such an early start tomorrow.'

'Of course not. I was thinking 6:30 a.m.' When she opened her mouth to say something his grin gave him away. 'Just kidding. Not before nine o'clock, promise. I said I'd take in a delivery for Etna anyway and I worked my butt off today so Harvey's more than OK with the later start.'

'I guess I'll see you around then.'

He didn't want this to end, not yet, but they'd already reached the archway that led down the path behind the bakery to the sisters' cottage. After a few more steps they came to the adjacent path he needed to take to access the entrance to the flat above the tea rooms. 'You will. And for what it's worth, I'm sorry about the ribbing too.'

'Ribbing?'

'About the man in the photograph. It really isn't any of my business so I apologise for teasing you about him. It was insensitive and rude.'

'It was just a photograph,' she said, not quite meeting his gaze.

'Who is he?'

She grinned. 'I thought you just said it wasn't any of your business.'

'I'm trying to be nice, if it helps.'

'I appreciate it, and I'm sorry, I probably didn't need to be so touchy. He's a man from my past, someone I met in Italy.'

'He's Italian?'

She nodded.

'And you're not over him.' He pulled a face. 'There I go again, overstepping.' It wasn't what he usually did but it was as though being close to her released a valve that usually stayed in place to prevent him from blurting out anything that came into his head.

Thankfully she looked amused rather than annoyed. 'You think you've got me all figured out, don't you?'

'Not particularly, I'm just curious.'

'About the photograph.'

The photograph, other things too. Maybe this was what his dad had meant when he accused him of hiding himself away, not taking a chance on the real world. He'd come to the village expecting nothing other than hard graft and Etna's attention before he found more supply work in September. He definitely hadn't expected Jade.

'So, what's your story?' Jade asked him all of a sudden. 'We've all got one,' she persisted. She was turning the tables to put the conversation onto him.

'Nothing to tell,' he claimed, enjoying the game.

'Spoilsport.'

When a bit of colour flushed her cheeks he said, 'Tell me I'm wrong about the Italian and if you say you're over him I won't ever mention him or the fact you carry his picture in your bag again.'

She began to laugh, an exasperated but jolly sound. 'Goodnight, Linc.'

'Hey,' he called after her when she turned and started walking away, towards her cottage. 'We're in the middle of a conversation, you can't just leave.' But he was laughing.

She turned back still smiling but didn't say anything. She didn't have to. The look she gave him was enough to tell him his feelings weren't all one-sided. And he made his way back to Etna's with a spring in his step that had been absent for as long as he could remember.

Coming to Heritage Cove may just be the best move he'd made in a long time.

41

Chapter Four

In the cottage, aware of the sounds of renovations coming from the bakery beyond and knowing full well that Linc was there, Jade got to thinking about the way she'd flirted with him after the pub quiz a few nights ago. Flirting was all well and good but Jade had been doing that since her twenties and as fun as it was, she wanted and needed more now. The unfortunate thing was that every time Jade caught a glimpse of Linc, no matter how quick it was, it made her want to hang around and keep him company, talk some more. With him it seemed easy. And in some ways, he was perfect. She could have a bit of fun, then once he left the village she could get back down to the business of running the bakery and the rest of her life plan that she was ready to make a start with. Now more than ever.

Jade and Celeste were similar in many ways. Celeste had the same willowy height as her sister, inherited from their mother's side. Of Irish descent, they both had porcelain skin and green eyes, as well as a row of freckles across the bridge of their nose. But the similarities ended there. Celeste had had her hair shaped into a pixie cut that suited her slightly edgier and more confident personality, and Celeste had never ever talked about wanting to settle down. She was all about work, she thrived on it, and when it came to her personal life, she was content to have a fling here and there – she'd had one in Bordeaux with the most handsome

Frenchman you'll ever see. He owned a winery, he wanted her to stay there with him in his farmhouse, and he might have persuaded Celeste if their accommodation hadn't been booked elsewhere. Then there was the divorcee in Budapest who was clearly letting off steam after the demise of his marriage of fifteen years. Celeste had enjoyed being wined and dined, being spoiled – at least until he'd spent one date talking all about his wife. Her guess was that he'd go back to her in the end as though he didn't know how to be on his own.

Jade rinsed out the dishcloth and hung it over the rail next to the sink to dry. She'd finished wiping down all of the kitchen surfaces in the cottage, which was their workspace during the day. They'd had the official inspections to ensure their preparation practices and spaces as well as food safety procedures were adequate. They'd got the go-ahead and, so far, the arrangement was working well while the bakery was closed. They were running a minimal business and because they were used to being somewhat busier, they'd found themselves getting very organised very quickly. This morning, nice and early with a full day ahead for them, Jade and Celeste had made up an order of fresh bread rolls for the school's summer holiday programme, another of pastries and a selection of cupcakes for Aubrey House, the residential home, which was having its annual summer party for residents and their families. Alongside all that going on, Jade had been organising cake samples for Barney and Lois to test this afternoon, and while Celeste headed off to make the delivery to Aubrey house, Jade could focus once again.

She took out the recipe for a lemon-elderflower cake she was making for a fiftieth birthday celebration at the end of the week. She'd already lined two cake tins for the tiers as well as put out a couple of individual silicone cupcake moulds to do the sample miniatures. This morning she'd held back two cupcakes – one vanilla sponge with spiced rum buttercream, the other a rhubarb base with delicate creamy frosting – and she was all set with a sample of fruit cake too because last month she'd made a wedding cake and kept a couple of small versions aside that she'd been infusing with brandy every few days to get the premium taste she was looking for. She'd prepared even more miniatures this morning too, as she'd made a carrot cake to order, a beetroot chocolate cake and a vanilla sponge with ginger frosting. She wanted Barney and Lois to try a good variety of flavour combinations before they made their final selection, which, according to Lois, was to be simple and elegant with fresh flowers for decoration.

As she worked, whisking the eggs, yogurt and milk together and then beating the butter and sugar, Jade's thoughts drifted to the photograph of Dario that she no longer kept in her bag, because Linc finding it had made it more real. And what's more, it made it even sadder that she was carrying it around with her as if she couldn't let go, couldn't accept the holiday romance for what it had been. Short-lived, all-consuming, but now it was gone. And so was the photograph. She'd put it away with the others in the box at the back of her wardrobe, along with the necklace Dario had given her on her birthday, the ticket stub from their tour of the Teatro La Fenice, the magnificent opera house with its sumptuous interiors embellished in gold, a place Jade had been in awe of and wanted to return to again and again.

Jade added the wet ingredients to the dry and folded them in, thinking back to those heady days experiencing the world, the trip that reached its climax in Venice, the floating city with its winding canals and striking architecture, and the man Jade had thought might just be the one she was supposed to be with. The bustling zigzagging alleyways in Venice and the mayhem of the city that had been on the girls' wish list from the start of their trip had left its mark on Jade for good. Because Jade wanted the dream. She wanted the career and the personal life; she just didn't know whether she was ever going to get it.

'Knock, knock!' A voice came from the open back door of the cottage now, tugging Jade from her reverie. Probably a good job too. She needed to concentrate and her mind had wandered hundreds of miles away.

'Come in,' Jade called, knowing it would be Melissa as planned with her secret ingredient to add to this masterpiece.

'It's warm in here.' Melissa wafted a hand in front of her face. The door was open in an attempt to get a through draft while Jade was baking, but she'd been hard at it for hours and so had the July sunshine, not jumping behind any clouds today. 'The elderflower cordial you wanted, made by yours truly,' Melissa announced proudly, setting a bottle down on the counter as Jade poured cake batter into the two awaiting tins as well as the cupcake moulds. 'Carol took me through the recipe. She can't wait to pick the berries as soon as they're ready – I swear she stops by every day to check on the bushes.'

'You love it as much as she does.'

'Guilty,' Melissa grinned.

Melissa lived with Harvey at Tumbleweed House, which once belonged to Harvey's mum, Carol, until she moved to a smaller cottage in the village. Most of the land that had come with the house originally when

Carol's parents were the owners had been sold off, but half an acre remained and, along with it, the elderberry bushes that had been in Harvey's family for generations.

Jade eyed the bottle of cordial. 'I'm interested, how did you make the cordial if the berries aren't ready? Should I be concerned?'

'Not at all. The cordial is made using the flowers rather than the berries, and the flowers were perfect last month when they were open and wonderfully fragrant.' She perched on a stool and wiggled her fingers when she described the scent from the plant. 'The cordial will be the perfect ingredient for your cake, I promise.'

'You're getting into the elderflower business.' Jade slotted the cakes into the oven one after the other.

Melissa spent a lot of time away in her job as a flight attendant. Jade guessed that was what made it so nice to have a permanency in her life with Harvey. Finally. Because like Lois and Barney, Harvey and Melissa had once been together and drifted apart for various reasons before eventually finding their way back to one another. It made Jade wonder whether it could ever happen for her and Dario. Although given he lived in a whole other country she guessed not.

Melissa recounted how she'd made the cordial. 'It takes a ton of sugar, then citric acid to offset the sweetness. But because it's homemade I think it's extra special.'

'You should hang around to try some once they're done.' Jade checked her watch. 'Should be ready in about twenty minutes. I only need one for Barney and Lois's tasting. One for us, eh?'

Melissa pulled a face and looked at the tins behind the oven door. 'I've only just given you the cordial, shouldn't it be in the cake by now?'

'Nope. I'm going to mix it with some lemon juice and then when the cakes are cooked, I'll use a cocktail stick to poke holes in the surface and spoon over the mixture so it can seep into the sponge.'

'My mouth is watering already.'

Jade started to wash up the bowls she'd used and Melissa snatched a tea towel from the hook near the oven to help despite Jade's protests. They talked about Barney's wedding, Lois's outfit she'd shown them on one of their book-club nights – which didn't always involve a book discussion but always involved gossip – and when the cupcakes were ready, Jade took them out and did the honours with some of the liquid topping.

Melissa's eyes closed in pleasure at the first bite of the half a cupcake Jade gave her. 'We make a good team. With your baking and my elderflower cordial, we could take on the world.'

'I think it'll be the flavour of choice for Barney and Lois. I've made others but I get the feeling they'll settle on this one.'

'Hmm…delicate and different. Perhaps a bit like Lois, although not at all like Barney.' Melissa had known Barney since she was a little girl so if anyone could be a good judge of his character it was her. 'And if you mention the elderflower cordial came from Harvey's place, he'll be sold straight away.'

'I won't mention it at first. I want to give the other cakes a chance, make sure they're choosing the one they love the best rather than one that has the added meaning.'

'But isn't that the point of a wedding, to make sure there's meaning behind as many things as possible? Like something borrowed, I suppose.'

'I know what you mean, but let's just see what they go for without pointing them too far in one direction.' As well as this cake being for friends, it was another showpiece to add to her portfolio and it would be seen by not only very close friends and family but anyone who chose to come to the Wedding Dress Ball. Barney had already suggested she leave some business cards out on one of the upturned barrels in the barn that would serve as tables – he told her to use the one by the barn doors – to spread word about her business. And Jade wasn't going to argue with that.

The girls talked colour. 'I thought the pale icing would contrast well with purple flowers,' Jade explained. 'Lois wanted fresh but I'm investigating edible instead. I might even attempt to make some myself if I can master the skill well enough to show in public.' She dug out a plastic container from the bottom of one of the pebble-grey-fronted kitchen cupboards and showed Melissa the flowers she'd already found in a mixture of bright colours and used for previous creations. 'It always amazes me how people can craft so well with sugar or buttercream.'

'I'm sure you can do just as good a job.'

'I don't know. But whatever I do, I'll add some faux greenery as well, make it realistic.'

'You know you're going to be doing the cake for our wedding too, right?'

Jade's smile matched Melissa's at the reference to her own wedding. 'I'd be offended if I wasn't. You and Harvey are special to everyone around here, me included. Any ideas yet? A Christmas wedding could tie in with a whole different cake theme. You could bring in reds, whites, greens, have something quite spectacular. Start thinking.'

'Thinking about cake? Sure, I can do that any time.'

The timer beeped and Jade pulled out the two big cakes from the oven. With her trusty cocktail stick she prodded the surface and then poured the topping all over so that it could soak through. 'Come on, I'll let these cool. We can go and see the progress on the bakery.'

As they walked from the cottage, stepping on the paving stones across to the back of the bakery, Harvey was first out and didn't miss a chance to kiss his wife-to-be a hello.

Linc emerged from the kitchen soon after Harvey and almost collided with Jade.

'I thought I'd show Melissa the progress,' she stammered, stepping back before her face pressed against his strong chest. 'I'm desperate to see the cabinets myself.' Did she sound as lame as she felt? She'd kept away yesterday and the day before when the units were delivered, not wanting to get under Harvey and Linc's feet, but also not wanting to get tongue-tied like this. She'd peered in the window a couple of times of course but this morning was when they'd really got down to it, fitting bits together, slotting things into place, so this would be her first proper inspection. She hadn't even been able to sneak a peek in the front of the bakery because those windows had now been covered with paper so nobody could see inside until the grand reopening. It generated a buzz of excitement for sure and people were already speculating about it. Since the bakery had closed its doors Jade couldn't walk the length of The Street without at least one or two people telling her how eager they were to get their bakery back.

'Go ahead,' said Linc, nodding a hello to Melissa.

When Jade stepped inside the kitchen a huge smile spread across her face. Not only was the cabinetry there but they'd already begun to put some of it in.

Harvey wiped his hands on a cloth and pulled Melissa close to him as he watched Jade's reaction. 'You approve?'

'Approve? I love it!' She turned around on the spot, taking it all in. Slate-grey cupboards were in place against one wall, the pantry cupboard was being constructed by Linc right now as he picked up the drill and made a hole in the framework ready to hang the door. There was to be an enormous island in the middle of the kitchen with plenty of space to walk around it even with units against the walls and gaps for chrome wire shelving units that could house loaves of bread and be moved as required from here to the front of the shop. There were two long worktops still to install, stretching either side of the existing sink that stood waiting – it had been new a couple of years ago and would fit in well with the renovation – and on one of those worktops Jade and Celeste had discussed lining up mixers and bowls along with the beautifully shiny aluminium utensils racks Celeste had sourced. The floor wouldn't go down for a while yet but it was to be the same throughout the kitchen and the actual bakery, black and white as though it were tiles to the untrained eye when it was actually heavy-duty flooring fit to withstand weight, heat and a multitude of spills throughout the day. The kitchen worktops that had been installed thus far were stainless steel with kickboards to match and although not all were in place, Jade knew that once they were it was going to add even more elegance to this once-drab kitchen they'd inherited from the previous owner and made do with.

'I don't know what more to say.' She was in awe of the progress already made. This was what they'd dreamed about, and even though she and Celeste had been running the bakery for a while now, it was putting their own stamp on it, finally, that had the emotions flowing.

Celeste appeared at the back door just before Jade went through to the bakery itself, where the new shelves on the back wall had begun to be fitted. The natural-wood bread-display unit to replace the battered old one that had seen numerous repairs over time was still covered in see-through plastic but Jade could make out the details of its four shelves, a little like wooden boxes. At the bottom the wooden section had wire racks in it that would allow them to display baguettes standing tall like soldiers, eight or nine across, three deep. Above that there was another wooden container for loaves in all different shapes and sizes – bloomers, farmhouse, rectangular focaccias and rounded sourdough loaves, split tin, and Vienna bread. Next up was a shallower wooden shelf, ideal for showing off freshly baked rolls, bagels, buns, and the uppermost section was the same, perhaps for muffins, doughnuts, brioche.

'They've done us proud.' Celeste came through to join Jade. She ran a hand across the display unit, feeling the wood beneath its covering. She called back to the boys in the kitchen. 'You've done an amazing job, thank you!'

Melissa came through next and admired this part of the transformation. 'Harvey's loving every minute of doing this, you know. So is Linc, for that matter. And I can't wait until opening,' she smiled. 'I saw Tracy yesterday and she's counting down the days.' Tracy had been Melissa's friend for years and was a frequent customer to the bakery. Jade and Celeste were still making rolls and loaves for Tracy to serve at the inn and would continue to do so for the rest of the time their business was shut. Tracy prided herself on giving guests fresh ingredients and local produce wherever she could. She even got her eggs from Nola, whose daughter lived locally and had a lot of land out the back of her cottage. They kept the chickens there, supplying a handful of people in Heritage Cove, including the owner of the Heritage Inn.

'I made the delivery to Aubrey House and they were thrilled with the selection of food,' Celeste told her sister as they both stood marvelling at the transformation so far. 'And they're already talking about the Christmas party this year so we might get that gig too if we're lucky. I did suggest Etna do it alongside us but she told me she doesn't need the extra work at that time of the year.'

'She works hard enough as it is,' Jade agreed as they went back into the kitchen. She caught Linc's eye. 'When *is* she going to retire?'

He put down the drill he was using. He looked good in jeans today despite the dust all over them and covering the front of his charcoal T-shirt. But Jade had decided it was going to have to remain a case of look, don't touch, because she had a business to relaunch, too much else to focus on.

'Let me see.' He put a pencil behind his ear after he used it to mark a place at the back of the pantry cupboard, ready for shelving Jade presumed. 'Today's Sunday, tomorrow's Monday…never?'

'Much as I love our business, I don't think I'll be doing this into my seventies,' Celeste concluded before adding, 'Right now I vote we grab coffees for the workers and ourselves and we'll bring them back here to enjoy in the garden.'

'That sounds just what I need,' said Jade before making a note of the coffees the boys wanted, and when Linc accidentally brushed her arm with his when he prompted her to make sure Etna made his extra hot and didn't forget to add a double shot this time, she quickly found her purse and got out of there so he wouldn't register the way she'd reacted, like she was glad, like she wanted him to do it again.

Once they'd collected and delivered the beverages plus a bacon roll for each of the workers – on the house from an insistent Etna – the sisters and Melissa unfolded three deck chairs in the garden and positioned them in the shade. Despite the banging from inside the bakery and kitchen, it was nice to relax and take a bit of time out, but it wasn't long before the girls got onto the pressing issue of conjuring up a business name for the bakery.

'The sign writer needs to know,' Celeste prompted. 'Why is it so hard to think of anything?'

'Not hard,' said Jade, 'more like impossible.'

'Surely it's not impossible,' said Melissa, earning herself a look from both sisters.

'We're just going to have to go with Heritage Bakery.' Celeste shook her head in the absence of any better ideas. 'People know it, it says what it is, it keeps the tradition.'

'Lucy struggled to come up with the right name for her business when she took over,' Melissa put in. 'She wanted to honour its place in the Cove and retain its character and traditions. We're a bit set in our ways around here,' she added with a smile.

Lucy, who was now a bona fide local, had come to the Cove to stand in for Fred Gilbertson, the village blacksmith, on a temporary basis. She'd ended up buying the business from him when he retired, falling in love with Harvey's brother Daniel, and had become as much a part of things here in the village as anyone else. Her business had a simple sign on the side of her workshop that said "Lucy's Blacksmithing" and that was it even though she was more of an artist than the sort of blacksmith Fred had been. She'd kept the workshop as it was, adding in some display areas for her work, and she even still had the old forge.

Jade wondered whether fighting against tradition was the right way to go or whether people in the village would prefer them to keep things the way they were. 'Perhaps you're right, maybe we should stick with Heritage Bakery.'

'We'll have to if we can't think of anything.' Celeste tilted her head back to get a few of the sun's rays on her face, prompting Jade to ask if she should be doing that when she didn't have sunscreen on. She tutted at her sister's fretting and told her she wouldn't do it for long.

'Don't be defeated,' Melissa carried on. 'I can tell that changing the name is what you've both always wanted, and as long as it fits, everyone will get used to it. You're going to all this effort to put your stamp on the place – there must be a name that's perfect for you. The place will look more or less the same from the front and hasn't lost an ounce of character, but what you sell has already changed vastly from the items the bakery once produced – with its cream horns and not-particularly-tasty vanilla slices that I'm pretty sure weren't always freshly baked – so out with the old and in with the new when it comes to a name.'

'She's right,' Celeste sighed.

Harvey's voice carried from the inside of the kitchen. 'What about The Twisted Sisters?' They must've been talking louder than they realised.

'That could work,' said Celeste, meeting a look of disapproval from Jade.

'Buns of steel?' Melissa sniggered.

'Sensible suggestions only.' Jade sipped from an ice-cold can of lemonade; she'd been working too hard, getting too hot, to indulge in a coffee.

'Why don't you think about your favourite things?' Linc had come outside to retrieve the spirit level from the open toolbox.

Melissa smiled at him. 'Good idea.' She gave him an admiring glance when he bent down to pick something up off the floor and she winked in Jade's direction as he went back inside.

'Don't get any ideas,' Jade sniggered.

Melissa leaned forwards and whispered, 'He's not Italian, but he's hot.'

'Why not suggest him to Celeste?' Jade defended, not wanting to talk about the Italian who'd once been in her life. She'd told them too much in the pub that night, but no more.

'Oh, I think he's already got his eye on one of us,' Celeste said knowingly, 'and it isn't me.'

Jade moved the conversation on. 'Maybe he has a point. Perhaps we need to think about what we like. What are our favourite things at the bakery?'

'That's too difficult,' Celeste groaned. 'Unless you want to call us the bread roll, brioche, doughnut, apple pie, raspberry cupcake, peanut –'

'OK, I get it,' said Jade, stretching out a foot to gently kick her sister and make her stop. 'We both like our baked goods.'

Melissa thought harder. 'When I'm travelling I usually like to sample local cuisine and find things I didn't even know existed. It's all part of the adventure for me and the food becomes a memory as much as everything else. Greece, for example, is the first place I ever tried the gooey melted cheese of saganaki. I won't think of chilli mud crab in the same way again after tasting it in Singapore, and I'll never have sushi quite like the stuff I once had in Japan. What was the first item you put on the bakery menu?' she prompted. 'Or what was the first item you made so successfully it was almost like you'd found a signature dish or recipe?' She pulled a face, unsure of the correct terminology, but she was clearly enjoying this brainstorming.

Celeste began to laugh. 'Our first loaves left a lot to be desired. Some people think breadmaking is easy but, believe me, it takes time and practice to get it right.'

Jade thought about it. 'The first new item I introduced onto the menu other than what we'd already come up with based on research was the cinnamon-and-raisin puff-pastry twist. We were in the lead-up to Christmas and I wanted something other than mince pies, something that was a new twist, if you'll pardon the pun. That's what we decided to try and it went down a storm.'

'Now we're talking,' Melissa beamed. 'Puff-pastry twist, cinnamon twist…what about you, Celeste?'

Celeste looked across at her sister with a knowing glance. 'I think Jade knows exactly what conjures up the most memories for me.'

It took her a few seconds but suddenly Jade gasped. 'My goodness, I'd forgotten…the salted-caramel turnover!'

'Spill, both of you,' said Melissa with the distinct impression she must be missing something when both girls fell into fits of laughter.

Jade told Melissa the full story of when Celeste had tried to make a salted-caramel turnover, messed it up good and proper and got in a real huff. She'd slung the turnover attempt at the kitchen wall, hard, but it had missed her target and hurtled into the bakery, hitting a customer square on the head. 'I stood there waiting for the customer to yell at Celeste, who'd emerged from the kitchen with the look of fear in her eyes,' Jade said between bouts of laughter. 'The guy had a piece of puff pastry in his hair and when Celeste went to take it from him, he gently took hold of her hand and said that was what you called a classic meet-cute.'

Melissa squealed. 'How romantic!'

'He asked me out there and then,' Celeste admitted somewhat sheepishly.

'Did you take him up on it?'

'We went out on a date, he took me for dinner, we had a romantic couple of days.'

'And that was it?' Melissa looked from one sister to the other for answers. 'What was his name?'

'Quinn.' Celeste lost herself in a memory but soon snapped out of it. 'But he was just in the Cove for a brief holiday. He went back to the Navy after that and we kind of lost touch.'

Melissa swooned. 'In the Navy, wow.'

'It was a couple of days I'll never forget,' Celeste told her. 'But we lost touch, as I say, and I'm married to my job.'

It was the closest Celeste had ever come to wanting to see someone for more than a casual fling. The sisters had gone out for a drink a few nights after Quinn moved on from the Cove and, watching Celeste now as she reluctantly shared details of their date and the days following, Jade knew this had been a fling that affected her sister like no other. But he'd gone, Celeste had got back to business, and she hadn't mentioned him again. Sometimes Jade wondered if it would be better if she was more like her sister, able to let go, move on, focus on things she could control rather than those she couldn't.

'How about…The Caramel Turnover and Cinnamon Twist Bakery?' Celeste laughed. 'Yes, it's terrible, and we are getting nowhere fast!'

'I've another idea,' said Melissa mischievously. 'What about The Meet-Cute Bakery?'

'Nice try, but not a chance,' Celeste replied.

'I've got something,' said Jade with a smile that grabbed Celeste's attention finally. She threw her arms wide in a gesture of announcement. 'What about…The Twist and Turn Bakery?'

Celeste grinned. 'You know what…I like it!'

'Me too,' Melissa agreed, clasping her hands together.

'Then I think we've got a winner,' Jade agreed.

Harvey appeared next with Linc alongside and Linc looked across at her. 'Any time you want to thank me for getting the creative juices flowing, just let me know.'

'She will,' Melissa injected before she and Celeste whispered to one another, making some kind of joke about other sorts of juices flowing when it came to Linc.

Jade shot them a glare. She couldn't even look at Linc because he'd probably heard what they'd said. 'I need to get back to work, I've got to get those tasters over to Barney and Lois.'

'Say hello to them from me,' Celeste called after her as she went to the cottage to collect what she needed.

She left Melissa and Celeste with the workers and set off for Barney and Lois's place on foot. It wasn't far and at least the tasters weren't all that heavy in their plastic container. She passed the tea rooms and waved in to Etna, thinking how happy she always seemed. Jade had always felt a little bit sad for the woman. She'd lost her husband long before the sisters even came to the Cove but she'd never found anyone else and didn't have children. She was all alone apart from the odd family visitor and occasionally Jade would sit in the tea rooms and watch her go about her business, wondering whether this would be her and Celeste in years to come. There was a lot to be said for it, but Jade knew she'd feel something was missing.

'Penny for them.' It was Kenneth, cap on his head to avoid the harsh rays of the sun, making his way past the chapel as Jade crossed over.

'Sorry, I was in a world of my own,' she smiled, although she didn't lift her shades now her hands were full.

'Whatever you've got in there looks good.'

She explained it was cake samples and reeled off a list of flavours the happy couple were about to sample.

'I'll see you then,' he said. 'I'm off for a coffee and a slice of Etna's lemon drizzle.'

'I don't know where you put all that cake,' she called after him with a smile.

'The allotment keeps me fit,' he hollered back with a pat of a non-existent stomach.

Perhaps the key to a happy life was keeping the simple things close, Jade thought as she followed the bend in the road around past the pub on the opposite side. Etna had her tea rooms, Kenneth had his allotment. And both of them seemed content. She wondered whether their secret was letting go of anything that might be holding them back.

Maybe that's what she needed to do. She needed to move on properly and stop holding on to the memory of Dario and a love that had long gone.

And there was more than one way to move on. There was finding someone else, there was stopping dreams of what might have been, and there was going out there to get exactly what you wanted and needed.

And she didn't necessarily need a man to do that.

Chapter Five

Linc couldn't deny he enjoyed the flirting with Jade and he knew she wasn't immune to it either. It happened every time they were in the same vicinity. She'd definitely been caught off guard when he was able to help them dream up a name for the bakery business the other day.

'Where were you off to so early this morning?' Etna asked him as she came into the kitchen late morning on a break from the tea rooms while Patricia held down the fort. She found a folder from the sideboard and waved it aloft. 'Accounts,' she explained of the folder bulging with papers.

'I had an appointment.' He scraped a knife of butter across the surface of a second piece of toast after it popped up from the toaster.

'What for?'

He'd forgotten her caring nature also meant Etna enquired about what he was up to. 'Dentist.'

'You had a check-up last week, nothing wrong is there?' She put the folder she'd been holding down on the table. 'You've been twice, what are you having done?'

'Had to have a few x-rays,' he said off the top of his head.

'I suppose it's better to be safe than sorry,' she smiled at him. 'Now, would you like a cup of tea? I can stop for ten minutes.'

'No thanks, but I appreciate the offer.' He pretended to carry on reading the newspaper so she wouldn't delve much more. If he'd remembered about saying he was going to the dentist last time he would've thought of a different excuse today, because there was no way he'd ever tell Etna what he was really doing. She'd never approve.

'Have you got more work on today?' she pressed, reaching for her folder, ready to leave him to it.

He supposed her inquisition stopped him from keeping up the pretence with the newspaper and it definitely prevented him from thinking about Jade. 'There's still plenty to do at the bakery. The prep for the units is coming along – Harvey's been working with a kitchen fitter, learning the ropes as they put in something called a ladder frame, which is apparently the base to put the cabinets on.'

'It sounds as though you're learning a bit too,' she smiled contentedly.

'Keeping the brain active,' he grinned. 'I know that it's a key part of the installation because that frame has to take all the weight – the cupboards and everything in them, the benchtop. The windows at the front will also have a bit of a revamp, they'll be repaired where needed. According to Harvey, the girls wanted people to drive past and not realise anything had really changed, at least not until they were inside.'

'I'm glad they've decided to keep the frontage the same.' Etna checked her hair in the mirror in the compact hallway that led to the door and the stairs down to the outside. 'It fits with Heritage Cove and there's always the panic with these things that new ideas mean changes that don't quite gel with the rest of the village.' She put her hands up in defence before telling him, 'I know it's an individual choice, I'm just pleased that this time they've done just what I would've done. The question is, are they going to be ready for the grand opening in less than a fortnight?'

'We'll make it ready.'

'And you're coping when Harvey is off doing the day job?'

'Stop fretting.' But he was smiling. It was nice she looked out for him.

'You did work awfully late last night.'

'Got to get it finished. And I'm taking a break now.' He demolished the last piece of buttered toast. 'Talking of which, don't you ever think about taking a break?' She was seventy-two and still working as though she were thirty years younger. He was all for doing what you loved but when did she last take a whole day off for herself and not to do something for someone else or run an errand? When did she last take a holiday?

'Not needed, Lincoln.' He knew she was full-naming him to make her point. And she gave him a wink that reminded him of when he was a boy and she'd come to visit and sneakily pass him a big slab of milk chocolate that he'd hide up in his bedroom and enjoy for himself.

'I've got more work too, at the waffle shack.'

'For Daniel?'

'Yeah. Once we're done with the bakery it'll be on to that, if you don't mind me hanging around a while longer.'

'I'd love it, it's wonderful having you here.'

He got up and put his arm around her. 'Thank you. And talking of the waffle shack, now I'm up and about I might head over there and ask for some more details. Harvey's at the bakery waiting for a delivery and he has things in hand there so right now I've got a bit of free time until I'm needed.'

'You make sure you don't overwork yourself,' she frowned. 'You don't want to start the autumn term exhausted.'

'Tell you what – I'll take a break if you will.' He dropped his plate into the soapy water already in the sink.

She laughed and gave him a little shove on the shoulder. 'Not a chance.' With the folder clutched in front of her chest again, she hadn't finished worrying. 'Are you going back to supply teaching come September? You haven't thought about settling into a permanent position again?'

'I haven't thought about it yet, no.'

'Moving from place to place isn't always a good idea,' she went on. 'You're too young to be avoiding the world.'

'I'm not avoiding the world. I've been very sociable since I got here – the pub, the tea rooms, the bakery and, next, the waffle shack.'

'True. It's just your dad –'

'He worries, I know.'

As a music teacher, Linc had been able to find plenty of supply work and had found the relative anonymity, along with the lack of involvement in the politics side of the job, a welcome relief. His head hadn't been able to handle all those extra stresses of the job before now, but perhaps Etna and his dad were right. Maybe it was time he started to put out feelers for something more solid. He didn't want to move around forever and he'd covered the same schools more than once now anyway, meaning he was in fact beginning to get to know people. And his moving from place to place meant he didn't really get time to invest in his students and he was starting to miss that, miss seeing children who had a talent, or who struggled, flourish after their joint efforts to get them to a certain point.

He chanced mentioning again that Etna might want to take a break. 'Dad would love it if you went to stay with him.'

'It's just hard with the tea rooms. I keep telling him to come this way.'

'He's worried he won't see enough of you if he does.'

Etna and Joseph had always been close – more so since Linc's mum passed away, and again when Joseph was in hospital. Etna had visited whenever she could and Linc would be forever grateful he'd come through his illness and was now in good health. Losing one parent had been hard enough; he wanted his dad around for a lot longer yet. Unfortunately, since Joseph lost his wife and then had his health scare, he hadn't managed to quite find his footing again. He had people at the pub to talk to, the odd neighbour who popped in, but Linc suspected what Joseph really needed was a good dose of family. Having his sister around and sidestepping his usual routine might be all that was required to put a real spring back in his step.

'Nonsense,' Etna insisted. 'He'll see me. He can plonk himself in the tea rooms and keep me company.'

'Perhaps I'll suggest it again then.' Both of them were creatures of habit and those habits were hard to break.

'Your dad is lucky to have had you at his side.' Etna had stopped in the doorway and now came back over to the table. She sat down next to him. 'I still feel dreadful that I didn't do more to help you when your mum was taken ill and then your dad.'

'You did enough. You helped a lot with Mum, came whenever you could. We knew you couldn't do it all the time, not while running your own business. But you were there for us all.' He put a hand over hers. 'Everyone has their own life.'

'I could say the same to you.'

'Walked right into that one, didn't I?' He smiled briefly. 'But I wouldn't change a thing. I stepped up when I had to, that was all.'

'You know, your dad might not like hanging around with me, his bossy older sister.'

'You, bossy?' he teased. He could well imagine. With her being older too he expected she'd been in charge a lot when they were kids. But whilst Etna still ran a tight ship and liked to be in control, Linc could tell she was also very tired, as much as she'd protest that she wasn't. Her joviality in the tea rooms didn't always continue when she came home exhausted and if anyone needed a break, it was her. 'Have a think about my suggestion of a holiday,' he went on. 'You might find you enjoy it and come back even more raring to go. You and Dad could have dinner at the local pub every night if you wanted – they do the highly acclaimed carvery, it's within stumbling distance of Dad's place.'

'Sometimes I swear he and your mum chose the house for that very reason.'

'You might be right about that. Although Mum never went to the pub without having had a long walk first. It was one of her favourite things of all – a winter walk, a carvery dinner at the pub and a brandy by the fire before they'd leave for home. And in the summer months she'd walk the perimeter of the farmer's field beyond the pub and then settle in the garden with a gin and tonic, always –'

'Long,' Etna laughed before he could add the word himself. His mum always liked her gin served in a highball glass pre-filled with ice, with a squeeze of lime juice and a twist of lime added.

'You and Mum got along well.'

'I was very fond of her. And she could talk, I loved that. We'd spend our evenings talking about anything and everything. I miss her.' She looked to him. 'I know you must too.'

Linc's mum had been gone eleven years but some days it felt as though she'd been in his life a lot more recently. He was glad about that because it meant his memories were still there, as vivid as ever, of the mum he'd nursed right up until the very end when she'd died peacefully with her husband and her children, Linc and his brother Zach, at her bedside.

Etna put on a smile. 'Listen to us, all melancholy…I'll think about your suggestion I take a break, how does that sound?' He nodded his approval. 'And while we're nagging one another, I want to know when you're going to get that guitar out for me.'

'All in good time, promise. I did have a brief play yesterday but you were still in the tea rooms.'

Linc had been playing the guitar since he was in primary school. He rarely used sheet music, instead playing tunes by ear. He'd played all through high school, even formed a band with some of his crazy mates and performed in school concerts. And with his life so messy over the last few years, playing the guitar had been a real escape. He'd come home from work, have dinner, and then while away the hours thinking up new tunes, playing favourites, disappearing into the music instead of his own thoughts. He'd brought his guitar here to the Cove and it was still a means to get away from anything going on in his head.

'I'll hold you to that, young man,' Etna smiled, picking up her folder again, ready to go.

'The windows are open all the time in summer, I wouldn't want to upset the neighbours.'

'Ppffft…don't you worry about anyone moaning about music, they'll probably enjoy it as much as birdsong.'

He walked her out and at the bottom of the steps that led up to her flat, she stopped. 'I'll give your dad a call later, have a bit of a chat.'

'Good, he'll appreciate it.' Linc locked the door behind them. 'While you're at it, can you reassure him I'm fine? He's texting me daily as if I'm twenty years younger and a wayward teen.'

'Don't knock it,' her voice trilled as he tugged on the work boots he'd left outside. 'He worries about you and wants to see you happy.'

He gave Etna a kiss on the cheek, sent her off to the tea rooms and made his way along The Street, across the field behind the bus stop and up towards the waffle shack.

When Linc reached the shack, a stunning wooden cabin set at the perimeter of the village green space, the place was busy. On the veranda out front was a family of four, each with waffles piled high with all sorts of things. One waffle looked like it had bacon on top, another had what could be chicken. Linc held the door open for a girl carrying out three plates filled with sweet waffles and toppings that made his tummy growl in hunger.

A tall man introduced himself as Daniel and Linc took a seat at one of the two remaining tables inside the shack while Daniel finished taking payment from a customer. He called over to a boy emerging from the kitchen and then took off his apron before coming to meet Linc properly.

After they'd shaken hands again Daniel, tall with dark brown cropped hair and thick eyebrows that settled into a more relaxed expression now he'd taken a break from the mayhem, told him, 'Etna has a lot of good things to say about you. First off, welcome to Heritage Cove.'

'Cheers.' Linc waited for the trio of giggling tween girls to leave the counter armed with their takeaway waffles in cardboard trays. 'Popular place.'

'Luckily for me,' Daniel admitted. Shirtsleeves rolled up to reveal strong arms, he didn't look the type to run a waffle business but he certainly seemed to be in his element. 'I launched right before Christmas and I wondered if it was a novelty and business would recede but so far it's the opposite. Which is why I need to do some work with the outside, provide a more attractive seating area for my customers.'

'Which is where I come in.'

'Exactly.'

The boy behind the till needed more takeaway waffle trays and Daniel darted off, grabbed a bag full of them from a cupboard by the kitchen, left the boy to stack them and came back to Linc. 'Harvey's pretty happy with the way you've taken to the work at the bakery, so there's your second reference.' He broke off to briefly speak to the young girl who'd gone back behind the counter and was busily scooping out ice-cream onto a golden waffle and then beckoned Linc to follow him through to the back.

69

'I can come back another time if it helps,' Linc offered as they went through to the compact kitchen space.

'It won't be any quieter,' Daniel assured him as he pulled a bowl of batter out from the fridge. 'Luckily I'm good at multitasking.' He made up a few more waffles that his staff came to collect and then, after ensuring he could take five minutes at least to show Linc the space that needed work, they left out of the back door to the waffle shack, the heavenly sweet scent lingering and following after them.

They were standing in a particularly overgrown and shabby area with only a couple of rubbish bins at the far end. 'This is the part of the business that I've been attempting to bring up to the same standard as the rest since I opened up last year. It might look like I haven't done anything at all with it but I've tried to make a go of clearing it on several occasions, but whatever's growing here is a nightmare to get rid of.'

The space didn't show that Daniel had made any progress given the thigh-high weeds and brambles swaying in a slight breeze that didn't detract from the harsh rays of the sun above on what was the most glorious day since Linc had arrived in the Cove.

Daniel pointed to the boundary, barely discernible, with a rickety fence at one end and absolutely nothing the rest of the way along. 'I'd like to turn this into a proper seating area. As you probably saw on your way here, plenty of customers take their waffles outside and sit on the field to eat, which will always be fine by me – it attracts new customers when they're spotted – and I have the veranda, but that's a squeeze and when it's busy I need extra tables. I'm already turning down bookings for parties, and I don't like doing that.'

'I always thought waffles would be more of a winter thing.' Linc remembered Etna telling him she'd had some freebies last year by way of an apology from Daniel for some of the "misdemeanours in his youth". Etna hadn't told Linc exactly what had happened; discretion was certainly her thing – she always had been able to keep a secret. Knowing this, he'd been tempted to tell her everything he had going on in his life but he wasn't sure how she'd react, so given he was living under her roof he'd decided to keep quiet. That way she wouldn't feel forced to reprimand him, lecture him or tell his dad what he was up to. He wasn't ashamed of it himself but others might see it differently and he could do without the judgement.

'They're an all-year-round thing,' Daniel explained. 'Business has taken off in a way I never expected. I thought I'd have a lull, particularly in summer, but good weather, bad weather, it doesn't matter – people want those waffles. I'd kind of hoped in a way that things would quieten down a little so I could go on holiday with Lucy, my girlfriend, but there's no way we'll be doing that this year.' He spoke more quietly. 'I've got a couple of really good staff, but they're young, and I'm not sure I'm quite ready to trust them to be in charge of the shack in my absence just yet.'

'Fair enough. Can't imagine Etna leaving her tea rooms in the care of anyone, let alone staff young enough to be her grandchildren.'

'Lucy has her own business too so she's happy to stay put this year. We compromise with a few afternoons out but perhaps next year we'll get that holiday.'

'Lucy's the blacksmith, right?'

'She sure is. And a good one at that. You should stop by, see what she does – it's a whole lot more than you'd expect.'

They got into more details of what Daniel needed doing here. He'd hire a digger for the groundwork, the whole fence would need to come out and he wanted bushes put in its place. The ground would then be paved and he'd have half a dozen picnic-style benches with some smaller bistro sets along the very edge for smaller parties.

'I've already talked all this through with Harvey,' Daniel said, pointing to the corner at the very rear. 'I'm having a built-in fireplace out here in the seating area as well as outdoor heaters dotted around.'

'It sounds like it'll be a real extension of the inside.'

'That's what I'm hoping for.' Daniel was about to talk more when he was called back to the shack again. 'See, this is why I can't go on holiday.'

Linc hadn't ever wanted his own business. A handful of private guitar lessons was as close as he got to that, but for some, it was all they wanted. He'd watched Jade and her sister – well, mostly Jade – since he arrived and she was the same, very happy to be her own boss, make the big decisions, take all the risk. He had to hand it to them all, his auntie Etna included, it took a special person to be that way.

They went inside and after Daniel had jumped in to help with the sudden rush at the waffle shack by taking over serving at the till, dealing with a phone call and then accepting delivery of ice-cream from someone called Zara who ran the local ice-creamery, he and Linc discussed a start date based on Daniel's plans and Harvey's. And Linc hadn't realised before but all this busyness, these distractions, along with an unfamiliar village, were doing the trick. His mind hadn't felt this clear in ages; he felt more himself than he had in a long while.

'Harvey says you're on track to complete the bakery renovations,' Daniel went on.

'We're a tiny bit ahead of schedule, actually. Thanks to the odd early start.' The corner of his mouth twitched, a hint of a smile as he remembered Jade's reaction the first day they met.

'Harvey will do well with this renovations business,' Daniel assessed proudly. 'And his fiancée Melissa has given notice for her job as cabin crew. She'll bring the feminine touch to the business – it'll be a real success, I'm sure.'

'Sounds like a good partnership.'

'How about you?' Daniel had taken two cans of Coke from the fridge and handed one to Linc. 'Anyone waiting back in Cambridgeshire for you?'

'No, I'm young free and single.' And his previous relationship didn't get any air time if he could help it.

Daniel's face brightened as another customer came in but Linc soon realised it wasn't a customer so much as a personal visit, judging by the hug the owner of the waffle shack received from the attractive blonde. This had to be Lucy. He'd seen her at a distance but this was the first time they'd met.

After Lucy said hello she introduced the young boy who'd come into the shack with her as Peter. 'I found him outside,' she told Daniel with a smile. 'I was on my way back from delivering some items to Tilly's Bits 'n' Pieces when I saw Giselle pull up. She had the baby in the back of the car and he'd only just fallen asleep so I said I'd bring Peter up here with me before I headed back to work. She said she'll see you tomorrow when she picks Peter up.'

Daniel ruffled the boy's hair and pulled him into a hug that he tried to resist but clearly didn't mind one bit. 'How's your mum coping with you two kids?'

'The baby keeps her up a lot,' Peter told him, dragging out the last two words to better make his point, but he loves the car seat.'

'If I remember rightly, you always did too,' Daniel grinned. 'It's great to have you here again. I'll warn you though, the sun doesn't go down until ten o'clock or thereabouts – I think we might still be making waffles at that time. Are you happy to have a late night and, in the meantime, work for your keep?'

Peter beamed. 'Yes!'

Linc must have looked as though he was trying to work out the relationship between Peter and Daniel because Peter turned to him and said, 'Daniel is my other dad,' as though it made perfect sense.

'You have two?'

Peter thought for a minute. 'Actually, I have three: Daniel; then there's Stu, my almost- stepdad when he eventually marries Mum; then my biological dad, who I've never met.'

'Sounds complicated,' said Linc, pretty confused already.

Lucy did the honours and explained Peter's claim while Daniel went to help the girl behind the till – Brianna, as Linc overheard – with the credit-card machine, which was playing up.

'Daniel and Peter's mum, Giselle, were married once,' Lucy began, amused by Linc's obvious surprise. 'But their friendship was strong and lasted even when they went their separate ways. Giselle helped Daniel out at a particularly difficult time in his life – I'll leave him to give you the details, should he choose – and in turn Daniel helped Giselle out when her life became more and more difficult without Peter's biological father anywhere to be seen.'

Linc tried to get it all straight in his head. 'Definitely complicated.'

Lucy smiled at Peter and gave him a nudge. 'Definitely. But Peter is pretty happy, aren't you, mate? Especially when waffles and staying up past your bedtime are involved.' She leaned in to tell Linc, 'Daniel went some time without seeing Peter so when they're together Daniel likes to spoil him.'

'They look as though they get on well.' He watched Daniel hand Peter an apron and help him tie it on. The arrangement and how it obviously seemed to work gave Linc a new appreciation for the way families could form unconventionally and it gave him all the more reassurance that what he'd been up to was a good thing rather than anything to be ashamed of, as his last girlfriend had insinuated. He'd stopped telling people about it after her reaction, which was far from approving and had dented his self-belief, made him question his motives.

Peter ran off to wash his hands in the kitchen and was soon helping out Troy, the other member of staff, wipe down the biggest of all the tables and clear the detritus now the party had headed off.

'How old is he?' Linc asked Daniel when Lucy went on her way having delivered Peter safely.

'He's eight, almost nine.'

'He seems a great kid. Having more than one dad doesn't appear to cause him any angst.'

'Yeah, I guess he could be really messed up with the way things have gone, but he isn't. A lot of that is down to Giselle. She's a very good friend of mine, hasn't had the easiest time.'

When another group of customers came into the shack Linc decided it was time to leave Daniel to it. 'I'll be off. This place is one of the busiest eateries I think I've been in,' he grinned.

'It keeps me sane,' said Daniel, before adding, 'Take some waffles on the house.' He indicated for Linc to follow him through to the kitchen before he left.

'When they smell this good, how can I say no?'

They went into the kitchen, where Peter was washing up at the sink and Troy had started to make the batter for savoury waffles. The kitchen smelt glorious with the salty sizzle of freshly fried bacon hanging in the air as Troy added it along with grated cheddar cheese and spring onions to a batter mixture before pouring it into the heated waffle iron.

Linc enjoyed his savoury waffles with sharp cheddar cheese and bacon sitting on the bench on the veranda of the shack while Daniel got back to work, and it was just the snack he needed before he headed over to the bakery to take charge of what was going on there. Being the one at the helm felt good when so much of the past year had been out of his control. And seeing Daniel around Peter today had reminded him how much he valued family. One day he might even want one of his own, but in a weird way Orla had put a stop to any such desires he might have had when in fact she'd been trying to do the exact opposite.

*

'You look more shattered than I do,' said Etna that evening when Linc emerged from the bathroom after an

76

extra-long shower. He'd stood in there soothing his aching muscles after a full afternoon that lasted well into the evening at the bakery. He'd put in more cabinetry, installed shelves, positioned the new downlights and dragged out a load of debris to the back garden ready for Harvey to sort through and get rid of. And, disappointingly, the only time he'd seen Jade was as she carried a cake box out to her car and drove off somewhere else.

'Thanks, love you too,' he called back over his shoulder as he went to his room, a boxroom that he could only shut the door of if he went right inside and up to the very edge of his bed, and this time at least he managed not to trip over the guitar case jutting out from beneath the single bed he was almost too long for.

He pulled on jeans. The weather had gone from a sunny summer's afternoon to a gloomy evening that had him putting the lights on already. He'd chopped the dinner ingredients as soon as he got in, though, in case Etna came back when he was still in the bathroom, since she had a tendency to do things herself before anyone else could. Tonight, he was making them Moroccan chicken with roasted vegetables and couscous, and after bashing his elbow on the wardrobe door in the tight space as he pulled a T-shirt over his head, he was about to head out to carry on prepping when he heard a yelp that had him sprinting into the kitchen.

He couldn't see Etna at first. 'Where are you?'

'Down here,' she whimpered.

He saw her around the other side of the bench, slumped on the floor. 'What happened? Did you slip?' He went to help her up.

'I stumbled,' she groaned, the obvious source of her pain being her ankle given the way she tentatively tried to touch it and wouldn't let him move her. 'I think it's twisted. Ouch, it hurts.'

'Come on, let me help you up.'

'I can't, it's too painful.'

'So, you're going to sleep down there tonight then?' When she pulled a face at him he said, 'Didn't think so.' He hooked an arm around her and had her put both her arms around his neck, placing her weight on the foot that didn't have an issue, and with a bit of huffing and puffing from Etna he finally helped her over to the sofa.

In the absence of any ice cubes in the freezer he pulled out a packet of frozen peas and once he'd elevated her leg with the use of a cushion beneath, he positioned the packet he'd wrapped in a tea towel gently around her ankle. 'How does that feel?'

'Better.'

'I'll give the doctor a call.'

She dismissed the notion with a grunt. 'They won't be able to do anything more than you're doing. A bit of rest and I'll be fine.'

'It might be a good idea to get it checked, make sure it's only a sprain.'

'You're fussing.'

'I tell you what. We'll have dinner first and then, after we've eaten, see how it feels.' He sensed it wouldn't feel any better at all by the way it seemed to have swollen up already, but letting her think she was the one in control was the only way to placate her.

He took charge in the kitchen and Etna was only allowed to move slightly once dinner was ready, just enough so she could eat from a plate on a tray on her lap. And after they'd eaten, when it was clear she was in just as much pain as before, not taking no for an answer, Linc helped her down the stairs and to his car so he could take her to the urgent care centre and at least make sure nothing was broken.

'I can't take time off,' she insisted to him yet again as the nurse typed notes into the computer.

'I don't think you'll have much choice in the matter,' said Linc. 'And I'll pick up the prescription for your painkillers before we go home.'

'I don't need pills.'

'I'll get them just in case.' She'd winced in discomfort enough times as she was examined. 'And you heard the advice – you need to rest that ankle. And I don't much fancy carrying you up the stairs to your flat every day; I'll get you home but once you're up there, carrying you down again to go to the tea rooms risks one or both of us doing a whole lot worse than you've done already. You'll have to take the time to heal, it'll be worth it.'

The nurse gave Etna crutches and had her practise using them a couple of times before sharing a look with Linc that said she'd seen Etna's type before – resistant to stopping their routine, oblivious to how much ignoring the advice would be worse in the long term. It was up to him to make sure Etna did as she was told.

'Now look who's being bossy,' she sighed as he led her out to the car slowly while she tried to master use of the crutches.

'It runs in the family,' he smiled.

Chapter Six

Jade welcomed a day away from the Cove to attend day three of a professional skills course she'd signed up to and started a couple of months ago. She and Celeste had been so busy with bakery orders over the last few days that they'd not seen many people at all apart from Harvey and Linc as they worked away in the bakery and Patricia in the tea rooms when they went to get coffees. Patricia had told them that Etna had had a fall and hurt her ankle and so Jade had handed a box of glazed doughnuts to Linc to pass on to Etna, who hadn't been quite up to visitors that day. He hadn't had a chance to stop and talk either though, since he and Harvey were busy with the cabinetry and trying to meet their own deadline.

Celeste was happy to manage the fort in the Cove today and keep their bakery business going by delivering bread orders to some of the locals – five loaves would go to the Heritage Inn, a selection of loaves and rolls would be delivered to the pub, and then she had a list of baked goods to deliver to other addresses dotted around the village. She'd also deal with any pop-ins when residents hadn't placed an order but would come to the cottage on the off-chance there was anything going. The girls didn't keep much pre-baked given the small space they were operating in compared to usual, but sometimes the caller would get lucky. The day before yesterday Tilly had come in wanting something sweet and Jade was just finishing spreading icing along a batch of freshly made finger buns. The order was for six, to go to the White Clover charity organisation situated on the outskirts of Heritage Cove for their afternoon staff meeting, and so Tilly grabbed the couple remaining, taking one for her and one for her assistant Dessie at Tilly's Bits 'n' Pieces.

Now, it felt good to get away from the renovations and focus on the cake part of the business, the side Jade was keen to develop further. And she wanted to do it before she launched into her own personal plan that had nothing to do with The Twist and Turn Bakery, as the girls had finally decided to call it. She only hoped Celeste would be as on board with this plan as she was with anything to do with the bakery.

Both Celeste and Jade were what you might call jolly bakers – they loved what they did – but as Jade arrived today in a professional environment with a talented instructor, she felt a tiny burst of pride and energy that the odd cake commission had led to plenty more and that she had the drive to get even more serious about the art of cake decorating. She wanted to get better, she wanted to do more, and the fit-out would mean more space for her to work, to display cakes, to store the ingredients and the tools she needed. She and Celeste had been under one another's feet some days, containers had been crammed into storage spaces that were impossible to search through with any speed when she wanted to find a particular tool, but the renovations would mean much smoother operations, with dedicated cupboards and drawers as well as a separate oven for this aspect of the venture.

Today's course would also put Jade one step closer to gaining a qualification in cake decorating. Some thought she didn't need it – last Christmas her cakes had been so popular she'd had a write-up in the local paper – but she knew she'd only made a dent in the learning she could do and she was eager for more. It wasn't so much about the qualification per se, although that would be good to put on their website and social media pages as well as display in certificate form in the bakery; it was more about tapping into the invaluable knowledge base and experience that this course brought with it. Nancy, the host who had been there every day, had twenty years of cake making under her belt and could pass on plenty of tricks of the trade. So far, they'd gone through baking the cake itself – in a few varieties – they'd covered marzipan techniques, layering and filling, ganache, and flawless covering. They'd discussed stacking cakes, edible bows, they'd practised shaping sugar flowers by rolling fondant, trying out roses, anemones, peonies, they'd made wired leaves and cherry blossoms.

The first thing Jade and the one other attendee did today was make a cake of their choice. Nancy was there to offer guidance but Jade worked methodically and confidently and soon found herself lost in the process. When Barney and Lois had sampled the cakes she'd taken them a week ago, both of them had readily agreed that the lemon-elderflower was the one. And they'd decided that even before Jade told them the cake had been flavoured with the cordial sourced from Harvey's place. Jade hadn't missed the emotion in Barney's voice when he concluded that that completely sealed the deal because using something that came from Harvey's home made the cake all the more meaningful. Harvey had been like a son to him for many years with his and Daniel's father being someone who didn't share a whole lot of love. That day, Jade had grabbed her notebook and sketched out a rough design for the happy couple, noting down details they envisaged. Most of her cake commissions were done in the same way, just on paper, and thankfully Jade had never had anyone disappointed with the end result. But today was a first, because she'd be making a prototype for Barney and Lois.

Jade made the lemon-elderflower sponge, slightly nervous in a different kitchen, anxious to master an oven she wasn't used to and have everything she needed to hand. She left the cake to cool, cleared her workstation and then it was back to Nancy's work area, where the host showed techniques for making sugar flowers and gave advice on piping dots, beading, ruffles and pleats.

'Who's the cake going to be for?' Nancy asked, standing at Jade's workstation. She was as sweet in nature as the sugary designs she perfected with ease.

'It's for two very special people,' Jade explained before recounting Barney and Lois's story and the rocky road they'd had up until they'd finally got together again after all those years.

'It sounds as though your heart will be in this, which leaves me in no doubt over how stunning the finished cake will be.'

Jade blushed beneath the praise as Nancy moved on to ask the other attendee about his cake. It turned out he was baking for his younger brother's wedding as they couldn't afford a professional cake baker, and the guy seemed all kinds of nervous that he'd mess it up. Nancy soon had him at ease before she began the next demo to show them both the best way to make buttercream flowers.

'You'll both get plenty of time to practise,' Nancy assured them, 'and you can use what you've learnt to decorate your cakes. Just remember, these aren't the finished products, so relax and enjoy the process.'

Up until now, Jade had made a few vague attempts at fashioning buttercream flowers on her cakes but mostly she stuck with ordering pre-made blooms or attempting basic sugar flowers. Nancy took them through which nozzles to select and when, the consistency the buttercream needed to be, how to make the leaves and how to achieve a curve in the petal. Her advice was to not make every single rose the same. 'Think about real flowers,' she said, pulling over the vase of gorgeous cream roses she had at one side of the kitchen. 'Look at these: none of them are the exact same size, the petals vary in shape – some curl in places whereas others stand up stiff and straight – some are fully open, some have only just begun to unfurl.'

At last, it was time for them to have a go themselves and with the cake safely out of the way, Jade started to practise. She squirted a piece of buttercream onto the square of parchment on the rotating cake stand and then onto that she put the base for the delicate yellow rose she was about to create. She filled one half of a piping bag with buttercream and added the tiniest drop of yellow colouring to achieve the desired shade, then, using the teardrop-fashioned nozzle as Nancy had demonstrated, she began to work on the rose petals.

'Relax a bit, enjoy it, and gently pipe as you turn the stand,' Nancy advised, inspecting her work. 'The layers will look natural if you have a bit of a wobble, don't worry.'

Jade could feel the tension as she tried to pipe, the board turning, and added petals at each rotation. 'It doesn't look like yours.'

'Years of practice,' Nancy laughed. 'Don't worry, we've got all afternoon and by the time you leave here you'll be happy with a beautiful selection of roses.'

Jade wasn't so sure. The first rose she'd created looked like a load of layers of buttercream lumped together and nothing like the delicate flower she'd wanted to make. And it most definitely wasn't wedding-like.

After a couple more hours, however, Jade began to relax and enjoy it, and before long she actually had what looked a lot more like the yellow roses she'd envisaged. She gently lifted them from their parchment and positioned them on top of the cake and Nancy showed her how to add the yellow centres and pipe green leaf details between the flowers.

'The best thing about the leaves being piped around your roses,' Nancy informed them, 'is that they hide a multitude of sins. See the bottom of this rose…' She pointed to the one Jade was least happy with.

'Not my best work,' Jade frowned. The petals overlapped nicely up the flower but the base was jagged and didn't look natural at all.

'So, add a few leaves…'

Jade picked up the piping bag filled with green icing and began to laugh. 'You're right, it looks quite professional now.' She looked for any other areas that needed a little manipulation without overwhelming the cake with too much greenery. She began to get a bit braver and mixed a little blue food colouring with red so she had a beautiful purple shade and then added it to some more buttercream to make petunias. She wasn't sure they could be identified as the flower they were supposed to be, but they were perfect for this cake and she knew Barney and Lois were going to love them.

Nancy clapped her hands together. 'I adore the purple, what a contrast! You've created something I'd be proud to serve up at any party or wedding.' She was equally complimentary about Brian's techniques. Jade wondered if she was being overgenerous but when she'd cleared up her workstation and returned to see the finished cake after not looking at it critically for a whole twenty minutes, she saw it as perhaps other people would. And she didn't mind admitting it would look perfectly in place on a wedding table.

Jade left the course with her head bursting with new knowledge. It would take years to fully master a lot of these techniques as well as Nancy, but the last few sessions had been a start and she buzzed thinking how much the cake side of their business might take off. Rather than the odd local commission or cakes to display in the bakery window, word could spread far and wide and grow the business tenfold.

She arrived back home and carefully carried the cake from the car, across the garden that separated the bakery from the cottage, and straight into the kitchen. She slotted the cake onto the bench just inside the back door, opened up the box and took another look at her creation. She thought she might burst with pride. The lemon-elderflower sponge was covered in the palest buttercream frosting with the merest hint of yellow and finished with piping around the sides, looping at intervals to give it an air of sophistication. On the top at one side, she had a whole host of the roses she'd created in a yellow so pale it was almost cream – some big, others small, some unfurled into full bloom, a couple

86

just beginning to open up. The purple flowers were indeed a wonderful contrast and the leaves between blooms looked natural and a part of her plan rather than piped to disguise any mistakes. The edible flowers actually looked like they could've been plucked from a cottage garden, she thought. People would never know! Barney and Lois were going to be so surprised and her heart beat faster thinking how she was going to show it to them as soon as she got herself over there.

But first, she wanted to freshen up and make herself more presentable. She closed the box and hotfooted it upstairs to the bathroom. She pulled off the denim shorts that had received a dusting of icing sugar despite being covered by an apron, and the light blue T-shirt she'd worn in the kitchen all day. Dumping the dirty clothes in her laundry basket, she put on more deodorant, re-dressed in a white linen top and a denim skirt and called out a hello when she heard Celeste come in downstairs. She couldn't wait to show the cake off to her sister – she'd be so proud. She touched up her make-up a little, wanting to look professional when she took this prototype cake to the happy couple who had no idea they were about to get this service.

'Did you see it?' she called out, trotting down the stairs, hardly able to wait to show Celeste her handiwork.

But she didn't get an answer, and when she glanced towards the back door she saw the top of the box that held her cake flipped up. She walked towards it with a feeling of dread in the pit of her stomach and recoiled when she saw a great big wedge had already disappeared from it. A knife lay discarded in the sink, covered with some of the lovely icing she'd so carefully spread onto her creation.

It was then she looked up and out of the window and saw the culprit sitting on a deck chair in the garden without a care in the world apart from the big slab of cake he was demolishing.

Linc.

She marched outside.

'Hey!' He brightened when he saw her coming and then hungrily dug his fork back in. 'Great cake. Celeste told me to help myself. Really good,' he said between mouthfuls as Jade stood stunned into silence.

The sun glistened on his tanned forearms with every flex of his tendons as he lifted the cake to his mouth to enjoy another bite. He only stopped when at last he clocked her reaction. There were only crumbs left on his plate by now and Jade got the impression he would've licked them up had she not been standing there.

'Why do I get the feeling I'm in trouble?'

'What makes you think you can help yourself to my cake?' she yelled.

'I told you, your sister said to help myself, so I did.'

She pinched the skin at the top of her nose, her eyes closed, attempting to stop herself blowing her top. 'I doubt that.'

'Are you calling me a liar?'

Just then Celeste emerged from the back of the bakery and into the garden where Jade was confronting the cake thief as he sat nonchalantly as though he'd never done a thing wrong in his life. 'Hey, sis, how was the course?'

'Great until someone ruined my cake!'

Celeste looked from Jade to Linc and the plate on the ground beside him. She looked confused. But then pulled a face.

'Did you tell him to help himself?' Jade demanded.

'Not exactly.' Celeste took a deep breath and looked at him. 'Tell me you took a big chunk of the red-velvet cake with chocolate icing, Linc.'

Linc shook his head. 'Definitely not chocolatey, nor red. But you did tell me to help myself to cake from the kitchen.'

Celeste closed her eyes briefly, realising the mistake. 'He's right, I did. But the cake I was referring to was beneath the cloche at the far end of the kitchen.'

'I just heard cake.' He realised his apparent error. 'I'm sorry, really I am.'

But Jade wasn't going to listen, she was too angry. She stomped back into the kitchen, seething. She looked at the cake that had been hacked and destroyed. All that hard work.

Celeste came in after her. 'Wow, did you make those flowers? They're stunning.'

'What's left of them,' she grumbled.

'This is all my fault. I should've been a bit more specific when I told Linc to help himself to cake. I didn't realise you'd be coming back here with anything, let alone a masterpiece.'

Her compliment placated Jade for a few seconds but disappointment took over. 'I worked all day on it, I was so excited to show it to Barney and Lois. It was a prototype, for their wedding.'

Celeste rallied. 'And you can still show them.' She gave her sister a hug. 'All's not lost. The way I see it, this is a bonus for the happy couple, am I right? Nobody gets to see their cake before the actual cake is delivered. There's still plenty of detail left to impress them, and now we get to see what the inside looks like too, with that delicate sponge,' she winked. She picked up the knife, gave it a quick wash and dry, and then, with the sides of the box folded down, she trimmed the edges of the cake neatly. 'If you think about it, it's artistic with a piece taken out.' When Jade shot her a look she said, 'OK, it's not, but take it to them, they'll still get to see the prototype.'

'I guess they can imagine some greedy guest couldn't wait,' she sighed. It had been a genuine accident on Linc's part, but still, did it not look so professional that he'd question whether he was really meant to help himself? It had her worried her skills weren't quite up to par for the wedding of the favourite resident in the Cove when she'd left the course today filled with confidence.

'Go on, get yourself over to Barney and Lois's,' Celeste urged. 'That'll cheer you up. I'll put money on them having a good reaction.'

Linc had already disappeared from the garden and was nowhere to be seen so Jade took the cake and got into her car. She'd intended to walk over there but she didn't want to tempt fate. The way things were going, she'd probably trip on a paving slab and face-plant in the cake, rendering it unrecognisable.

*

Barney and Lois lived in a cottage around the bend on the way out of Heritage Cove. It had a low-hinged wooden gate at the front that led past the small box garden to the front door and, on one side, a row of hardy juniper trees that formed an archway in the middle and led through to a courtyard and the back of the house. Jade had driven down the track that ran alongside the cottage and parked up in the gravelled courtyard opposite the barn that came with the property and was the venue for the annual Wedding Dress Ball and, this year, Barney's wedding too. The cottage had beautiful surrounds, with rolling fields that gave a true sense of space even though The Street wasn't all that far away.

'This is a pleasant surprise,' Barney beamed, welcoming Jade inside the home he shared with the love of his life.

'Not intruding, am I?'

'Never,' he dismissed. 'My door is always open, everyone knows that.' And she could already hear voices as it was.

She went inside to find Lois chatting to Etna, who was sitting at the dining table as Lois busied herself making the tea. The kitchen and dining area as well as the lounge were all together in this open-plan arrangement Barney favoured. The cottage still had smaller proportions in other parts, but this area he liked this way because it was sociable. And that was Barney all over – a much-loved member of the village, he was always one to stop and talk to whoever he could.

'Cuppa?' Lois offered Jade.

'Not for me, thanks.' Cake box in her arms, guarding it protectively after it had already fallen victim to Linc's abuse, she turned her attentions to Etna. 'How are you?'

'Better for those glazed doughnuts you left for me. I never got a chance to thank you, I'm sorry, I found I had to dose up on painkillers for a few days.'

'I'm just glad to see you up and about. I'll bet the doughnuts speeded up your recovery,' she winked.

'Something like that.' She indicated her foot. 'It feels almost normal now but I'm still being careful. And after days holed up in my flat, Barney and Lois offered to put me up for a while. It's lovely to have the company. You know me, I like being around people.'

'We're enjoying it too,' Barney assured his guest. Lois had set down a cup of tea on a saucer in front of

Etna while Barney brought over a cup for her and himself. 'It's lucky she had Linc staying with her, otherwise who knows how long she might have been lying on the floor. Reminds me of when I had a fall and Harvey found me.' He gave a shudder. 'Getting old can be scary.'

'No need to be dramatic. I would've dragged myself to a phone,' said Etna with an eye roll. 'But Linc really has been wonderful. He's really stepped up. He always does.' She tried to sip her tea but it was much too hot. 'You know, that boy nursed his mum when she was sick; he looked after his dad too. He didn't deserve me and my woes as well,' said Etna, giving Jade an unexpected insight into Linc's character.

'He's a hard worker,' Barney approved.

'He's working hard on your bakery,' Etna smiled at Jade, 'and he's made a start up at the waffle shack, which was a surprise extra job. He's also been getting up at the crack of dawn to start at the tea rooms and darting between there and the bakery so he doesn't let any of us down. Poor Patricia had twenty tourists turn up this morning and she says she doesn't know what she would've done without Linc. It might have been easier if I'd been out of action in the autumn rather than peak summer season.'

Jade's insides had flipped not only at the mention of Linc's name but at hearing how he'd jumped in to help out wherever he could. It sounded as though it was something he never hesitated to do with his family, and it painted him in a whole new light. She cringed at how she'd gone right off at him earlier over an innocent mistake.

'More doughnuts?' Barney asked Jade, cutting into her thoughts, when he finally acknowledged the box she was clutching.

'Actually, no. I've brought along something I hope you'll enjoy a little more than doughnuts.' She briefly explained all about the course she'd been doing. 'Today, we got to make a cake of our choice and I decided to try a prototype of your wedding cake.'

Lois gasped. 'We get to see it beforehand?'

'And taste it, I hope,' said Barney.

'There's just one issue with it,' Jade hesitated. 'I added lots of intricate detail – buttercream roses and purple petunias I worked for hours on, some piping around the sides – but unfortunately someone cut a huge chunk out of the cake when I wasn't looking.'

'That's terrible,' cried Etna. 'I hope your course teacher reprimanded them and told them not to come back.'

'It wasn't anyone on the course.'

'Then who would do something so preposterous?' Etna asked, livid on Jade's behalf.

'It was Linc.' She explained the mix-up, the way Celeste had told him to help himself.

Barney began to laugh. 'I bet you gave him a good talking to.'

'I kind of yelled at him.' She looked at Etna and pulled a face. 'After everything you just told me, I feel terrible. It was probably the first time he'd sat down for a break all day.'

Etna swished away her concern. 'He's got a thick enough skin; he won't take it to heart.' She watched Jade for a split second until she said, 'Come on, let's see this cake.'

93

Jade opened up the box to a reception of gasps and congratulations. They all loved it and were more than impressed with her work, no matter whether there was a piece missing out of the cake or not.

'It's artistic,' Lois observed, regarding the gap where the snaffled slice had been.

'That's exactly what Celeste told me before she took charge and neatened it up.'

Etna chuckled. 'Patricia had to request Linc to please present the cake in the tea rooms a little more delicately. He was cutting off great hunks of sponge and dumping them on the plates, no care taken. I guess that's what happens when one minute you're working on a renovation and the next you're leaping in to serve delicate food.'

Now Jade felt even more guilty and as Lois and Etna chatted away about the cake, the sponge, the way it was decorated, the intricacy of the flower petals, Barney whispered to her, 'Etna has been driving that poor boy crazy.'

'Linc?'

'She's been calling him and texting him constantly to check things are running smoothly. Some people are house-proud, Etna is tea-room-proud. I reckon he was doing fine when she was sleeping on those painkillers, but since she became more with it, she's been non-stop. I suspect she's done the same to Patricia. We thought we'd have her here with us for a while and let everything settle, and she's good company for two oldies.'

Over a slice of cake each they talked more about the wedding and how the barn was going to be decorated for the big event.

'We're hoping for a gloriously sunny day so we can throw open the barn doors,' Lois told them, 'but if it's not, the inside will be just as beautiful with all the usual twinkly lights wound around posts and beams and strung across the tops of the walls. We'll have a string quartet followed by a livelier band, there'll be white linen hanging from the rafters to create the perfect cloud effect, and we're having plenty of fresh flowers.'

'We've already put in an order with the florist,' Barney confirmed. 'I'm told Valerie was delighted to hear we were ordering so many.'

'There'll be flowers on every table, every upturned barrel,' Lois cut in. 'And all the chairs will have big white bows at their backs. We still want hay bales dotted around too, just like when the Wedding Dress Ball runs every year.' She put a hand to Barney's shoulder, the significance of the annual event not lost with the preparations for the wedding. The ball was an event Barney had started to raise funds for the charity White Clover, which supported families after the death of a child. Barney and Lois had been estranged for years following a painful history and the loss of their baby son, Harry, and with the event such a fixture for the village, it had seemed the perfect venue and occasion to get remarried. The arrangements would honour what had gone before, the significance of the event would acknowledge what they'd had and lost and the future they'd solidified by coming together once again.

'We usually have a guestbook, so we'll do that again and keep it with all the others.' Barney tipped his head towards the bookcase that housed what looked like photograph albums standing in a row, each of their spines with a different year on it to represent the ball that had run that particular summer. 'Looking back over the years is a special thing to do, you know.'

'I'm sure it is,' Jade smiled.

'It's going to be wonderful,' Etna beamed. 'And this foot had better be one hundred per cent, as I'll be dancing, just like every other year.'

'Good for you,' said Lois before she thanked Jade yet again for bringing the cake over today. 'I feel spoiled already and I know – not that I needed any reassurance – that the guests are in for a real treat. I love being in the kitchen and cooking, but making fancy flowers that I could easily confuse with the real thing seems nigh on impossible to me. You have a great deal of talent.'

'You should see Nancy the demonstrator's work,' Jade replied. 'She assured me I'll be just as good with practice. But I'm thrilled you love the cake as it is.'

'Despite the chunk missing,' Etna grinned. Jade had a feeling she'd love it if Jade mentioned Linc's name again. She hadn't missed the look his auntie had given her, as though she was wondering if there might be something brewing between the pair.

Jade picked up her car keys. 'I'd better be off. I'm going to see Valerie and the baby.' Valerie worked in the florist set back from The Street on a side street beyond the pub and she'd had a baby two months ago. She'd been a wreck for the first six weeks. Her husband was back at work and doing long hours but her parents had been with her for the past fortnight and, as she'd told Jade, she now had her head straight and was ready for more visitors.

'How are they doing?' Barney piled the empty plates together and put them into the sink for washing. 'She looked like any new mother would when I saw her last – elated, strung out, happy but exhausted. We missed her when we went into the florist, and I hear she was disappointed that maternity leave means she won't be involved with the flowers for the wedding.'

'When I spoke to her yesterday she said she felt human so fingers crossed that's still the case by the time I get over there,' smiled Jade.

'Give her our best,' said Lois, already making Etna another cup of tea even though she'd taken long enough to finish the first. Perhaps between Lois and Barney they were determined to keep Etna so busy she didn't have a chance to even think about the tea rooms and get onto Linc. 'And take the rest of the cake, we've had our treat. I want to save myself for the real thing now.'

'I was going to leave it for you. Are you sure?'

'Of course.' She took the tea over to the table and sat with Etna.

'I'm sure Linc would love some more,' said Etna, watching Jade as she closed the box. 'It's a fine cake.'

'Talking of cake, I hear your lemon drizzle was a hit with Kenneth the other day,' said Lois. 'I saw him in The Street and he wouldn't stop going on about it.'

If Jade hadn't been watching Etna so closely she might have missed the glimmer of embarrassment masked quickly by her sharing of her recipe secrets rather than any focus on the man who perhaps wanted to tend to a lot more than his allotment.

Jade left them to it. Her temper had faded, they'd all loved the cake despite its missing piece, and she happily made her way over to Valerie's.

But her contentment dimmed the moment she stepped inside Valerie's home and the scene of domesticity greeted her – the steriliser steaming away, the freshly laundered Babygros in a pile on the arm of the sofa, the spongy wipe-clean change mat leaning against the sideboard – it reminded Jade that she might be successful in her work life and getting better all the time, making a real go of the business she ran with her sister, but her personal life was light years behind and only she could remedy that. If only it was as simple as taking a course, brushing up on skills and spreading the word.

'I've brought cake,' Jade announced as Valerie jostled baby Thomas against her shoulder.

'You're my hero, I'm starving,' Valerie smiled. Her dark brown hair was tugged into a loose ponytail but she looked relaxed and in control.

Jade found a knife but had no luck with plates.

Valerie handed her the baby. 'You take him, it does him good to get used to others apart from me. I'll find plates and sort the cake. Are you eating some?'

'Why not, but just a small slice.'

'I, on the other hand,' said Valerie after she found a couple of plates and picked up the knife, 'can eat a wedge. Do you realise how many calories you burn breastfeeding? I'm permanently hungry – I can't stop looking in the fridge or the cupboards for what's next. I'm eating way more than normal – the baby sucks it all out of me. And I've been expressing too, making up bottles so my mum can give him a feed when she's here, or anyone else for that matter.'

'Are you fretting about leaving him when you return to work?'

'A little bit,' Valerie admitted. 'I know he'll get used to being without me. I'm torn between wanting him to be fine and wanting him to scream the house down because only I will do. That sounds a little crazy, I know.'

'Not crazy, just like a new mum, I suppose.'

'I'm disappointed to miss out on the flower arranging for Barney's wedding, but I'll be raring to go by the time Melissa and Harvey tie the knot,' she beamed.

Valerie perched on the sofa and enjoyed her slice of cake at Jade's insistence. Thomas was happy enough, she could keep hanging on to him for a bit. And he smelt better than cake. She inhaled his uniquely babyish smell from the top of his head, felt the softness of the whorls of hair the same colour as his mum's. And when Valerie had finished her cake and asked Jade if she'd mind holding him a bit longer while she nipped to the bathroom, Jade had no problem with that.

As the girls chatted, Jade enjoyed her slice of cake and they kept Thomas entertained on the mini gym with its rattles and mirrors and scrunchy pieces he found so interesting. Jade felt a tug inside of her that it wasn't so long ago she thought she'd have all this. She and Dario had fallen hard for one another, both of them head over heels. She'd thought they were on the exact same page. But either they weren't or they'd moved onto different chapters, hers here in England, his in Italy.

When she came back to England Jade had thrown herself into her work, telling herself it didn't matter, that it was a holiday romance, and that maybe, as it was for Celeste, the focus of their business would be enough.

But it wasn't. She'd known it and it was moments like this, as she scooped Thomas up when he became fractious and he settled in her arms, smiling up at her and squeezing her finger with his tiny fist, that reminded her she wanted and needed more. Her heart ached for what might have been, what could have been, had she and Dario handled things differently. And her brain jumped up a gear knowing that, at almost thirty-four, if she wanted a child of her own, she might not be able to wait for the perfect man to come along.

But she was smart enough to know there was more than one way to have a baby.

Chapter Seven

The work at the bakery had been full on. The new flooring was laid the day before yesterday – durable, non-slip, and its black-and-white-tiled effect in keeping with the olde-worlde feel the owners wanted. And today the final coat of paint was going on the walls.

As well as working at the bakery, Linc had been going to and from the tea rooms to help Patricia out. Etna wasn't around at the moment. Lois had driven her down to stay with her brother Joseph and it sounded as though they were having a great time. He'd taken her to the pub, they'd managed a couple of countryside strolls and they'd fed the ducks at the pond Linc remembered standing by as a little boy.

Linc had settled into a pattern, balancing time between the bakery, the tea rooms and the waffle shack, although he wouldn't be sorry to see Etna's return and the completion of this place. Holding down three jobs was too much even for someone who wouldn't mind not having to think about their own life.

'When are they fitting your dentures?' Harvey asked Linc as he passed him the pot of oyster-white paint. It was specialist paint, hygiene-coated or something or other, so if food did come into contact with it, it could be wiped clean very easily.

Linc frowned. 'Dentures?'

'You, disappearing off all the time to the dentist. You've got to be having serious issues given the amount of time you spend at the surgery.'

'It isn't just the dentist.' Linc had to think quickly. 'I've been at the tea rooms a lot, remember.' He prised the paint lid open with the tip of a screwdriver.

'Yeah, but you had another hour and a half for an appointment yesterday. It's not a problem,' he added quickly in an effort not to sound as if he was coming down heavy on his employee. 'I'm just wondering what the issue is.'

Linc suspected he was going to have to start thinking of some new excuses. 'That's the last visit I'll need.' He made a mental note to make it a bank appointment next time, or perhaps a trip to help his dad out – maybe even interviewing at a school about a permanent position.

Harvey didn't pry any further because there was a knock at the back door to announce the arrival of the display cabinets that were to go in the front of the bakery along with the natural-wood shelving and units that had already been installed against the wall. Harvey went off to help the delivery men bring them inside and Linc reminded him where the plastic sheeting was. They'd need to cover these new cabinets up so no paint could possibly make its way near the gleaming glass or highly polished chrome.

'Has it been nice getting Etna off your back for a while?' Harvey asked when he came through to the kitchen area again.

'I feel guilty saying it, but yes. And more than that, I think she needed the time away from here, she needed a rest even though she'd never admit it. She really doubts the tea rooms can ever survive without her. It's why she's never taken much of a holiday before. I get it, and

I'm sure you do – wanting to control your own business. She knows she's responsible for its success or failure but that doesn't mean she doesn't need time out.'

'Is she close to your dad?' Harvey was busy adjusting one of the drawers below a section of the kitchen bench; it wasn't sliding in and out quite as smoothly as it should be.

'She is, and this has been concentrated time together for them both. I wondered if Dad would find her too bossy, but it seems he's enjoying every second. Puts my mind at rest anyway.' He paused after rolling the paint up one section of the wall. It wasn't a vibrant colour but it wasn't stark either – the girls wanted a balance, something fresh and bright that would carry through to the front of shop, which would be painted in the same shade. 'Dad was sick a while back. He's recovered now, but there was a time when I wasn't sure he would. Etna has always felt bad about not being able to help out much, meaning the responsibility fell on me, but I never minded.'

'I'm sure you didn't. If something happened with my mum, I'd be there for her too. And Barney, for that matter.' He didn't need to explain the connection there. Barney had been more of a father to Harvey than his dad had ever been – a dad who, according to Etna, had been violent and put the family through hell.

'I think it was Etna's guilt that made her leap at the chance to get me here to the Cove.' Linc stepped onto the ladder to reach the top of the wall with the paint. 'Not that I mind, it's been good to spend time with her and do something totally different.'

'Hey, no arguments from me, you saved me from letting Jade and Celeste down when I failed to manage all of this myself.'

The painting took most of the day and, luckily for Linc, Harvey's girlfriend Melissa stopped by at the same time that Patricia called needing an extra pair of hands in the tea rooms, and she headed next door instead of him. She probably gelled more with the customers too and had a lot more chitchat than he ever did.

By the time they'd finished the final coat on the walls Linc's body was crying out for a long soak in the bath, but with plans to meet Harvey and Daniel at the pub this evening, he settled on a shower so he was in and out of the flat in record time.

*

Harvey bought the first round at The Copper Plough. They asked Benjamin if he could join them but the chef laughed at the suggestion, asking whether they'd seen the heaving beer garden filled with hungry punters.

They took the table at the back of the pub near the door that was open to let a draft come through. The evening was fine and sunny and perfect for outside but with the boys having all been on their feet all day, none of them were keen on standing-room only when they peered out the door and saw it was just as busy as Benjamin claimed.

'The waffle shack is doing steady business,' Daniel told them, 'but I'm looking forward to getting that back area sorted.'

'Is that a hint to go faster?' his brother asked him.

'Always,' said Daniel. 'Just kidding. I know the bakery has taken up most of your time. I just hate turning down bookings or telling people I don't have space. Some are happy with takeaway, but not all.'

Linc set down his pint after a few refreshing glugs. 'Etna's back tomorrow night – Dad's driving her up here – so I'll be down a job. It means I can put in a lot more time at the waffle shack instead, and we're almost done with the bakery.' It felt strange that things were coming to a close so soon. He'd be sad to leave the Cove behind. Who'd have thought he'd fit in so easily and be out drinking with locals after a few short weeks as though he'd known them for years.

'You'll lose your bachelor pad,' Harvey pointed out.

'It's hardly that, but I can't deny it's been great having my own space again – even though I'm too knackered to really appreciate it half the time.'

'What's the plan for you after this?' Harvey set down his pint. 'Back to school in September? You do supply teaching, don't you?'

'That's right. It's suited me up until now. I appreciated the anonymity of different schools for a while.'

'You teach music, right?' Daniel asked.

'Yeah, love it.'

Daniel tore open a packet of peanuts. 'Then you might be interested in what I heard today. Jane Wideman, head teacher at the nearest secondary school to the Cove, was in the shack and completely stressed out. She told me her head of music just informed her he won't be returning for the autumn term. He's going to live in Wales and run a B&B. He's almost sixty, so it's a case of semi-retirement rather than anything sinister at the school to trigger a sudden departure.'

'Do you think he realises that running a B&B will probably make teaching a bunch of rowdy teens look easy?' Linc laughed.

Harvey waved across at his mum, Carol, who'd come in with Lois for a pub meal and a chat. 'You've got a good point there.'

'So, what do you think?' Daniel probed.

'Of applying?' Linc contemplated the suggestion with another gulp of his pint. 'It's a big step. I wouldn't be quite as close to Dad's place if I came here.'

'Perhaps if you come here your dad will visit Etna more, you never know. And you're only an hour or so away from him.'

'True.'

'Why don't you have a chat with Jane?' Daniel pulled out his wallet, ready to get in another round. 'I can get in touch with her and pass on your number if you like.'

'It's worth talking with her,' Harvey encouraged. 'Nothing to say you have to take the job if it doesn't sound like what you want.'

'OK, pass on my number, we'll see what happens.'

When Daniel went off to get a round in and Harvey chatted with Lois and his mum, Linc sent his dad a message suggesting he stay a few days after bringing Etna home tomorrow. Perhaps it would give him a bit of a change of scene too, and it would be good to spend time with his dad here in the Cove.

'I've had another thought,' Harvey told him when he returned from the bar. 'If you do consider this job, a move this way – unless you're thinking of commuting, that is – then Melissa has a cottage she rents out. The current tenants are a family who've bought their own place and are moving out pretty soon. The cottage does need a lick of paint and a bit of maintenance but I can take care of all that. And it's a nice place, reasonably priced.'

Linc wasn't so used to everything falling into place quite so neatly. 'Thanks for the heads up, certainly worth thinking about,' he agreed.

They chatted amongst themselves; Harvey recounted his days at the very school they were suggesting Linc apply to and Daniel had plenty of stories too. And before long it was Daniel who asked Linc about his real reasons for heading to the Cove and working through the entire summer holidays. 'Didn't you want to go off somewhere exotic, make the most of your long break?' he wondered.

'I needed a distraction.' Linc turned a beer mat over and over beneath his palm. 'I've been keeping myself busy for a while now rather than actually try to be a bit more settled or move my life forwards in any way. It sounds dramatic, but I'm not sure where I'm heading.'

'You want a change of career?' Harvey asked.

'No, not at all. I like teaching. But my head was all over the place with Mum, then with Dad, and then with other stuff.'

'Must be a girl involved,' Daniel deduced.

'There's always a girl involved,' added Harvey. 'Take me and Melissa as an example, we've had our problems, then you and Lucy went through it.'

'Let's just say she needed a little convincing I was worth getting to know. I was a bit of a bad boy in my past,' Daniel grinned, before telling Linc how he and a group of friends had once broken into the tea rooms. 'We didn't do any damage, just sat and had tea. But Etna caught us red-handed.'

'Don't tell me, she let you off with a warning.'

'Are you kidding? The police came,' he added to Linc's astonishment. 'Scared the life out of me – she was furious. She didn't press charges but she did make us wash up everything we'd used and we had to pay to repair the damage to the door. But it could've been worse. In my defence, it was a long time ago.'

'Etna loves him now,' Harvey added for good measure. 'Especially after the apology and the free waffles when he opened up the shack. Those went down a treat.'

'She's a good sort, your auntie,' Daniel nodded.

Conversation stalled and Harvey turned the talk back the way it came, to why Linc had felt the need to take on extra jobs through what should be a summer of rest before the new term.

'Mine might be a story for another time,' said Linc.

'Come on, we're all mates now, what are you running from?' Daniel sat back, enjoying his pint but ready to listen.

Linc supposed it might be good to finally get it all off his chest with people who didn't know him all that well and so he found himself sharing details about him and Orla, how they'd been together for a while and everything was comfortable, right up until it wasn't.

'I thought that one day it might get serious,' Linc told them, 'but I wasn't at that point and I know now that that should've been a warning sign that I was never going to be. I should've told her that at the time, but I didn't. I stayed with her, and I didn't see how serious she'd become about us. More so than I realised.'

'And so, you ran,' said Harvey.

'It was more than that.' He toyed with the beer mat again, its rounded edges already torn where someone else had probably done the same, perhaps trying to share a story with someone else as they did so. 'I was about to finish things between us when she got pregnant.'

Harvey stopped drinking and Daniel's pint didn't quite reach his mouth. 'Yeah, that'll add a complication.'

'I would've stepped up to my responsibility even though it was wrong when I wasn't entirely sure I loved her enough.' He kept his voice low in the busy pub. 'She lost the baby at nine weeks.' Even though he hadn't been ready for a baby and wasn't even sure he wanted to be with Orla, he never would've wished what happened on her. 'She was understandably devastated, desperately sad, and I did my best to support her but I didn't know how to. She kept pushing me away and in the end she went off to stay with her friend in America.

'She didn't contact me at all and part of me was angry she hadn't let me in, but I thought perhaps she realised she didn't really want to be with me long-term either. When she came back, she came to see me. All she kept saying was that her head was really messed up and she hadn't been herself before she left. She wanted to try for another baby. She wasn't really hearing what I was saying, that I didn't think we should be together. It was crazy, it was like anything I said filtered through her mind and disintegrated into dust as though the words had never been there at all.

'My dad was pretty sick at the same time that this was going on and my life was all over the place, with trying to look after him and keep working. Supply teaching was a godsend, it let me work in stints around when Dad was having better days, take time off when I needed to. Orla started to turn up at Dad's house when I was staying there, sometimes when I wasn't but didn't answer my own front door. She'd come at all hours and hammer on the door and she didn't let up for a long while.'

He paused when someone squeezed past their table to get outside. 'Eventually Orla came to talk to me and revealed she'd been seeing the doctor and was on medication. By that point I was angry, which was probably more to do with the stress over Dad than her. But it was on that visit she told me she had to be honest and she admitted that when she'd got pregnant with our baby, she'd done it on purpose. She'd lost a baby five

108

years previously with a man she was engaged to and I think she was so desperate to find someone and have a child that when we got together, she saw it as her chance.'

Linc shook his head and stared into his pint. 'I couldn't blame her entirely because I saw how much she was hurting, but what she did left its mark, it stopped me being willing to trust quite as easily as I once did.' He sat back, hands on his thighs. 'So, there you have it, my life in a tattered nutshell.'

'You really should play the violin, you know,' said Harvey, and it was his comment that released the tension, at last had Linc laughing.

'Yeah, it's pretty woeful, I'll admit. My mate Toby thinks I should take a leaf out of his book and sleep around to avoid complications; even my dad thinks I'm existing, not living.'

'Has there been anyone since?' Daniel asked.

'I dated someone for a couple of months before I came here, but it didn't work out. No idea why.' He had, but he wanted to stop the conversation there. No way was he ready to share that much personal information about himself. Perhaps another time, maybe never.

'So, you're in the Cove to escape,' Harvey concluded.

'Not the way I'd put it, but I suppose you're right. Thanks to you and Daniel, and I suppose Etna, manual labour is keeping me busy – and this, well, it's good to be out and about with people my own age. I'm feeling better than I have in a long while.' His emotions had taken a battering over the years and he'd always found it hard to take time to focus on that side of things. Strength had only ever made sense to him in a physical realm, not any other.

109

'And thanks to you,' said Harvey, 'the bakery is looking grand. The girls can't wait to start getting it ready for opening.'

'Talking of girl trouble,' said Daniel to Linc, 'I hear you might have clashed with Jade again.'

'You heard about that?' He hadn't seen Jade since he wrecked her cake. She'd avoided him as much as possible and he'd been far too busy to stop, let alone be sidetracked by a beautiful woman.

'Yeah,' Daniel grinned, 'and don't look now but she just walked in.'

Linc didn't dare turn around. He had his back to the door, so could avoid her at least. The last thing he wanted was her having a go at him in a pub full of people.

Harvey was laughing. 'Celeste told us you'd been filling your face with the wedding cake prototype she'd slaved over all day and you were sitting there in the garden enjoying it until she found you.' Daniel and Linc couldn't help but smile either. 'Did it at least taste good?'

'It did until she yelled at me.'

Harvey checked his wallet for cash. 'I could do with a bowl of chips. Interested?'

Linc nodded and stayed where he was while Harvey made for the bar and Daniel went to use the bathroom.

He didn't have to wonder long whether Jade would spot him because the others had only just left him and there she was, sitting in the seat next to him, looking stunning in a simple pair of slim jeans with a loose cream shirt, slightly sheer, enough that he could make out a lacy camisole beneath. His eyes were drawn to her neck and the delicate silver chain with a cupcake decoration on it.

'Come to yell at me some more?' he asked before she could get a word in. He loved how she scrunched up her nose and the row of freckles went out of shape when he asked the question.

'I've come to apologise for overreacting.'

'I deserved it. You'd spent all that time and effort on something that I have to say was amazing in both taste and appearance. And I'm not saying that to get you on side either. I'm sorry I stuffed my face before I thought to check it was OK to dive into a cake that, to be fair, didn't look anything like leftovers or something someone might have whipped up to share around. In my defence, I was salivating when I saw it.'

His description got her grinning. 'Say more things like that and I'll go easy on you from now on.' Before he could add anything else, she said, 'Etna told me how much help you've been to her and that you'd been working flat out all day.'

'Don't let me off the hook because you feel sorry for me. I don't need pity.'

'Celeste neatened the cake up and I took it over to Barney's place anyway – that's when I saw Etna. Both he and Lois were thrilled with the results, so no harm done.'

'I tell you what. If I'm ever offered cake again, I'll check I'm hacking into the right one before I help myself.'

'Deal.'

Melissa and Lucy pulled over another table to join theirs as Harvey and Daniel returned, Celeste grabbed some more chairs and soon the group were all sitting together and talking as though they'd known one another for years. They demolished a couple of bowls of chips between them, drinks flowed and conversation soon turned to the bakery after Lucy arrived to join them.

'I hear you chose a name,' said Lucy after she'd kissed Daniel hello.

'We did,' Jade smiled. 'And the sign is finished, it looks amazing – dark-wood edges, a cream background with a type of cracked effect to make it look old like so many of the homes and businesses in the Cove, and they've added in an illustration at the bottom.'

'I'm glad you're keeping the frontage the way it's always been,' said Lucy. 'It's a bit like why I kept some of the things the same at my place. I kept the solid fuel forge in my workshop because I didn't want to strip out all the character from a place that had been around for so long, but at the same time I made it my own with my work on the shelves and the new sign out front. People like some change, but you need to hold on to what's special.'

'Lucy's Blacksmithing is a real part of the Cove,' Jade told Linc, prompting Lucy to tell him a bit about the business, how she wasn't a farrier but wanted to keep the word *blacksmith* as part of the business name, to maintain tradition.

'Did you make the sign yourself?' Linc had seen it when he first arrived and Etna gave him the low-down on the local businesses and residents. Lucy's Blacksmithing, on the opposite side of the bend to the Heritage Inn when you came into the Cove from one direction, had a sign swinging from two chains attached to a bracket that was fixed to the workshop. The flat above could be accessed from steps leading up from The Street, or by going through the workshop, but the blacksmith's business itself had the one entrance door, to one side of the sign.

'I sure did. And I also made the trellis for the pub.'

'I'm impressed.' He'd seen that too, the intricate work that had gone into something that all the locals now got to admire with its clambering purple and white flowers. 'I'm feeling like the odd one out now though.'

'Why?' Melissa pondered.

'You all have your own businesses – waffles, blacksmithing, a bakery…' he pointed to Harvey next, 'and you're in the home-renovations business. I'm not sure I'll fit in unless I start something myself. Even Melissa is giving up her job to go into business with Harvey, I hear.'

'She's got an eye for it,' Lucy claimed. 'She helped me choose colours for my flat, which hadn't stood the test of time at all. Even the ugly gas heater in the lounge went and instead I have a beautiful log burner with a gorgeous varnished shelf above that Melissa found for me online.'

'You wait,' Melissa smiled at Linc. 'You might doubt whether you'll fit in here, but Heritage Cove has a way of drawing you in and never letting you go.' She held up her drink in a toast. 'You have been warned, Lincoln!'

He rolled his eyes at the full address but took it in good humour.

Harvey hugged Melissa to him and kissed her forehead. The pair were getting married at Christmas and Linc had never seen two people so in love – although Lucy and Daniel weren't far off, the way they couldn't keep their hands off each other. He thought again about the photograph that had fallen out of Jade's bag that day and wondered who the guy was, whether she was still pining for him every time she was in the company of couples like they were now.

'Have you been down to the cove yet?' Celeste asked him, interrupting his thoughts.

'No, I haven't had a chance.' His admission was met with cries of disbelief as though he'd somehow wronged each one of them. 'Etna did tell me it was a sight to behold. But I've been busy working three jobs, remember.'

'I don't think I've ever gone more than a few days without going down there since I arrived in Heritage Cove,' Jade told him, and he wasn't sure whether it was the drinks or the disbelief that he hadn't seen it for himself, but she went on to suggest there was no time like the present. Palms flat on the wooden table, she added decisively, 'Let's all take a walk down there now. It's even better at night.'

'Too late for me,' said Harvey, arm around Melissa and ready to set off home.

'Me too,' said Celeste when she returned from taking a couple of empty glasses to the bar and got the gist of the conversation.

They began to file out and Daniel and Lucy were next to admit they were beat and a beach walk would have to wait. And when they stepped out of the front entrance and made their way down the path, passing between the iron lamp-posts, Linc said, 'Looks like it's just you and me then.'

But Jade didn't answer and so he said, 'I suppose it is pretty late. Perhaps I'll leave it until tomorrow.'

She spun round more quickly than he suspected she intended and they both stopped on the pavement. 'It's beautiful at night and I'm happy to show you. I could do with the fresh air; I didn't even make it out for a walk today.'

He couldn't believe his luck and his heart went against all of his instincts not to get involved, not to leave himself open to any more hurt, when he said, 'Then that's settled.'

They were still looking at each other when Celeste interrupted as she walked back to them both as they lagged behind. 'Do you have a key?'

Jade nodded and they kept walking. Daniel and Lucy crossed over to go to Lucy's place, Harvey and Melissa were next to say goodnight as they turned down the lane to go to Tumbleweed House, and when they were almost at the archway that separated the tea rooms and the bakery and led down to the cottage at the rear, Celeste told Jade she wouldn't wait up and waved them goodbye.

'And then there were two,' Linc breathed into the night air. He looked up into the blackness of the sky, the stars twinkling by now, a crescent moon fragmented by a few wisps of passing cloud. 'It's a nice night, and warm. But I honestly don't have to see the cove tonight, I can wait. I don't want you to feel obliged.'

When she smiled her green eyes twinkled with the yellow glow from the nearby street lamp. 'I promise I'm not just doing it for you. Going down there clears my head and it's way better when there's nobody else around.' She gulped as though she'd just realised her remark sounded a little suggestive and that she might want them to be alone as much as he was starting to.

'Lead the way,' he said, wishing he could put an arm around her and hold her close.

They crossed over and, past the chapel, took the track that had hedges in some places and brambles that loomed taller than he was in others. The moonlight above was just enough for now although he was glad

115

someone else was here to be a guide. He knew a bigger beach was further on out of the village but he'd heard plenty about the cove itself and the stretch of sand and sea that locals favoured because of its relative seclusion owing to the questionable walk to get down there.

They gingerly made their way to the very end of the track, where they turned to the right and followed it down towards the sands.

'Tourists still come this way occasionally,' Jade explained.

He stumbled on a large stick he hadn't seen. 'Do any come back?'

Her laughter told him she was as happy to be here alone with him as he was with her. 'It's fine when you know the way but most don't want to trek down there with inflatables, picnic baskets and without their cars.'

They reached the part-sand-covered steps bordered with a rickety wooden handrail that Jade warned him not to bother holding on to if he wanted to be saved. 'It needs replacing but locals know the deal. Nobody would ever put their hand on it for balance, put it that way. I think the council are repairing it early October, but don't tell any tourists, we want them to stay away as long as possible.'

'I'll bet.' He kind of understood why. It was secluded, secret, an escape tonight. It was impressive even when he almost tripped and had to wonder how far he'd fall if he wasn't careful. He got out his phone and used his torch app to light the way until at last they were at the bottom and Jade jumped off the final step onto the sand.

The night breeze caught her hair as she turned back to look at him. 'Come on, you wuss!'

'Hey, you wouldn't say that if I fell.' He'd wanted to check how far she'd jumped but it was a pathetic foot at most so he put his phone away and followed after her.

They walked across the sands, their feet sinking into the soft surface and slowing their pace as the sand spilled into his shoes. Before they reached the water's edge, he followed suit when she sat down. The cool grains beneath them allowed wiggle room to get comfortable as they looked out at the wide oval coastal inlet with a sea as calm as he felt being down here.

'It's a hidden gem,' he readily admitted. 'Thanks for volunteering to bring me down here.' He might not have ever believed its beauty if he hadn't seen it for himself.

'My pleasure. Didn't look like anyone else was going to offer. Maybe I felt sorry for you.'

His laughter rippled across the water. 'Or maybe you plan to drown me in return for stealing a piece of your cake.' A whoosh of waves as they crashed on the shore and then receded to do it all over again soon grabbed their attention. It was soothing, mesmerising, a way to calm the soul. 'Looking at the sea makes me think of freedom, of seeing the world, travelling far and wide.'

'I'd highly recommend it.'

'Maybe one day I'll take an extra-long holiday, go somewhere exotic. How long were you and your sister travelling for?'

'We went for a year.'

He whistled through his teeth. 'I don't remember Etna telling me the bakery was closed for any length of time. It's the sort of thing that would create a local outcry.'

She laughed. 'You're right. We got the previous owner on board so as not to upset the locals and she ran the place in our absence. I think it was like a final goodbye for her before she moved on.'

'And did you plan your travels or wing it?'

'It was mostly planned, but not always. We worked some of the time so that dictated part of the route as well as giving us some cash to fund our wanderlust. We started in Paris and fully embraced the well-trodden tourist routes – the Eiffel Tower, Champs-Elysées, Louvre, Place Dauphine and Arc de Triomphe. From there we ventured further around France to some of the smaller yet no-less-beautiful places.'

'Now, France I have been to,' he said. 'I once did a cycle ride in the Champagne region. It was stunning.'

'It really is.' She grinned. 'Can't say I'd want to do the bike ride though.'

When she smiled at him, he felt the connection between them both and hoped she did too. As much as he'd resisted getting close to her, or to anyone for that matter, he couldn't help his feelings. 'It wasn't so bad. We got glasses of champagne at every stop.'

'No way, that doesn't sound very sensible, you'd dehydrate!'

'What can I tell you? I haven't always been so practical and responsible as I am now.' His dad's words rang in his ears again. He'd forgotten what it was like to have fun – his dad had said that to him once, out of concern that his son had gone from carefree to someone who had been so on hand to help and save them all that he'd forgotten how to act his true age. Now, watching Jade's face come alive with the memories, he wondered if perhaps his dad had a point. He was only in his early thirties, way too young to be avoiding moving on with his life as though he was scared at what came next, that it might hurt him even more than what had gone before.

Jade had taken off her sandals and dug her toes into the sand. 'Give me cheese, wine and grapes rather than a bike, although Celeste and I did hire those bicycles with a big basket on front while we were over there – we'd cycle country lanes and pick up baguettes and cheese, as well as the odd bottle of wine. It was a freedom I can't explain. We found some idyllic villages that way and locals were so welcoming, many of them keen to show us that France was about more than the tourist hotspots. We found the most exquisite patisseries and bakeries, ate the finest pillowy chocolate pastries.' She closed her eyes in memory and he was hooked listening to her, addicted to the fascination of it all. 'We moved from France on to Spain, we worked with a family who needed home help and childcare. We ate tapas, learned to cook traditional paella with our native hosts in Valencia, and we hiked through some of the most spectacular terrain in Switzerland and Austria.' She locked eyes with him. 'I'm rambling, aren't I?'

'I'm happy listening.'

She shifted uncomfortably but looking out at the water had her calm again. 'All this talking about travelling is making me yearn to see some of those places again.'

He nudged her with his elbow when she quietened, perhaps hesitant to go on. 'Tell me more.'

She filled him in on the café culture in Vienna, explained how they'd fulfilled their curiosities in Krakow learning the history neither of them had had much interest in at school. 'And then we really let loose hopping between the Greek islands, which was an unplanned detour we squeezed in last minute when a job we had lined up fell through. Or at least it did on our part, less than twenty-four hours after it started, when we realised the family didn't need a home help.' A smile crept across her face. 'The couple were looking for some kind of arrangement.'

'You mean…sex?'

'Yep.' She began to giggle. 'It soon became obvious they wanted us to indulge in a whole lot more than washing bed sheets or cleaning their home while they worked.'

'Did you report them?'

'No, we'd found the job responding to a noticeboard advert locally and to be honest I think they would've had us work there without the added extras if we'd just told them no. But by then Celeste wasn't having any of it, she said she wouldn't sleep at night thinking Rupert would creep into her bed.' She was laughing uncontrollably now. 'I was more scared of Ursula than him – I'm pretty sure she was a man beneath the kaftan – but whatever, it wasn't something we were interested in so we got out of there.'

'And were the Greek islands as amazing as we're led to believe?'

'Better. You know all those whitewashed buildings you see in the brochures? It's exactly like that, with trails of deep-purple bougainvillea and so much sunshine.'

'Where did you go after that?'

'Germany was next. We saw castles, swathes of land so vast it was like being in a fairy tale. And then, finally, it was Italy.' She cleared her throat.

'And the discovery of coffee.'

'Something like that.' She scooped up sand into one hand and let it fall between her fingers. 'But it worked out for the best when Etna wanted to be the one to install the coffee machine at the tea rooms rather than us at the bakery. She loves her machine these days. I don't think she realised what a disservice she was doing by serving up instant coffee to her regulars.'

Linc laughed. 'She does like to keep everyone happy. She's got to know people's orders too. Some guy came in earlier and all she said was "Good afternoon, Kenneth, flat white?".'

'It's nice she remembers, it's a real personal touch that makes people come back time and time again. And talking of Kenneth,' she smiled, 'I think Etna may well have a soft spot for him.'

He looked across at her. By now he'd relaxed onto one forearm, legs outstretched. 'Is that right?'

'Don't mention it, I think she's a bit embarrassed. And I might be reading way too much into it.'

'I won't say a thing. But good for her, she deserves to have more than just her business.' Jade looked away and he hoped she didn't think he was talking about her too. 'Where did you go in Italy?'

'Venice mainly. And, yes,' she said before he asked more, 'it's as spectacular as we're led to believe.'

'I've heard it's overrun with tourists.'

'Yes, that too unfortunately, but it didn't ruin its beauty.'

When she didn't elaborate any further about Italy in the same way that she had with the other places, he didn't push it. It felt too good to be here with her and he didn't want to scare her off. 'It sounds like the trip of a lifetime.'

'It really was. We left travelling very late, Celeste and I, and then it became a case of doing it now or never...and I didn't like the sound of never.'

'It must take all of your time, running your own business. It doesn't leave much time for a personal life.'

121

She hesitated a fraction of a second, enough to tell him either there was more to her story than he knew, or that she would prefer him to mind his own business. 'Not much, no.'

'So, what made you two come to the Cove?' He decided steering the subject away from Italy might be the best way to avoid having her clam up.

'Listen to you,' she said grinning, 'saying "the Cove" already.'

'When in Rome…' Oops, another Italy reference he should be avoiding. 'What made you come here though?'

'We were in London, both working for law firms, a big mortgage each, and one night over a bottle of wine we admitted to each other that while we liked the pay check at the end of the month, it wasn't where our passions lay. We'd been dreaming of running a cake shop since we were young girls. I don't know what ignited it apart from our gran baking with us after school for something to do. She was always a keen baker and I guess she passed that on to the both of us. Celeste joked that night over wine that we should give up our jobs and get on with it, open a bakery, live life on the edge.'

'So you did.'

'No, not quite. It was almost another three years before we took the plunge. We took our time looking into what it might actually involve. We looked at premises on and off but nothing felt right. And then we both came to the natural conclusion that we wanted to get away from the city. We also began to talk about travel and we'd started to make tentative plans when the bakery here came up for sale. We couldn't let it slip out of our grasp. It was the change we wanted, more affordable than anything in or nearer to London, and the

122

thought of living so close to the sea made us feel we'd be able to put down roots. So, we grabbed it while we could. If the previous owner hadn't agreed to step in, we wouldn't have gone travelling as we planned, but she did and so we got to do both. I'm glad, though, because travelling allowed us to really think about the vision we had for the bakery, it allowed us to alter the menu after months of stepping back and researching in person or online and to really discuss it at length in a way we might not have done if we'd been here and leapt in with both feet.'

'It sounds as though it all worked out.'

'Yeah…' Her voice trailed off and again he wondered whether there was something he was missing.

'Daniel told me there's a job going at the school,' he said to change the focus.

She plucked a shell from the sand. Her attention drifted between him and the sea. 'Are you thinking of applying for the job?'

'I might do. The music teacher is leaving and Harvey said he'd put me in touch with the head teacher.'

'That'll be Jane,' Jade smiled. 'She comes into the bakery often. I did her niece's birthday cake earlier this year, lovely lady. I think the school went into special measures for a time but since she took over, she's turned it around. They're classed as outstanding now.'

'Good to know. So, you'd send your children there?'

She frowned. 'I don't have any.'

'Obviously. But if you did…'

'If I did, yes, the local school would be a fine place to send them.'

She seemed a bit bewildered by his question, and quite rightly. It was weird asking her something like that and he wished sometimes he wouldn't think out loud. It didn't always help.

With the sounds of the sea all around, the air fresh and not another soul in sight, he didn't mind being down at the cove one bit. And while he was putting his foot in his big mouth, he figured he'd ask, 'Do you think you might've once had kids with the guy in the photo?'

She was quick to look at him but not so quick to answer. 'It was only a photo,' she said eventually. He sensed a sarcastic comment or a none-of-your-business remark had been on the tip of her tongue before she decided against it.

'That you carry in your bag.' He shrugged. 'People don't generally do that unless that person is significant.'

She hesitated before telling him, 'At one time, yes, I think I would've had a family with him.'

'What's his name?'

'Does it matter? It wasn't meant to be, that's all.' Another wave crashed against the shore and fizzed away. 'So, you're seriously thinking you might move here permanently?'

Nice change of subject but he'd go with it. 'It's something to consider. I'm kind of hoping my dad might think about it too.' The thought had only come into his head tonight, down here on the beach with thoughts of his dad coming for a visit and experiencing the Cove for himself.

'Do you think he would?'

'Possibly. He's content where he is now but I know he's missing company. He and Etna have got along better than I would've ever imagined these past few days.' He began to chuckle. 'Honestly, you should listen to them. When one is on the phone the other can't shut

124

up in the background, it's as though they're picking up from when they were little.'

'That's nice. It sounds like what I have with Celeste. I mean, going into business with a friend or a relation isn't for everyone but it's working out well for us. We have the odd run-in but on the whole it works well.' She seemed way more relaxed talking about work than anything verging on personal.

'And she's happy with the direction you're going in with the cake side of things?'

'Very. I think the different parts of the business will help us have a little bit of it for ourselves.'

'It sounds the perfect arrangement.'

He lay flat on his back on the sand and looked up at the sky. 'I could fall asleep here.' When she said nothing he added, 'Try it. Lie down next to me and look at the stars. You keep going on about this place and how great it is at night, looking at the sky is all part of it.'

She relented and lay down, a waft of citrusy shampoo mixing with the salty tang of the sea as she settled mere inches from him. 'I think this place has hidden powers.' She nudged him when he sniggered. 'Melissa was the one who put me onto it. It was apparently her go-to space over the years right from when she was young. I don't often get to come down in the day with the business so busy.'

'I might need to come down again, in the light next time. It's way too dangerous otherwise.'

'You get used to it.' She sighed. 'It's different down here at night with only the sea to listen to.' He could hear the smile in her voice. 'And you, of course.'

'And being here with me is a bad thing?'

She turned her head to face him, bringing them so close he could feel her breath on his cheek. 'I'm not sure yet…'

Neither of them was looking at the sky anymore. He was looking deep into green eyes, at dilated pupils. He was taking in the elegant planes of her face, the way wisps of hair fell across high cheekbones and onto soft lips before lifting slightly every time the wind found them.

Jade was easy company, they talked properly, and despite some of her misgivings, he could feel a trust building between them. He almost felt ready to confide in her. The last girl he'd been involved with after the split with Orla had lost interest when he told her what he was doing, what he saw as a good deed and as helping. She'd not only thought he was a weirdo but told him as much when she said they could no longer see each other. She suggested he had psychological problems, even recommended he see a counsellor. The remarks had niggled him even though he knew them not to be true. He was doing a good thing, but not everyone would see it so clearly.

When he reached out a hand and moved the strands of hair from Jade's cheek as the wind picked up, she caught her breath. His hand lingered against her skin and he moved a little bit closer. She didn't back away. Their lips were almost there, almost touching.

But another wave crashed, her eyes flashed with doubt or fear, and she pulled away.

'I need to get back.' She'd jumped up and was brushing the sand off the bum of her jeans.

They made their way to the top of the beach in relative silence, back up the track and towards The Street, crossing opposite the bakery. And when they

126

were level with the archway that led down the path behind the bakery to the sisters' cottage, they walked down there together so he could take the adjacent path that would lead him to the entrance to the flat above the tea rooms.

'Thanks for showing me the cove,' he said, conversation strangely absent compared to not so long ago when she couldn't stop talking about her travels. 'Now you lot can stop looking so shocked at me never having ventured down there.'

She smiled up at him and he didn't want tonight to be over. 'Goodnight, Linc.'

She turned back once to smile at him briefly before she put the key in the lock at the cottage and disappeared inside.

It was much darker now the moon had hidden itself behind a thick cloud and didn't seem to want to come out again, but Linc whistled all the way to the flat and up the stairs, and, once inside, he flung open the windows to let in some air. He downed a glass of ice-cold water and took out his guitar. He strummed out a few tunes, singing along to a couple of them, and when he'd lost himself in the music for long enough, he took out his laptop.

It was late but he was buzzing. And he wasn't sure whether it was being included with the boys at the pub, or Jade and her company, or the cove with its tranquillity and seclusion and the claims it could clear your head in a way that nothing else could with the fresh sea breeze, but finally he'd do what he'd been asked to do some time ago. And once he began to write, he couldn't stop. He'd been asked to put together a blog post about his experiences, almost a diary account of what it was like to do this good deed that so many people wouldn't talk about, let alone approve of.

And the words flowed better than the first two times he'd tried to do this, his feelings pouring out onto the page in this personal account he hoped would help others, whatever part of the process they were involved in.

Chapter Eight

Jade and Celeste stood in the bakery's kitchen taking it all in. They'd seen the job in progress of course and before Harvey and Linc had cleared out all their tools and finished the painting, but yesterday they'd been busy with their home baking and Harvey had told them it was probably a good idea to give them a chance to wipe everything down, for the paint to really be a good dry not just dry, whatever that meant, and for them to make sure everything was as perfect as it could be before the sisters made it back into their business by filling the kitchen with all their equipment and paraphernalia.

The moment the girls stepped inside the Twist and Turn Bakery now that it was completely finished and there was no sign of the renovations team was an experience unlike any other. It was morning and neither of them had been remotely tempted to sleep in today with so much to do. Both were dressed in shorts and T-shirts, ready to put in the work it was going to take to get this place ready for action, despite the cool outside as summer forgot its promise of long, lazy sunny days and instead acted as though it were autumn with a howling wind and blustery rain. They moved about switching on all the lights in the kitchen right through to the bakery and, standing together in the kitchen again, neither of them could stop smiling. The whole place held a sheen, an air of pride that it was ready for them, and they both knew it wouldn't be long before the smell of fresh paint and carpentry was replaced with what should be there instead – the smell of delectable baked goods.

Jade went over to her baking corner with its separate oven wide enough to fit two or three tins inside, deep enough to fit more depending on what she was baking. Before, she'd either had to fit in with whatever was going on in the other ovens, or wait. This corner area was spacious and Harvey had been the one to suggest the shelving above and the carved-out centre section at Jade's eye height. It had a slanted wooden backboard and weighted pieces of string so that she could lean a recipe book in place and hold pages open as she worked. No more finding tins or using anything she could get her hands on to keep the book in place as she baked, this was perfect. Her hands would be able to work, her eyes could see the detailing and look up at the recipe.

Jade made her way around the kitchen. The enormous ovens had been pushed back into place and cleaned outside as well as inside. She could already envisage loaves and rolls baking in the different sections and the scent wafting everywhere when they were ready. She ran a hand across the smooth, clean front of the trusty bread slicing machine. The old machine they'd inherited when they bought the place had been smaller, its position on a benchtop. It was rickety, hard to use and rusty in parts, and it was no surprise when it gave up on them within a fortnight of them opening their new business. The girls had invested in this top-of-the-range free-standing machine capable of slicing hundreds of loaves every hour, not that they needed that kind of capacity throughout the day but its reliability during the morning baking rush was welcome. They usually filled the shelves with the most popular sellers they knew would go within the first couple of hours of opening, then baked and kept shelves stocked throughout the day, easing off mid-morning, going with demand throughout the afternoon and winding down come the approach to closing. Jade imagined the warm, yeasty smell in the air and the heat from the ovens, loaves passing from back to front as they were sliced thick or thin as appropriate before being bagged, chitchat echoing around the bakery floor and smiles exchanged as customers caught a glimpse of the girls in the kitchen busying themselves with an order.

The aluminium benchtops were pristine and Jade could already see each of them emptying flour onto the surfaces, spreading it around, taking dough and kneading it, shaping out rolls and loaves ready for the tins and trays, all the while talking about whatever came to mind. They were both good at that, talking and working, it was probably why they worked well in business together. If one of them found it hard to multitask, this relationship might very well never have got off the starting blocks. When Linc had asked whether Celeste minded that Jade was going to give more focus to the cake baking and make it a real part of the business rather than an aside as it had been up until now, it had solidified the fact that it was quite the opposite. Both girls knew the business had to evolve as they saw fit and Celeste had actually said in words that it was good there was some kind of divide. Celeste was perfectly capable of baking cakes, she'd done it often enough, but it was Jade who had the passion and talent to take their cakes to the next level.

Celeste brought her own talents to the business and as Jade walked through to the bakery and admired the glass-fronted display cabinets, the beautiful wooden shelving ready to house their products, she thought about how much research her sister put into this business, how it was Celeste who often went the extra mile. They both put the effort in, but it was Celeste who had been more experimental, trying out different fillings in the middle of loaves that somehow just worked. Celeste was always the one well aware of what items were the most popular and those that were the least, adjusting their workload and schedule appropriately. They both handled the accounts side of the business between them, but it was Celeste who had made contact with local businesses and services in the area who'd gone on to put in bulk orders on a regular basis. And in turn Jade took care of the legal side of their business. People were always surprised to hear just how much documentation was needed when it came to running a bakery, but it was a legal requirement to have written procedures in place to ensure food safety. Jade ensured licences were up to date, that they were always ready for a health inspector to stop by and that they'd never be caught off guard and their reputation would remain intact.

'You're quiet,' Celeste remarked as Jade came back through from the bakery.

'I'm still taking it all in.' She'd been off in her own little world walking around the space that was fresh and ready for them. 'Sometimes I can't believe this is all ours. We went from being little girls wanting a bakery of our own – to this.'

Celeste began to laugh. 'There were a few steps in between, remember, like totally different careers for the both of us. This is harder in some ways but easier in others.'

Jade put her arm around her sister and hugged her. 'It's because we have drive and passion – that makes it easier.'

They went back through to the bakery itself, chatting about how customers would soon congregate choosing whatever they liked. In here they'd even carved out a space in the very corner with a couple of stools where Jade would be able to talk to people enquiring about cakes for special occasions. It had some bench space with a wooden top that matched the wood of the shelves, and there'd be room for her to open up folders and show examples of her previous work to generate ideas, as well as her ledger with dates and outlines of the customer's requirements to ensure she delivered. She had another pad of plain paper too and with a pencil she usually offered up sketches if a customer had particular cakes in mind, to ensure they were thinking along the same lines.

Celeste walked along behind the display cabinets, each with an internal thermostat to ensure they maintained the perfect temperature for whatever was inside and interior LED lighting that would soon highlight pastries, delicate cupcakes, pains au chocolat, croissants, iced buns – all the things that deserved to be shown off. They were often the items people hadn't even come in for. Customers would drop in to fetch a loaf or couple of loaves for the family and they'd be unable to resist the treats staring back at them.

'The bakery has our stamp on it now.' Jade stood by the window that was still covered in paper, preventing anyone from seeing inside until it was time for the grand opening. Her eyes welled up at how much this bakery meant not only to them but to the residents of Heritage Cove. When the girls had mentioned they were doing it up, or people had passed by as they closed the bakery for the last time until the reopening and pinned a notice on the door to say what was going on, there were a few concerned residents checking they weren't going to become part of a chain bakery, that they weren't changing the façade too much, that they weren't going all new age with this. And, now, Jade couldn't wait for opening day because she and Celeste had done every single one of them proud.

'I can't wait to get baking in my dedicated cake area,' Jade smiled, earning herself a nudge from her sister.

'You'll get there eventually but for now, enough dreaming, more doing.' She went out to the kitchen and lifted up one of the cleaning trugs they'd left on the benchtop nearest the door and pulled on a pair of Marigolds.

Jade found her own Marigolds and cleaning trug, because her sister was right – it was time to get practical, to ensure everything was perfect in anticipation of the opening. She started with the cake corner. She wondered if the sides of her face were going to start hurting she was smiling so much, but the hard graft at last took over. She squirted cleaner and wiped the already gleaming tiles behind the benchtop with a damp cloth and it wasn't long before her mind drifted back to Linc the night before last and their walk down to the cove.

She was glad they'd gone down there but she didn't know whether she was glad they'd almost kissed. The moment had been over so quickly on her part when she thought about what she was doing. She knew Linc didn't fit in with her life plan. Not at all. She couldn't get involved with anyone right now. But his touch had felt so good, had left her skin tingling as he moved her hair away from her face. She'd almost wished he'd do it again when they said goodnight but she'd shut herself inside the cottage and leant against the back door for a moment knowing she couldn't get that close to him again. She'd gone upstairs and flung open the window to let out some of the summer heat the room was holding on to. She never minded birdsong, the repetitive strains of the song thrush that carried on until all hours as though these birds assumed the residents of the Cove needed singing to sleep. But that night she'd only just climbed into bed when she heard a gentle sound coming from somewhere and it wasn't a bird. At first she'd thought it must be from a radio or a CD drifting from another open window somewhere but when she looked out and saw a light on in Etna's flat in what she knew to be the spare room – Linc's room – and his window flung open too, she realised it must be him on the guitar. Etna had told her he played when he wasn't too busy, but Jade hadn't realised he played this well. It wasn't a tune she recognised, but it was beautiful. A little melancholy but not in a miserable way – in a way that soothed and hinted there was more to get to know about the newcomer to Heritage Cove.

She tried to refocus and cleaned the tiles, the worktop, the shelves, the front of the oven that, when she opened it, was so new it even had a tag still on one of the shelves inside. She pulled it off and then turned her attention to the cabinets on the island in the middle of the room. Everything had been left pretty clean anyway but it was like moving into a new house or a rental property – you always wanted to do a once-over yourself – and with it being their business, they weren't going to cut any corners.

When Jade's stomach growled because it had been so long since breakfast, they were pretty much done. 'I think we need a quick break.'

'Good idea.' Celeste tugged off her Marigolds and began to wash her hands at the sink. 'I'll go and get us a coffee each and something to eat from Etna's tea rooms before we start bringing in the boxes of equipment to wash everything.' She was drying her hands on the paper towels from the dispenser on the wall when she suggested, 'Unless you'd like to go.'

'Happy for you to go.' Jade took off her own Marigolds and lathered up the soap between her palms but her sister was watching her. 'What's that look for?'

'Are we going to talk about the other night and a certain someone who might just be at the tea rooms now he doesn't have an excuse to be here?'

'He's working at the waffle shack, remember.'

'You know that for definite?'

Jade shook the excess water off her hands and plucked a towel from the dispenser herself. 'No, I don't. But there's nothing to talk about. Really,' she added at her sister's look of doubt. 'I showed him the cove in all its glory, then I went home. And he didn't need an excuse to come here. He was working on the renovation.' Celeste didn't look convinced. 'You go and I'll bring in a couple of boxes and some tea towels. It'll take us a long time to wash everything.'

'Fine,' replied Celeste, before heading to the cottage to get her purse, but not without yet another knowing look. Sometimes it was all it took and words didn't matter, and Celeste wasn't dumb, she knew her sister well enough to see there was an attraction between her and Linc, no matter how much Jade pretended there wasn't.

Jade began to bring some of the boxes in from the cottage and left them inside the doorway until she had quite a stack. They'd have plenty of room to do this massive washing-up session at least, with benchtops on either side of the main sink and the central benchtop as well as those running around the edge of the kitchen. And then they'd be able to find new homes for every utensil, every piece of crockery.

Glad she hadn't worn jeans just because of the gloominess beyond the window this morning, Jade wiped the sweat from her brow and wasn't sorry to see Celeste appear around the back with food, coffees and news of Linc. Not that Jade showed she was at all interested in the last item, but of course she didn't mind hearing what her sister thought of the newcomer to the Cove.

'He's in there again. The apron quite suits him.' Celeste handed her the takeaway cup of steaming latte.

'I thought Etna was back last night.'

'She was back late so she's unpacking and putting on a wash while Linc steps in at the tea rooms.' She unwrapped a ham and mustard roll. She'd got Jade the same, as well as a slice of Etna's cheddar, pancetta and thyme quiche to share.

'She's learning to trust others with her business, that's a first.' Ravenous, Jade ate most of her roll barely taking a breath.

'Linc's a nice guy.'

'I never said he wasn't,' she said and popped the rest of the roll into her mouth before adding, 'Why don't *you* go out with him?'

Celeste rolled her eyes. 'He reminds me a lot of Joel. Do you remember Joel?'

'The guy you were friends with at school and everyone thought you were a couple. That Joel?'

'Yes, and we were only ever friends. Some guys just fit into the friend mould, and that's where Linc will sit for me, I can tell. Besides, I wouldn't want to step on any toes.' She handed Jade a piece of the quiche. 'It'd be good if he applied for that job at the school, wouldn't it?' Celeste carried on. Clearly she wasn't ready to let this one go yet. 'He told me about it when I was at the tea rooms.'

'You two really did chat.'

'As did you, the night before last.' And then Celeste had had enough of hints, of looks, of tiptoeing around the point. 'He is clearly keen on you, Jade. And I know the feeling is mutual. I can't see why you wouldn't want to go for it with him.'

Jade put the rest of her quiche in her mouth to make it impossible for her to speak again until she'd finished.

Celeste leaned against the benchtop in the middle and removed the lid from her coffee. She blew across the top of the liquid. 'I hope you don't mind but I suggested to Linc he come on over when he has a chance, see this place taking shape as we put things to rights.'

'That's fine, he's allowed.'

'I know I go on at you sometimes –'

'So don't,' she snapped.

'You don't usually mind a bit of teasing, you normally laugh. What's going on with you?'

'Nothing – busy, that's all.'

Celeste put out her hand to stop Jade getting on with the job at hand when she picked up her Marigolds again. 'There's something you're not telling me. I can't believe I hadn't spotted it before now.'

'Nothing to spot.' With a glance at the boxes that still needed unpacking and everything inside washed, dried and put away, it was time to get to work. 'And I have no problem with Linc coming over.'

Celeste finished off her slice of quiche and her coffee before she took the rubbish to the bin just outside the door. 'I only want you to be happy,' she muttered, 'but I'll shut up for now.'

Jade let her sister have the last word and opened up the first box, which had a lot of her equipment for cake making. 'I'll do all these tins by hand, but in one of these boxes there should be utensils – measuring spoons, spatulas, jugs, et cetera – perhaps we'll get that all into the dishwasher.' She spoke as though Celeste hadn't got it in one that there was something else on Jade's mind, something big. She needed to talk to her sister about it but right now, focusing on the bakery was easier.

Without a word, Celeste looked through the boxes – thankfully they'd had the foresight to scribble what was inside on the top flap – until she found one containing what Jade had described and after it was all ensconced in the dishwasher bar the few items that needed handwashing she moved on to another box and they worked in silence for a while until she pulled out some silicone snowflake moulds and a set of Santa cookie cutters. 'We said we'd keep your equipment in the corner cupboards, the bakery stuff we both use in the main area, but how about dedicating a double cupboard to occasions like Christmas?'

'Good idea,' Jade smiled in an attempt to ease the atmosphere. She set the fluted cake ring she'd just washed onto the drainer. 'It'll make it easier. Try the cupboards next to the baking area, there's a double set that will be perfect.'

Within a couple of hours the kitchen at the bakery didn't look much different but progress had been made. They were going to be a lot more organised after this renovation. Knives, measuring spoons, palette knives, piping-bag nozzles, cookie cutters and other accoutrements had already found a new home in the drawers; modern cupboards with internal wire display baskets made it easy to stack loose-based cake tins, silicone moulds in all shapes and sizes, rectangular, round and oblong tins, brownie tins and sandwich tins, and not only that, it was easy to see where something was and items were able to be pulled out without disrupting everything else. Previously it had been a case of finding somewhere to shove their equipment and a lot of the cupboards and drawers had been full to bursting point, meaning every time they wanted to find something it took forever and frequently involved unloading an entire cupboard's contents.

The new kitchen had a huge larder cupboard in place of the old one. At first glance you'd think it was the same arrangement inside – just shelves that went so far back things often got lost – but when you tugged the handle it didn't open a door but rather a pull-out storage system with half a dozen wire baskets, each capable of taking a decent weight, so perfect for various types of flour, sugar and any other dry ingredients they might need. Jade also had something she'd always dreamed of – a blind-corner kitchen storage unit – in the new baking area and she couldn't wait to fill its metal pull-out baskets that smoothly swung open to reveal everything inside. No more struggling to get the items at the back. She was going to put her special equipment in there – there was, of course, a lot of crossover with the main business, but she and Celeste had decided she'd need dedicated tools and accessories so that they never had a situation where they were both battling for a particular shaped tin or piping nozzle or tray.

'Knock, knock!' came a voice from the back door.

When Jade looked up and locked eyes with Linc she couldn't quash the happy feeling swirling inside her. 'Come in, we're getting there, slowly.' It wasn't tidy with almost every cupboard door flung wide open and things strewn across the benchtops. 'Just a matter of finding a home for everything but at least we're thinking about it properly.'

'It's looking a lot more like your bakery already,' he smiled.

Jade wiped over the stand mixer and set it into its new position against the wall on the next benchtop along from the sink. This one had a pale blue body and over in the cake corner they'd have another one, except in pink. 'We'll have a better workflow with this new kitchen and, of course, that'll mean a better business.'

'The wall colour looks great too,' Celeste complimented when she came to dump all the mixer's attachments into the sink filled with hot soapy water and took over the washing-up task from Jade.

'It was a good choice,' replied Linc. 'And the smell will soon go.'

There was another knock at the back door and this time it was Etna. 'Can we come in?'

'Of course, welcome home, Etna.' Jade gave the woman a hug before she spotted the man hovering behind her. He removed his tweed cap and adjusted his glasses when his actions knocked them skew-whiff and Jade realised this must be Linc's dad. The smile was exactly like his son's, wide and genuine, and he had the same waves in his hair that indicated it wouldn't be straight if he let it grow a bit. Linc might not have been in the village all that long but his hair had grown already and its dark brown waves had started to give way to the odd curl. Perhaps now he wasn't working flat out he'd

141

be able to go for a haircut, although the floppy, laid-back look kind of suited him.

'It's good to be back in the Cove,' Etna smiled after she introduced her brother Joseph to the girls. 'It feels like I've been gone a month, not a few days.' There was a family resemblance between her and her brother as well, the same greying hair and blue eyes that danced as though youth was still on their side.

'I'll bet it was nice to take some time away though,' said Celeste.

'It actually was,' Etna admitted. 'But poor Joseph has had to put up with me bossing him around for the last few days.'

'Don't worry,' Joseph winked at the girls, 'I'll get my own back somehow.'

'Are you staying in the Cove for a while?' Jade asked.

'The Cove,' he repeated. 'Just the words conjure up a lovely day by the seaside.'

'You should go down there when you get a chance,' she recommended.

'You should, Dad, it's beautiful.' Linc's gaze darted towards Jade but she looked away before Etna or anyone else picked up on the vibe between them. She suspected Celeste had but was keeping schtum after her reaction earlier on.

Jade watched Linc, who couldn't stop himself walking around the kitchen inspecting joins, light switches, running his hand along cupboards and standing back to check the doors hung right. For a man who was a teacher he took a lot of pride in this side job for the summer. Or perhaps, like her, he'd felt awkward remembering their trip down to the cove together.

'I'm staying a couple of weeks,' Joseph informed them. 'Etna and I both agree that I should've done it a long time ago. I was digging my heels in, thought she should come to me, and now that she has – well, it's my turn to visit her here.'

Linc called over from where he'd been peering into cupboards to see what they'd done with the space. 'Harvey offered me a room at Tumbleweed House for two weeks, otherwise we'd be tripping over each other.' He pushed his hands into the pockets of his jeans and on one forearm he had a splash of something he'd likely picked up in the tea rooms – chocolate sauce, or icing perhaps. 'I don't mind a change of scene and I'll be working up at his brother's waffle shack most of the time anyway.'

'I've heard about this waffle shack.' Joseph's eyes lit up. 'I must say, for a small village you've really got your pick of places to go, from a tea rooms, a pub, a waffle shack and' – he looked around him – 'what I can tell is going to be a delightful bakery. They say village businesses are dwindling but it doesn't seem the case around here in *the Cove*.'

Celeste called out from where she was stacking loaf tins on top of a shelf. 'He's sounding like a local, Etna.'

'How about a tour?' Joseph, still curious about this place, clasped his hands together.

Like his son, Joseph was friendly, easy to talk to. Jade gave him a tour of the place, took him through to the front and explained how they'd left the frontage as it was previously so that it wouldn't look any different apart from the new sign. She pointed out the new shelving and what products would go there, the sorts of items that would soon be on display behind the glass-fronted cabinets.

'And what are you calling this new business of yours?' he asked after he and Etna had seen everything. 'Etna tells me you're going for another name.'

Jade smiled. 'Etna is worried it'll be something out there, something that doesn't really fit in with the village.'

'I don't *dis*approve of a change,' said Etna. 'So, what's it to be?'

'We're not telling anyone yet,' Jade said. 'Not until opening day, when all will be revealed.'

'Spoilsport,' Etna tutted.

'When are you back at work at the tea rooms, Etna?' Jade could sense that looking around someone else's business was making her itch to get back to her own.

'I would've been back the minute I arrived in the Cove if I'd been allowed.' She shot a frown in Linc's direction but it didn't take long to give way to a smile. 'I'll be back in the tea rooms full-time tomorrow.'

'Tomorrow?' Joseph guffawed. 'You've already been in there bossing Patricia about, tidying up the centrepieces on tables and clearing empty mugs. Yes, I saw you.'

She ignored the jibe and clutched her nephew's hand. 'Thank you, Linc, thank you for stepping in and helping me. I only hope I can repay the favour one day.'

'You already have by inviting me to come and stay and finding me work to keep me out of trouble, although it was a bit more demanding with the tea rooms thrown in,' he grinned. 'And don't think that being all nice to me now will stop me checking you're not pushing yourself too hard. Regular breaks are going to be part of your routine from now on, yes?'

'Yes,' she nodded, although each of them in that kitchen knew it wasn't going to be easy to have her adhere to the plan.

'Good luck enforcing that,' Jade whispered to Linc when Etna went over to look at the cake corner and Celeste explained the recipe holder Harvey had built into the shelf at eye height.

'Don't worry, I have a plan.' Linc's arm brushed against hers ever so slightly the way it had done once before and sent a shiver up her body.

'And what's that?'

'Dad's going to keep Etna company at the tea rooms. She likes to keep an eye on him anyway, in that bossy-older-sister way of hers, but he's told me he'll offer to help out claiming he's at a loose end and that should do the trick.'

'Did you look into the teaching position at the school?' The question was out before she had time to worry about whether he'd read too much into her query, think that she was more interested than she knew she should be.

'Daniel passed on my number,' he shrugged, 'so it's out of my hands unless they call me.'

Etna had done another circuit of the kitchen and the bakery with Joseph, both still admiring the newness as she talked about perhaps one day sprucing up the interior of the tea rooms, upgrading the kitchen units to some of these fancier ones the girls now had. She was particularly impressed with the corner cupboard and the way the shelves inside unfolded to provide a more efficient storage space.

'You know,' began Jade, 'your dad has that look newcomers get when they come to the Cove.'

'What look?'

'Tourists often come in here and they get a certain twinkle in their eye when they talk about the village and everything it has to offer, like it's a gem they've stumbled upon without realising they'd been looking for it.'

'You can get all that from a look?' he teased.

She shook her head. 'You mark my words, he loves it here.'

'Do you ever tell the tourists about the cove itself or keep that a local secret?'

'It depends – if I really like the look of them I'll whisper the secret in their ear, but otherwise, I don't bother.'

Celeste was busy telling Etna and Joseph what the grand reopening day for the bakery would entail.

'Do you need an extra pair of hands on the day?' Linc jumped in.

'You've only been free for, what, five minutes and already you're at a loose end?' Jade wondered.

'Something like that. Honestly, put me to good use if you need to. I'm not due at the shack until later on because we're still waiting for delivery of a skip.'

She didn't want to think too much about the uses she could find for him, because none of them involved this place. 'I think we're all set but thank you, I appreciate knowing we can call on you if we need to.'

'I can help you out right now, just say the word.' He regarded the boxes, many of which hadn't even been opened yet. 'You look as though you've got a lot to do.'

'Take him up on it!' Celeste urged. 'The more pairs of hands the better.'

'I suppose you could unpack some of the remaining boxes for me,' Jade relented. 'Leave the items on the left of the sink and I can wash them. Then you could empty

146

the dishwasher and put all the clean, dry items onto the benchtop in the middle. How does that sound?'

'Happy to help.' He sent a smile her way and one Jade had to admit she treasured, thrilled to be working alongside him for a while. And at least if he was here Celeste wouldn't be able to grill her about what had been on her mind lately. She had to come clean soon, but she wasn't looking forward to it at all. Because Celeste's disapproval might just cast too much doubt in her mind.

By the time Linc set off for the waffle shack when Daniel texted to say the skip had been dropped off, Celeste looked like a pressure cooker that was begging to have its lid taken off. 'Nice of him to help,' she said but Jade knew the simple comment was likely a prelude to a deeper conversation.

Jade stacked the final box with the others, inside a larger one, dumped them all in the shed after she'd moved the tins of leftover paint shoved in there out of the way, and locked up the bakery for the night. The girls went back to the cottage for a well-earned cup of tea and, with the back door open to let the fresh air filter through the kitchen, the lounge, and creep upstairs to cool off their bedrooms, Jade leaned back against the kitchen chair she was sitting in. 'I'm going to ache tomorrow.'

'Me too, but it'll be worth it.' Celeste took a mouthful of tea. 'Any regrets?'

'None, you?'

'Of course not.'

'You had me worried for a minute.'

Celeste tapped her fingers against the side of her mug, the ring on her right hand making the familiar sound it always did – a ting as the metal came into contact with the china. 'I wasn't just meaning regrets about taking on a business. I was wondering if you'd ever regretted leaving Dario behind.'

Jade had expected another comment about Linc, the man who lived locally for the time being, not about her ex who lived in another country. 'You haven't asked me about him in a long time. What's brought this on?'

'Because I know there's something bothering you.' She sat forwards in her chair. 'You always said you and he made the best decision, that it wasn't meant to be.' She hesitated before admitting, 'And I know you still carry a photograph of him in your bag.'

Jade didn't fly into any accusations of snooping. Her sister had seen the photograph months ago when she went to find the business card passed to them by the manager at Aubrey House residential home. Jade had dropped it into her bag and forgotten to take it out; Celeste had gone to get it and pulled out the picture, one eyebrow hooked questioningly, and Jade hadn't volunteered any information whatsoever. They hadn't talked about it since.

'Not anymore I don't.' She wasn't going to let slip that actually it had been Linc finding the photograph that finally prompted her to put it away along with all her other travel memories as though it was nothing in particular, just part of the grand trip they'd done once upon a time – another sight she'd seen, another experience she'd had. When she'd left Italy Jade had thought that despite their joint decision not to make contact, Dario would be in touch. She'd checked her emails constantly just in case, she'd had to resist searching his name online too many times, and she hadn't done very well with that at all; it was so easy nowadays to check up on someone. The last time she'd typed his name into the search bar she'd seen he'd done

148

exactly what he'd stayed behind to do – run the family business. There'd been a local write-up about it, most of which Jade couldn't fully understand with her limited grasp of the language, but she'd deciphered enough to know the article was an accolade. Dario was a success story; they were both masters of their own universes, as he'd once put it. Jade sometimes wondered whether Dario checked her name on the internet the way she'd done with him, or was it a girl thing? But his lack of contact, and, even more, the way Linc looked at her that day when they talked about the photograph, had at last made her realise how crazy she was to still be thinking about what might have been. And ever since she'd put the photograph away, her mind had cleared enough to focus on what her personal life could really be like without him in it. And she was OK with that. She was moving on, at long last.

'You got rid of the photograph?' Celeste double-checked.

'I put it with all the others, away, out of sight. I need to move forwards.'

With a sigh of relief, Celeste told her, 'Not before time.'

Jade rolled her eyes. 'Don't for one minute think this means I need help finding someone new.' Celeste never really went in for the whole matchmaking thing – at least, she hadn't until Linc had come along but Jade could tell that was exactly the way her mind was now working.

'Don't worry, I know you're old enough to run your own love life.'

'What about yours?'

'Oh no,' said Celeste with a shake of her head, 'this is about you.'

Jade laughed and pulled open a packet of biscuits, waving them in her sister's direction. Celeste took one and just about had enough tea in the bottom of her mug to dunk it. 'That's a revolting habit. You totally spoil a good biscuit, making it soggy.'

'Rubbish.' She popped the whole thing in her mouth and attempted to say, 'Best thing ever.'

Biscuit eaten, Celeste returned to the topic of their bakery and the amazing kitchen they'd begun to put in order. There was a lot of work to be done, but despite the exhaustion, they both felt the elation. And Jade was only glad they hadn't lingered on the topic of Dario or Linc. She didn't talk about Dario much anyway, not these days. She had at the time – when they'd first left Venice she'd gone on and on about him and it had driven Celeste batty until Jade stopped sharing and kept her feelings to herself.

She wondered, when Celeste found out what she intended to do, would she think she'd lost her mind? She might well do, and once she knew, she wouldn't be encouraging Jade to get involved with another man either.

Chapter Nine

'Thank you for writing the blog post.' The doctor Linc had seen the first time he'd come to the clinic caught up with him in reception following his scheduled appointment. 'You come across well, I knew you would.'

'You've got more faith in me than I have in myself.' But Linc tried to take the compliment. 'It was hard at first, putting my feelings into words, but I think in a way it's helped me too. I've faced a few conflicting opinions along the way and even though I did the mandatory counselling here, the process still messed with my head a bit.'

'You faced opposition to what you're doing?' The doctor passed some forms over the reception desk to Nadine, the lady who always welcomed you with a smile. In the time he'd been coming here, he'd got to know most of the staff well. The whole arrangement put everyone at ease, no matter the reason they'd come to the clinic.

'My girlfriend – who I'm no longer with, by the way – thought I was some kind of weirdo.'

The doctor's harrumph suggested he'd heard that and worse many times before. 'You know, that viewpoint says more about the other person than it does about you or what we do here.' He put a reassuring hand on Linc's shoulder. 'You're doing a good thing, a very good thing.'

Linc left his appointment and realised that the honesty and maturity behind his blog post made him feel ready to share exactly what he'd been up to with someone else. He could tell Etna – she'd understand the end result but perhaps not the process. He could tell his dad; he'd approve. He could tell the boys he'd begun to bond with in Heritage Cove, he could tell Jade.

Jade. She was the person he wanted to tell the most, but he didn't want to scare her off. Since he'd been in the Cove and the bakery had gone from being stripped bare to looking almost finished and ready for the grand opening later today, they'd begun to get on better and better. When they talked, they really talked, and he sensed she needed it as much as he did. She'd popped into the tea rooms more in the last few days, according to Etna, and Etna had said it was as though she was looking for something. *Or someone*, she'd added to him last night when he'd gone over for supper with her and his dad. He'd been living at Harvey's for a few days but didn't want to encroach on his time with Melissa, and besides, he wanted to see his dad as much as he could, gauge whether a house move in this direction could be a possibility.

Linc was about to start the car when his phone rang and after a brief conversation, he told the head teacher at the school that he'd go and see her tomorrow. He had an interview and she sounded keen already.

Linc drove back to the Cove rehearsing in his head what he'd say when they met, possible interview questions and responses. Over his time as a teacher, he'd planned and prepared his lessons according to the curriculum and outlined syllabus, but he'd also tried to inject a bit of personality into an otherwise banal formal teaching process without breaking too many rules. He'd run extra lessons to bring students up to par so they could join the orchestra, he'd shown engaging videos of music out there in the real world with some of the most renowned orchestras, pivotal performances. He'd had students watch footage of some of the more unusual instruments and the class had been enthralled to see a massive flute, a hybrid instrument known as the cello horn – its name self-explanatory – and, the star of the show, an enormous double bass made in the 1800s and standing over three metres tall. The instrument had a low-end rumble and could only be played by means of the musician standing on a special platform and pulling on levers to change the pitch of a string while drawing the specially made bow across to make a sound. In his permanent position, Linc had organised excursions – he could recall the passion in the eyes of the pupils in his class as they watched the London Philharmonic Orchestra at the Royal Albert Hall, or their enthusiasm on the trip that stuck in his memory as one of the best when they made it to Mozart's birthplace in Salzburg. The performances of orchestras and choirs amidst jaw-dropping Alpine scenery had been one of the highlights of his teaching career but it was easy to forget all the highs when he was operating on a conveyor belt, passing in and out of schools to cover when they needed, not really investing time in the environment and team because he'd soon be on to another place.

Linc had many of the essential qualities he felt were necessary for a music teacher and went over them in his head as he drove back to the Cove. He had the patience to guide and push, he enjoyed one-on-one instruction or working with a group, he encouraged music appreciation of any kind, whether it came from a string quartet, a gospel choir, old Western and cowboy music, traditional folk songs or a punk rock band. It didn't matter. Appreciation of music came from all directions and he wanted his students to explore possibilities and find a passion. Of course, not all of his students were interested in music, but when he found those who were it made his extra efforts more than worth it, especially when he encountered a kid who dismissed the idea of learning music and eventually came to love it.

Linc smiled as he arrived back in the village, proceeding around the bend and past the sign welcoming residents and newcomers, past the Heritage Inn on the corner. The Street looked different already beneath the sun that had come out as if especially for today after two days straight of bruised skies and miserable drizzle. Bunting was strung from one side to the other from lamp-posts. Tables lined the pavement in front of the bakery and already crowds were beginning to mill for the two-o'clock launch of the refurbished venue. He parked out the back of the tea rooms in one of the vacant spots Etna owned and as he twirled his car keys around one finger, he couldn't stifle a bit of a whistle. Hearing from Jane had made him realise how ready he was to shift things around a little, to move to another school for a permanent role again and perhaps settle into the next phase of his life.

*

'Would you look at this,' Etna smiled, linking her arm through Joseph's. Linc walked alongside as they made their way next door from the tea rooms to the bakery to join the big crowd swarming in eagerness. The signage was already up – Linc had seen Harvey and Daniel putting it up there this morning under Celeste's guidance

– but it was covered in paper, as were the windows, and it was all helping the excitement to mount. People were chatting amongst themselves, speculating over what the name might be, already talking about how they couldn't wait for the bakery to be back in business.

Linc waved over to Jade and, if he wasn't mistaken, she looked just as pleased to see him as he was her. He watched her stand on a stool, her sister on another, and Celeste hushed the crowds quickly by thanking them for coming, telling them she knew it had been hard for them all to see the bakery close for weeks but that the changes were well worth it. She was interrupted more than once – one person wanted to know if they'd still make a Victoria sponge; that request came from Mrs Filligree, who came in every Thursday to pick up the cake to take to her mother-in-law's house for morning tea, according to Etna. Someone else wanted to know whether they'd still make sandwiches and rolls and would the coleslaw bap or the roast beef and caramelised onion varieties still be available.

'We've got all your old favourites,' Celeste assured the crowd. Linc was impressed she could be heard over them. 'We'll have some new items too and, of course, cakes by Jade for every occasion you might ever need, so don't hesitate to make a booking with my sister to discuss your requirements.'

'Make the most of it, everyone!' Jade added. 'We'll be giving away a lot of free baked goods today!' She waited for a cheer to subside. 'You might have noticed my good friend Tilly weaving her way between you all. She's in charge of giving everyone a voucher for a freebie. Whatever you like – a loaf of bread, brioche, a gingerbread cookie or a cupcake – it's yours, and we hope it encourages you to come back for more.'

155

The applause and excitement mounted. The onlookers were like horses behind the starting gates, scraping their hooves on the ground, impatient to begin the race – this one being towards a bakery. The imagery had Linc amused as he wondered whether there could very well be a stampede. He decided he'd hold back a while. He swore he saw some folks' elbows jut out at the mention of the free stuff. 'Perhaps they think the bakery will run out of supplies if they're not first,' he said to his dad beneath his breath.

Joseph pulled down his cap that stopped the sun getting in his eyes. He'd had the same cap for years, almost as much a part of him as his grey hair and wrinkles and his favourite armchair. 'I'm not surprised, the smell is intoxicating, especially if like me they didn't have much of a lunch.'

'I think I'll hang back,' said Etna, managing to raise her voice above the hubbub. 'I don't want to get injured again.'

'Fair enough, sis.' Joseph grinned. 'But I'm anxious to get in there. Don't worry, I'll make a run for it for all three of us. What do you fancy? Farmhouse loaf? Jam doughnut? Iced bun?'

Linc was about to say he didn't mind when Jade clapped her hands together again to get everyone's attention. She'd moved the stool she'd been standing on so that it was near the bakery door while Celeste's was at the far end of the front window. They were both smiling, their hands reaching up to the paper covering the sign. A photographer for a local paper was clicking away on her camera, moving left and right and reminding the girls to look her way.

Jade managed to raise her voice above the crowd although it took a couple of attempts. 'And now, without

156

further ado…we give you…' She grinned at her sister and gave her a nod and they both tore off the paper as they yelled out, 'The Twist and Turn Bakery!'

Celeste disappeared inside the bakery to get rid of the paper and to pull off the window coverings so the shiny new inside could be seen beyond the criss-cross-glassed windows. Now that you could see the entire bakery, the sign blended in well with the deep timber panels and the Tudor-style exterior. *The Twist and Turn Bakery* was written in curly font in an arc with a basket of bread painted beneath, and with its dark-wood trim, a cream background and a cracked effect to give it an antique finish, the new sign and its bevelled edges was perfectly in keeping with a village that had so much character.

The continuing noise of the crowd prevented Jade from saying anything else but she took it in her stride, laughing and grinning and doing her best not to wobble on the stool. Linc was glad all eyes were facing her way rather than only his, because he knew he'd been staring this whole time.

'Before we declare the bakery well and truly open,' Jade bellowed the best she could, 'I'd like to add that we are truly blessed to have a home in the Cove with each and every one of you. And a huge thank you goes to Harvey and Linc for the work they've done over the last few weeks.' She beckoned Linc to come forwards but it took Etna giving him a shove for him to do so.

'Thank you,' Jade beamed at him when he drew closer and for a moment he thought she might kiss him until Harvey appeared at his side. Someone else took hold of Harvey's dog Winnie's lead as the girls told both men to climb up onto the stools in their place so they could get a round of applause too.

157

'I wasn't expecting that,' said Harvey when they'd had their cheers and the girls agreed they could get down. He ruffled Winnie's head and the Labrador's tail wagged at the attention.

'Harvey is starting his own renovations business and he comes highly recommended,' Celeste called out from behind a cupped hand to the crowd.

Harvey leaned towards Linc, their feet safely planted on the ground again. 'I was about to say I'll tell the girls off for embarrassing us but maybe she'll drum up business so I can't be too harsh.'

Jade was busy ushering everyone into a queue while Celeste manned the bakery door, ensuring nobody went inside until there was a sense of calm.

'All this excitement for a bakery,' Linc said to Harvey.

'Should've seen the crowds when my brother opened the waffle shack. What can I say? People here like their food.'

Linc laughed when he saw his dad so quick off the mark he'd managed to bag fourth place in the line outside. He winked over at Linc and waved his three vouchers at him. Back beside Etna, Linc told her, 'Dad seems to be really enjoying himself. I'm glad he came.'

'Me too. It was about time. And look, he's chewing the ear off locals already.' Barney had either managed to run for fifth place in the queue or he'd played the elderly-resident card and had someone let him in before them and the two men were talking like old friends.

'Do you think Dad's asked him what the local beer is like yet?'

'I doubt Joseph would've even had to mention it. Barney is probably arranging to get him to the pub as we speak.' She smiled as they both looked over to Linc's dad before she turned her attentions back to her nephew. 'Where were you this morning? I thought you'd make the most of a lie-in after your efforts here the last few days and weeks?'

'You been checking up on me? Maybe I lazed in bed all morning at Tumbleweed House.'

Her look suggested she knew full well he hadn't. 'I know you're big enough to look after yourself, but Harvey was helping with all of this, getting the bunting up and the bakery sign, and when I didn't see you, I asked where you were. I knew you weren't at the shack. But he said you'd left the house before he did.'

'I had a few things to do, that's all.'

'Hmm.' She didn't look convinced. 'Secrecy, I'm not sure I like that.'

'Don't worry, I'm not doing anything untoward.' He didn't say anything more because his dad came over brandishing a paper bag for each of them.

'Thought I'd get these cinnamon-and-raisin puff-pastry twists – they're what inspired the name of the bakery, apparently.'

Linc took the warm, layered flaky pastry from the bag and smiled as he bit into it because he could remember the look Jade had given him when he'd suggested he'd played a part in getting her creative juices flowing when it came to choosing a name for the bakery.

'You look like the cat who got the cream,' said Etna as they stood on the pavement on the opposite side of the road from the crowds still queuing, happy faces emerging from the bakery with whatever delight they'd picked.

'Except he's the boy who got the pastry,' Joseph added.

'He can't stop smiling,' Etna persisted, watching Linc. 'I get the feeling it's a certain young lady you've got in your sights.'

He was about to deny it when Kenneth came over to say hello before he joined the queue himself. Instead, Linc said, 'Love is in the air, right?'

Etna shot him a look. 'I've no idea what you mean.'

At least they were both off the hook from any questions either way when Harvey, Daniel and Benjamin joined them. Etna excused herself and headed across the road.

Linc couldn't fully focus on what Harvey was telling him about the muck-up in his day job with a homeowner who'd started his own loft conversion without finding a suitable professional to help because his gaze kept drifting across to Jade and Etna, who were talking away after Jade handed out more vouchers. About what, he had no idea. But he did clock Jade looking his way a couple of times, at least until she went back inside and Etna headed next door to the tea rooms. The line outside the bakery had hidden the window of Etna's business but Linc could see people were inside, probably taking the weight off their feet after the grand opening, and knowing his auntie, she'd want to keep them all happy with pots of tea and a space to sit. They might be full up with freebies and more from the bakery but she'd probably talk to them for long enough that they'd order food in the tea rooms too. She had a magical way of keeping people there as long as she needed for business to turn over happily all year round.

Before Daniel headed back to the waffle shack he reminded the others, 'Drinks at the pub tonight for Jade and Celeste – we'll give them a proper toast.'

Apparently it had been Melissa's idea. 'Sounds good to me,' said Linc, happy to be a part of it all. It was easy to forget he didn't actually live in Heritage Cove. Yet.

Linc wondered if Jade would be as happy to see him later as he would be to see her. He was about to go on his way when he saw her emerge from the bakery to chase a customer carrying a hessian bag filled with at least three baguettes. From what he could make out, the man had paid but not waited to collect his change.

Linc intercepted her at the door as she got back to the bakery, breathless from the chase. 'You did it.'

With a smile, she agreed, 'It's been a great day.'

'But you're exhausted,' he added for her, noticing she had a few grains of sugar at the side of her mouth, a speck of flour on her temple. She looked as though today was running her ragged, but in a good way. 'And it's not over yet.'

'It's not. Still a few hours until closing but then I can collapse.'

He shook his head. 'Oh no, your presence is required at the pub. Celebrations are in order. I thought you would've been told.'

'Celeste mentioned something,' she sighed. 'I was hoping I could safely ignore it for an evening of solitude.'

He wouldn't mind sharing that with her instead, but the pub would do. 'Drinks are on everyone else, remember.'

She grinned. 'You lot obviously don't understand much about a bakery. We'll be up before five o'clock tomorrow, all systems go, while the rest of you are enjoying your shut-eye.'

'It is particularly quiet at Tumbleweed House.'

'Hmm…so, it's going well, living there?'

161

'It's a good temporary stopgap. And Harvey and Melissa are wonderful hosts, pretty relaxed. They were very generous to step in and rescue me from squashing into the flat with Dad and Auntie Etna. I'm trying to be a good house guest – even taken Winnie for a walk a couple of times. Mind you, Harvey mentioned something about helping with the elderberry harvest. Does that make sense to you?'

She recapped about Harvey's family having once owned and run an elderberry business. 'I think there's half an acre or so still dedicated to elderberries but it's not a business now, it's just something Harvey and his mum like to keep going. Careful, or you'll get roped in with the berry picking and you'll have purple fingers for weeks.'

'Thanks for the warning.' He leaned against the whitewashed wall at the side of the bakery as Jade hovered near the front door. 'Loved the cinnamon-and-raisin twist, by the way.'

'I noticed your dad chose three of those. I'm glad.'

'I feel honoured I tried the item that inspired the name.' A moment hovered between them similar to those they'd shared before and he wanted to reach out to her but didn't. 'Business is really booming,' he remarked instead, as excited chatter from a group nearby filled the air along with a summer breeze that was pleasant rather than cold. Pockets of people congregated on the pavements, others came and went from the bakery, and he didn't want Jade to disappear off just yet because chatting with her was so easy.

'I've already got two new cake-design meetings with customers lined up – one for a twenty-first birthday and another for a christening.' It seemed she wasn't ready to get going yet either.

'That's great.'

'And I can't wait to make my first cake in my new corner using the recipe holder.'

'That was particularly genius,' he agreed. 'I heard Harvey got the idea after he spoke to Etna one day and she was moaning about having to weigh down the pages of a recipe book in her kitchen. He suggested she try a recipe holder and she said they weren't much better when they weren't at eye height.'

'Talking of Etna, where's she gone?'

'Where do you think?'

She smiled as she realised. 'So much for taking a break. Do you think she'll ever do it – properly I mean, cut back on her hours?'

'I think the last few days have been a start but she can't extinguish the drive she has. She'll no doubt be in her element right now. I expect she and Patricia will be serving tea – not much food for a while as people's stomachs process their freebies – but they'll be talking all about this place and keeping the customers' attention until they can fit in that extra snack or slice of cake.'

Jade's laughter appeared to help her let go of some of the tension of the day. 'You'd think we'd be in competition but I often send people next door to take the weight off their feet after they've bought something in the bakery and, likewise, she often recommends us to her customers. She even lets some of them eat what they buy here in there.'

'You three seem to have an understanding. Talking of business, was she prodding you earlier, asking more details? I saw you chatting,' he said by way of explanation.

'Actually, she didn't talk business at all. She was telling me about you, about how you looked after your mum when she was sick. It sounds as though you had a pretty tough time, and then again with your dad.'

He swallowed hard. 'How did you get onto talking about me and my family?'

'We were saying how well you and Harvey had worked together, then how you'd stepped in at the tea rooms and that led to talking about you always helping other people.' She looked a little unsure whether to add anything else. 'She told me you need to help yourself as well as others. She began to go into great detail of your commitment, your family values' – she smiled – 'your caring side.'

He couldn't hold back a grin either. 'Apologies for that, it sounds like she was trying to sell me to you and I promise, I never put her up to it.' His gaze was drawn to the sugar grains at the side of her mouth when the sun made them stand out beneath its rays, and when she didn't answer, and before he could think it might be inappropriate, he reached up and with the pad of his thumb brushed them away. 'Sugar,' he explained. He thought he heard her sigh but maybe it was wishful thinking.

'Thank you,' she answered without breaking eye contact. 'I'd better go.'

'I'll see you later.'

He watched her go into the bakery and when he went on his way, he had one intention in mind, and that was to let her know how he felt. He couldn't ignore it any longer and enough people had told him he should be looking for his own happiness as well as being there for everyone else.

And so tonight he was going to do it. He was going to ask her out.

Chapter Ten

Jade had never felt so glad to be standing beneath the jets of a shower as she did after the grand reopening of the bakery. As much as they'd planned a slightly more relaxed few weeks while the business was closed, it had turned out to be anything but. They hadn't baked anywhere near as much but instead they'd been trying to work in the kitchen at the cottage, juggling deliveries for their orders, they'd been keeping an eye on progress at the bakery as Harvey and Linc got it finished and then there'd been the last couple of days, getting it all put back to rights. Not an easy task at all. Today the adrenalin had kept their energy levels up but right now, Jade would much rather go to bed than venture anywhere near a pub. Then again, every time she thought of the way Linc had reached out and wiped the sugar remnants from the side of her lip she couldn't put him out of her mind, and going along tonight meant she'd get to see him again. And that made her happier than she'd care to admit. Confused, certainly, but she'd ignore the latter emotion for now and try to go with the flow.

'You'll enjoy it once you're there, once you've got a glass of wine.' Celeste peeked in on her sister as Jade pulled out the hanger with her new summer dress. 'Oh yes, wear that, the colour makes you look hot.'

Jade knew exactly why her sister was saying that. Thank goodness she hadn't seen her and Linc talking earlier or she'd have a lot more to say about the matter.

She shut the wardrobe door and put her arm into one sleeve of the red dress she'd picked out with its delicate blue-centred daisies printed on the material. She put her other arm in and wrapped the material around her body before tying it at the front. The dress settled nicely around her hips and, on a balmy evening, would keep her nice and cool no matter if they were in the beer garden or inside The Copper Plough. Already it felt good to be wearing something fresh after getting so hot and bothered in the bakery in three-quarter jeans and a T-shirt.

When the girls arrived at the pub, they couldn't see many others so they headed straight for the bar.

'On the house.' Landlord Terry winked when he poured a glass of pinot grigio for each of them. 'You deserve it today. And thank you for the scones – Nola and I had them for our break this afternoon and, don't tell her,' he added, leaning over the bar and lowering his voice, 'but they're way better than the ones she tried to make last week.' He pulled a face.

Glasses of wine in hand, they turned to see Tilly heading back inside from the beer garden, her mid-brown hair curling up evenly before it met with the collar of a retro mint-green dress with little red petals. She floated towards them in her peep-toe sandals. 'We've got two tables right at the back,' she told them after hugging them hello. 'Just follow the noise.' She squeezed through towards the bar.

'I'm not sure I can do rowdy,' Jade whispered into Celeste's ear.

'Me neither, I must admit, but we don't have to stay all night.'

But they needn't have worried because the only noise they could hear was the beautiful guitar playing towards the back of the beer garden, and there was only one person Jade knew who played like that.

'A man of many talents,' Celeste nudged her sister as they approached.

Linc was playing a classical melody she didn't recognise and it brought an air of romance to a gorgeous summer's evening. People stood mesmerised; some stood that little bit closer together than they otherwise might have done. Jade didn't let on to Celeste that she'd heard him play once before, from her window that night, and the music had had the same effect on her then as it did now, making her want to close her eyes and let it wash over her.

The playing paused when their arrival was noticed and all attentions turned to the sisters and their successful launch of the Twist and Turn Bakery. They had drinks offers coming from all directions, seats were vacated so they could sit down, and when Linc looked over Jade smiled back.

'I'm glad we came,' Celeste confided when everyone seemed to, at last, get back to their own tables or groups of friends and leave them to it. 'People are so lovely, aren't they?'

'They sure are.'

'And Linc – do you think he's lovely?' Celeste had her glass of wine between her fingers, cupping the vessel as she watched for her sister's reaction.

'Would you stop it. He's a nice guy, I'll admit it. There, happy?'

Celeste shrugged. 'And do I smell the perfume you hardly ever wear?'

'Yes, you do. No point having it sitting in the bottle and going off.' Her parents had given her a bottle of Chanel Allure eau de parfum on her last birthday and its concentration of oils compared to the eau de toilette version made it not only pricy in comparison but richer in scent. Tonight, she'd wanted a reward for their efforts over the past few weeks – a treat, a reminder of her femininity and something to make her feel special. Not that she didn't feel all those things every time Linc's gaze drifted in her direction.

Celeste swayed a little in time to the music, or perhaps that was the wine's doing. 'All right, I promise to hold off on any more comments, at least for tonight.' When she saw Zara, who ran the local ice-creamery, she went over to chat with her.

'How's the wine?' Linc's smooth voice fell over her as he came up to the picnic bench where she'd settled and didn't intend to budge from for the entire night. She hadn't realised the music had stopped.

'Going down a treat.' She raised her glass to his when he lifted up a pint of beer. In place of his guitar playing, a robin was singing high-pitched and confident notes as it perched on the perimeter fence next to the lamp-post that had already become illuminated despite it not being fully dark yet.

'Glad you came?'

'I am, to be honest. Although I won't have too many or my head will hurt when my alarm gives me the rude awakening in the morning.'

'Yeah, I've been witness to your fury – those poor loaves and bread rolls, not to mention the cupcakes, if they're on the receiving end of your temper.'

She gave him a playful shove on the arm. 'I wasn't that bad. OK, I was a bit, but I apologised. Both times.'

'Early mornings must be hard in the winter.'

'They are, believe me – it's pitch-black leaving the cottage and for a good few hours after that, and then when it gets really cold and icy it's difficult to motivate myself to climb out from beneath my duvet. The festive recipes keep us going, though, and Etna brings round the odd hot chocolate or coffee to keep our spirits up. You'll have to come back to the Cove and see The Street all lit up for Christmas.'

'Unless I stay…' She'd been hoping he'd say that but did her best not to look too happy. 'I'm talking with Mrs Wideman tomorrow, or should I say I'm having an interview? I'm not sure. All I know is we're meeting at the waffle shack so it can't be too formal.'

'It does sound rather laid back going to the waffle shack. Perhaps you could win her over with Daniel's menu, there's plenty to choose from.'

'I know, he's forever offering me something on the house. I'll be enormous if I keep taking him up on it.'

Not from where she was standing; he looked as fit as the day he'd arrived. 'You could, alternatively, play her a song on the guitar. Perhaps that could form part of the interview.'

'I like the way you think.'

'You're brave to play here.' She looked around at the crowds, the vast audience. 'It doesn't bother you?'

'Not at all. I'm more nervous playing to a bunch of disinterested teens than I am to a crowd of people influenced by the evils of alcohol,' he said with a raise of eyebrows that almost met the floppy hair across his forehead. 'I was happy to play when Terry overheard me talking about the guitar the other day. He and Kenneth were in the tea rooms and Etna suggested some live music at the pub and volunteered my services.'

Jade laughed. 'She doesn't want to let you go, that's why. She's doing all she can to keep you here with us.' The word *us* hovered in the air between them and mingled with the thick, sweet scent that wafted in the breeze from the tall orange honeysuckle bush.

'Kenneth is in the tea rooms a lot,' Jade remarked.

'They're definitely keen on each other,' he agreed. 'Question is, who will make the first move?'

She had the feeling he might be hinting at each of them rather than his auntie and the local. 'It's good to see her so happy,' she said instead of trying to read a deeper meaning. 'And whatever else happens, they've got a good friendship. It's not nice to be lonely; I'm glad she has company.'

'Me too. And I think company is the reason she was so ready for me to come and stay, and now Dad. She might love the business but she knows there are other things just as important.'

'Talking of work, tell me, what do you enjoy about your job the most?'

'Is this practice for my interview?' When she pulled a face he said, 'I love it when I find kids who are passionate about music.'

She sipped the cool, crisp, spritzy wine. 'And what happens with the ones who aren't?'

'Sometimes their heads can be turned.' He outlined some of the extra-curricular things he'd done in the past, the personal touches he added to his lessons. 'I haven't been able to do that so much without a permanent position.'

'And that's why you're interested in the one here?'

'It feels like the right time. But still, even with a permanent position, I need to be careful not to overstep and be too pushy, but keeping kids interested is half the battle in my job.'

170

'I'm sure it is. We have quite a few parents in at the bakery after the school run and you hear a lot, working behind the counter.'

'Believe me, I know. I heard a lot – some of which I'd rather I hadn't – working in the tea rooms.'

'Like what?'

He came closer to ensure nobody heard but her and when he whispered in her ear, he was so close she could feel his breath in the place just below her earlobe, tickling and making her shiver as he told her he'd heard two mothers having a conversation about getting Botox and one of them floating the idea of a boob job.

'At least it added an element of fun to your day,' she suggested.

He swigged his beer. 'Definitely. And I heard another guy tell his mate how much it hurt to have a back, sack and crack wax.'

Jade only just swallowed in time before she laughed. Otherwise, it could've been very embarrassing when her wine ended up spraying everywhere. 'There are some conversations you really should have in private. I wonder if he was even aware that you'd heard.'

'I don't think he cared. He wasn't making any effort to be discreet.'

'Perhaps he's proud he managed to have it done,' she sniggered.

They didn't get to talk much more because Carly, who was Nola and Terry's daughter, came over and asked to join them. 'Seriously, I can't take much more of Mrs Filligree's interrogation,' she said, elbows on the table and the base of her hands against her forehead.

Jade looked to where Mrs Filligree now had someone else's undivided attention. 'What's she interrogating you about?'

171

'The damn eggs.'

'Eggs?' Linc wondered.

Jade stepped in to explain. Probably easier with Carly still sitting low on the bench and hiding. 'Once upon a time, Melissa's family kept chickens and supplied locals – including Mrs Filligree – with eggs, then Nola took over the job and kept the chickens at Carly's cottage because she couldn't keep them here at the pub. These days, it's Carly's job to look after the chickens and the locals.'

'Don't tell me, you're not that into it?' Linc guessed.

Carly shook her head, sending her red curls bouncing. 'I never minded having them there but that was when Mum looked after the chickens. Nowadays, she and Dad are so busy with the pub that I'm the one doing most of the work. My parents still do all the egg deliveries to people in the Cove but all the rest is a lot of hard work.'

'Your kids love looking after the chickens,' Jade reminded her. Her son and her daughter both had the same fiery red hair and came into the bakery after school every Friday for a sugary doughnut. She'd tried to tempt them with cookies last time but it seemed doughnuts oozing with jam were the favourite. 'They tell me about them all the time – when they're naughty and don't want to go into their coop, whenever one escapes and you have to chase and catch it.'

With a sigh, Carly admitted, 'They do love the little guys, but now the kids are settled at school and I'm returning to my job come October, I could do without the extra workload. And really, I'm very OK with buying my eggs from the supermarket.'

A gasp sounded behind them and Carly cringed before turning round to greet Barney, who'd been enjoying a pint with Linc's father a few tables down but must've come over to congratulate the sisters on today's opening and overheard their conversation. 'Fresh eggs are infinitely better than anything you get from the supermarket.'

Carly pulled a face at Jade that said *Sprung*. 'It's the extra work, Barney, that's all. I know it's good to eat fresh.' She exchanged a grin with Linc and Jade. Barney did like to keep the community in order.

Terry the landlord picked that moment to jostle Linc out of his seat and back to the guitar playing. 'He's filling my beer garden with people,' he winked at the rest of them as he headed for the inside, different-sized glasses slotted between his fingers.

'Would you reconsider rehoming them?' Barney asked Carly after the interruption.

'I would consider it, although it's not that simple. As Jade said, the kids love them – I can't imagine their little faces if I told them they'd lose them.'

'Who says they have to lose them?' Barney persisted. 'I've got a lot of land at my place.'

Surprised, Carly sat up a bit taller in her seat. 'You're offering?'

'I am. And Cora and Justin would be welcome to come over anytime to see them.'

'That would be amazing.' Carly looked as though this man had made her night. 'Are you sure?'

The guitar filled the air again, making people smile when Linc began to play an Oasis hit tune. Some were even beginning to sing along, swaying in time with the music. 'Come on, I'll buy you a drink and we'll carry on our discussion. Make sure we bypass Mrs Filligree,' he suggested when Carly got up, much happier than she'd been when she sat down.

Others filled the table the minute there was a space but Jade didn't mind and she didn't feel she had to chat all the time either. She was quite content to sit back and listen to Linc as the skies grew darker and she even shivered.

Valerie was next to come over, apologising she hadn't seen much of Jade, offering her congratulations. 'I can't stay any longer, even though I'd love to.' Baby Thomas was strapped against her chest in a special carrier. She had hold of his little feet as though feeling him against her body wasn't quite enough. 'This one is starting to fuss.'

'He's done well.' Jade could just about reach her finger in to stroke his cheek as he turned his head from side to side, perhaps hungry. With the air growing chilly, she wanted her bed as much as this little one probably did, especially now the music had stopped again.

'He's always good in the carrier. We've danced, haven't we, Thomas? We've done the rounds to talk to everyone, but now it's time to head home and say goodnight to Daddy.' She began to smile at Jade. 'You can't take your eyes off him. Want to borrow him one night? He wakes up like clockwork for a 4 a.m. feed. He's all yours, just give me the nod.'

'That's not too early for us, we'll be baking soon after that time.'

'Perhaps he's going to be a baker when he grows up.' Valerie had her chin lightly resting against the top of Thomas's head.

'Send him my way, I'll teach him everything I know.'

Before Valerie could escape, Tilly and Celeste took an opportunity to fuss over Thomas.

'He's gorgeous,' Tilly enthused.

'He totally is,' Jade agreed, waving mum and baby off as they left for home.

'Did your uterus skip a beat?' Tilly giggled once they'd gone off down the path that ran alongside the pub and led to the pavement on The Street. She finished her glass of prosecco.

'Quiet, you.' But it had. Of course it had. Jade had wanted a baby for a long time. It was the part of her life plan she'd begun to put into action right after they returned from Italy. Celeste knew about the big step she'd taken back then, but she suspected her sister had forgotten all about it.

'She needs a man before she can have a baby,' Celeste said, coming to join them. 'I'd suggest trying that first.'

'Look around…' Tilly lifted her glass as she turned, as though she'd been given a project she could finally get her teeth stuck into, and when chef at the pub, Benjamin, walked past with a bowl of freshly cut chips she almost knocked into him. Luckily, he was amused – and strong enough that the food stayed in his hand. 'Benjamin's single,' she whispered, although her whisper was decibels higher than anyone else's might be.

'Benjamin's a friend, nothing more,' Jade replied. He was a lovely guy and she hadn't said anything to her friend but over the past few weeks she'd noticed him watching Tilly whenever they were in the pub, coming over to where they were sitting to say hello any time he got the chance.

Tilly gestured to the crowds in the beer garden using her hand, although it was so dark by now that Jade had no idea what or who she might be gesturing at. 'Plenty of other men to choose from, take your pick. Get yourself a baby daddy!'

'Oh my goodness, no need to tell the world my desire to have a baby.' Glad Tilly's glass was now empty, she added, 'No more drinks for you, eh?'

'Tilly's fun when she's drunk,' Celeste giggled.

'Actually, she is,' said Jade in a low voice. 'But I wish it wasn't me we were talking about. Besides,' she said to them both as they moved further away from anyone else, 'I would never do that to a man, I'd never trap him.' She wished she hadn't run out of wine – at least then she'd have her glass to hide behind, the alcohol to make her braver. 'Perhaps I have another plan.'

Celeste showed the first signs of curiosity, her mind clearly going to the place she thought her sister had left behind. 'Tell us more. I mean, I should be involved seeing as we live together and run a bakery together.' Jade hesitated enough that Celeste's brain whirred into action and she lost interest in finishing her own drink. 'You're not doing what I think you're doing, are you?'

'What?' Tilly looked from one to the other. 'What is she thinking of doing?'

It looked as though the moment had arrived, the moment she'd admit everything, and perhaps at long last she was ready. 'Sit down, both of you, and I'll tell you.'

Tilly, clearly tipsy, tiptoed as if in a comedy sketch over to the nearest vacant table. 'Spill your secrets.' She beamed a smile at Benjamin, who must have picked up on how drunk she was because he'd brought over a jug filled with iced water and three glasses.

As Celeste poured them each a water, Jade told them how she'd grown tired of waiting for Mr Right, that she knew time was not on her side now she was approaching thirty-four.

'I want a family, plain and simple,' Jade concluded to the two shocked faces, neither of which gave much away.

Celeste managed to mask any approval or disapproval. Perhaps the information needed time to percolate.

'I don't want to settle for any man just because I want to have children,' Jade went on. 'It wouldn't be fair to do that to him, to the child, or to me.'

And although Tilly wasn't at all sober, she was still able to think. 'There's something I'm missing, isn't there?'

'There is,' Jade exhaled. 'I need to bring you up to speed.' It would also give Celeste a chance to digest Jade's plan, part of which she already knew about, and let it settle in her mind.

And so, beneath the night sky, Jade told them both everything – how devastated she'd been to break up with Dario when they left Venice and how she'd returned to England grieving over what might've been.

A few months after the sisters arrived home in England, when her head was a lot straighter than it had been at first, Jade had looked into getting her eggs frozen. She knew she wanted a family – she had no doubts in her mind – but after Dario, she felt as though finding someone else and falling in love was impossible. Celeste had urged her to wait before she did anything and she had, she'd gone to counselling, she'd seen a gynaecologist to check everything was in working order, but she never changed her mind. Celeste had supported her during the process, she'd been there for the daily injections to stimulate the ovaries, been by her side at ultrasound appointments and for blood tests whenever she could, and she was there to drive her home after the egg collection. They'd talked and talked over those weeks when the process was in full swing, but once it was done, the talking stopped. Jade had suddenly become content that she had safeguarded her future dreams, she was far happier than she'd been in a long while, and although Celeste never said as much, Jade wondered whether her sister was thinking her actions had been more of a knee-jerk reaction to the split with Dario than a firm plan.

Both sisters had thrown themselves into the business and it wasn't until they started to put their renovation plans in place, including expanding the cake-making side of things, that Jade began to think more about her plans and dreams on a more personal level, about the family she longed to have. The timing would work once the renovations were finished and they were on track with the bakery. She and Dario had severed contact; the happy ending they'd both discussed on more than one occasion, with children a part of the bigger picture, was over. Gone. And the day Linc had found the photograph of Dario, prompting Jade to finally put it away with the rest of the travelling memories, had been another sign that she was ready. She wanted to get started with the IVF.

'I was worried about telling you my plans.' She watched her sister, trying to gauge her reaction. 'I know you were behind me when I went through having my eggs frozen, you were one-hundred-per-cent supportive, but the next stage makes it real.'

'What is the next stage?' Tilly asked. She seemed to have sobered up a lot with the topic of discussion.

'Basic biology.' Celeste reached out her hand and clutched her sister's in support, although Jade suspected she needed as much emotional support to get her own head around it. 'She needs a sperm donor.'

Tilly puffed out her cheeks. 'That's some news. Why didn't you ever say anything to me?'

Jade shrugged. They were good friends, but it was so personal she hadn't been ready until now. 'I'm telling you now that I think I have things sorted in my own head.'

'Well, we are all behind you,' Tilly assured her. 'And if anyone can make it work, it's you.'

Celeste rallied. 'My only doubts are because I worry about you, but you've had this in the back of your mind for a long time, I need to remember that. And if it's what you really want, I will be there for you. So, this is why you've been acting a bit odd?'

'I've had a lot on my mind,' Jade nodded.

'I don't suppose we could ask Linc if he needs another job, could we?' Celeste quickly realised her suggestion had been taken the wrong way. 'I don't mean as a sperm donor! I mean as a baker – I'm going to need help while you're off having a baby.' She began to smile. 'I'm going to be an auntie.'

Tilly was smiling too. 'What happens next? How do you choose the sperm donor?' She'd almost sobered up but when her glass missed the edge of the table as she put it down and she had to rescue it from the ground, Jade knew she'd have a whopping hangover in the morning.

Jade took out her phone and brought up the website of the clinic she'd chosen to use so she could show the girls some details, hopefully get their backing all the more, because now she'd told them, she knew how much she

179

really wanted that. She found the appropriate screen and showed them how you could select a donor by narrowing down the search. If you wanted, you could select race, eye colour, height, hair colour. Each donor had a number and if you delved further you could find out hobbies and interests, medical details including screening tests, a description of them and their personality traits, their skills, their job.

'There's a lot to think about, plenty to consider,' she explained to them both when she put her phone down. 'And it isn't cheap. Neither was the egg collection,' she informed Tilly. Celeste already knew, of course, that Jade had used her own savings, and she still had more – she'd always been sensible with finances and they'd worked some of the time they travelled, which meant she hadn't made too bad a dent in her bank account. 'I have enough money for a couple of attempts. I mean, it might not even work, but I have to try.' Her voice shook; she hadn't realised how emotional she'd become talking about it with them both.

Celeste and Tilly both reached over for a hug, uttering their encouragement and support.

'How will it work with a business to run?' Tilly asked. She ran her own shop, Tilly's Bits 'n' Pieces, so she knew what it was like – they all did.

'I will have to do what everyone else does and look into childcare, juggle both. The good thing is that if the cake side really takes off, I can work slightly different hours to the bakery.' She and Celeste had already talked about that a long time ago, they'd discussed taking on another worker should they need it, and so it wasn't a total surprise and Celeste still seemed on board with the idea.

With a deep breath, Jade said, 'I'm about to fall asleep on my feet.' She realised Linc had disappeared already too and, disappointed, all she wanted to do now was go home.

'I'm ready to go too,' Tilly yawned, eyelids heavy.

'Me too.' Celeste smiled at her sister and gave her another hug before they set off.

Jade smiled a little when they nodded goodbye to Benjamin and his eyes lingered on Tilly. He was definitely starting to care for her more than he was letting on.

The walk home seemed endless even though it wasn't far at all and as they passed the tea rooms Jade began to wonder what had happened to Linc. Why had he disappeared so quickly from the beer garden, and why hadn't he even bothered to say goodbye?

But it had been an eventful day and with an early start looming, her thoughts soon fizzled out the minute her head hit the pillow.

Perhaps getting everything out in the open was what it took to get a good night's sleep.

Chapter Eleven

'Easy!' Joseph told his son when Linc came into the tea rooms for his lunch break after working at the waffle shack, took the mug of coffee Patricia had made him and plonked it on the table so hard it slopped everywhere. 'What's going on with you? You're like a bear with a sore head this morning. You didn't sink that many beers at the pub last night, did you?'

The last thing Linc wanted to do was discuss with his dad what was bothering him. He felt as gloomy as the overcast day outside. It was as though summer couldn't be bothered to hold up its end of the bargain. 'No, unlike you and Barney. You should both know better at your age.'

'He's good company.'

'He is,' Etna agreed, sitting down with the both of them. Patricia was enforcing regular rest times for her boss and this was one of them. 'He's excited about his wedding. Did he bend your ear about it?' she asked her brother as all three of them nursed a coffee.

'He told me all about it, invited me along,' Joseph smiled, 'and he told me all about the Wedding Dress Ball, although I said I'd heard plenty about that from you over the years.'

Linc had to admit the coffee calmed him down. It was a good one, made out of the fancy machine – way better than one you got at those chain cafes selling stuff that tasted like dishwater and had no right calling itself a coffee.

Etna and Joseph were on to talking about the wedding, the ball, what it all would entail.

'We could go together,' Joseph suggested to his sister.

'You should be warned, brother dear – I like to dance.'

'Even with your ankle?'

'Stop fussing about my ankle. It's fine, I've not had much bother from it at all the last couple of days. And I don't have to dance the whole time. How about you, Linc? I assume you'll be going along to the wedding – it's an open invitation to anyone coming to the ball, it seems.'

'I don't think any of it is my scene.'

'Rubbish. I've heard you talk about school functions where you've enjoyed getting in amongst it and you told me it was hard as you had to hold back and be responsible, and that the kids had laughed at your dancing.'

He couldn't help a smirk. She was right. His dancing wasn't the best but he had enjoyed every function he'd been charged with overseeing. When he'd heard Barney last night at the pub talking about the event, he'd thought it would be the perfect place to invite Jade and perhaps they could slow dance – now, that he could manage. He could hire a tux, dress to impress. He hadn't thought much beyond that until he'd overheard her conversation with her sister and their friend who owned a shop. Before that, he never would've picked her as one of those girls who, similar to his ex, was desperate enough for a family that she was willing to trap some poor bugger into parenthood.

'If you're in the Cove,' Etna went on, 'it wouldn't be right for you not to come along. And, remember, the Wedding Dress Ball is for charity. We raise a lot of money every single year.'

'What charity?' He thanked Patricia for the oat biscuits she brought over to their table and helped himself to one. Earlier, she'd tried to persuade him to have a big slice of millionaire's shortbread but it was far too sweet for him.

Etna broke off part of her biscuit and popped it in her mouth, sending a thumbs up in Patricia's direction. 'The charity is White Clover. They support families after the death of a child. Oh, they do such wonderful work for people who really are quite lost.' She went on to confide about Barney's story to Joseph.

'How incredibly sad.' Joseph shook his head, his look suggesting he was grateful his own sons were still alive and in his life despite one of them working away so many months of the year.

'Fine,' Linc relented, 'I'll come along.' How could he refuse when it was for a good cause? If he was going to be staying in the Cove, he wanted to get to know people and it was probably the best opportunity he was going to get.

Joseph picked up his cap from the table when he knocked it off. 'You'll need a date, son.'

'I hadn't heard that,' Linc batted back. 'In fact, I heard it was perfectly acceptable to go along on your own.'

'He's right,' Patricia called over. 'Singles, couples, doesn't matter, everyone welcome.'

Joseph stirred the remains of his coffee and Etna thanked Patricia, who'd efficiently appeared to clear away the empties and didn't miss a chance to remind Etna she had to have the full fifteen-minute break before she came back to help.

'I'm happy to head there on my own,' Linc assured his dad and his auntie.

'I know someone who might well be happy to be asked.' It was as though Etna, lipstick in place, eyes twinkling, was in a staring contest with her nephew and she wasn't going to be the one to look away first.

'Who?' Joseph looked from Linc to his sister. 'You've only been here five minutes, son.'

Linc didn't miss a trick. 'I know Kenneth is going,' he said, taking the focus away from him and putting it onto his auntie. 'I heard him talking about it a couple of days ago.'

'Kenneth?' Joseph was all ears.

'Kenneth is a friend,' Etna assured him, her discomfort masked by her ability to talk and explain someone else in the Cove to her brother. 'I'll introduce you when he comes in.'

Linc checked the time, finished his coffee and took his mug over to the counter at the front. 'I'll leave you two to it, I've got an interview to get ready for.'

'But you didn't answer my question about this girl,' his dad said, catching him as he made for the door. 'Who is she?'

But he declined to answer and as they both called out their good-luck wishes, he left them to gossip or whatever it was they'd occupy themselves with for the rest of the time.

He headed to Tumbleweed House for a shower first – this might be an informal interview but he'd been wrestling with roots and weeds and having a turn on the digger out the back of the waffle shack and although passable to sit in the tea rooms with family, he wasn't sure he looked or smelt like someone anyone would be willing to hire right now.

After his shower he made his way back to The Street, past the tea rooms and bakery, crossed over and walked back up towards the Waffle Shack. He purposely hadn't looked in at the bakery, even though the smell had definitely teased him enough and made his stomach remember how good everything from there tasted, in case he caught Jade looking his way. After Linc had heard the girls talking he'd considered cancelling today's interview and leaving the Cove as soon as he could, but ever since this potential job had arisen, he'd begun to think it could be good not only for him but also for his dad if they had a change and moved up this way. His dad might accuse him of existing rather than living, of narrowing friendship groups and not opening himself up to opportunities to be happy, but his dad had been doing the same thing since his mum died. Joseph was going through his daily routine assuming he had no choice, but hopefully this time with Etna was showing him that really wasn't the case. He'd drawn comfort from his routine for years, and perhaps it was time he made some changes too.

The thing that had been so much worse than what he overheard was seeing Jade with the baby. Watching how she cooed over him and touched his cheek, Linc had felt something in him pang as though to remind him he might want a family of his own one day. He just wanted it under the right circumstances. And that was why he hadn't wanted to catch her attention earlier. He didn't want to talk to Jade and have to bury all the feelings he knew he had for her.

Linc crossed the green space that led up to the waffle shack and shook off thoughts of anything other than the interview. He wasn't nervous; he usually handled formal meetings well, including the inevitable grilling for a new job. He didn't have a problem just being himself and had the attitude that if it was the right fit, it would all work out.

Daniel already knew he was coming in today to meet Mrs Wideman and told him he'd reserve the table at the edge by the side window so they had less chance of being disturbed. Linc pushed through the door and although he was ten minutes early, it seemed the head teacher was even more prompt. With a nod in Daniel's direction, he went right over and introduced himself. Mrs Wideman had told him he was welcome to dress informally as she would but he'd still made a bit of an effort with a well-ironed pale blue button-down shirt, tailored cotton-linen navy trousers and a pair of Timberland shoes that were at least not covered in dirt like the boots he'd been wearing while he worked out the back of this place.

'Please, call me Jane,' Mrs Wideman insisted when they made their introductions. She had a warm smile and she wasted no time telling him she had waffles on the way. 'Order something too, please, or I'll feel rather greedy.'

That in itself told him it was going to be a good interview and, over waffles drizzled in maple syrup, they talked shop. She asked him to tell her all about his career so far – he suspected starting with that the second Daniel set down her waffles and cutlery wrapped in a serviette was more to give her a chance to enjoy her food before

187

she had to really concentrate on getting the most out of him. When it was her turn, she told him a bit about the school, about the role, what the teacher who was leaving had done so far and about some of the students. She seemed forward-thinking and, whilst following government guidelines, wanted to inject her own personality into the place, which spoke volumes to Linc. He guessed a lot you couldn't really tell until you actually worked somewhere but it was enough for now and as soon as the interview was over, Jane, whose elderly mother had come up to the waffle shack to meet her, told him that although of course he would have to go through all the official channels and apply formally for the position, she would strongly support his application and would fast-track the process since the new teacher was needed in September.

'It's like you're heaven-sent,' said Jane before she left. Perhaps the waffles had gone to her head – that or Daniel had added a tipple to the maple syrup. 'I was in a flap when Mr Simmons announced his sudden departure. We thought he'd do at least two more terms but he wants his B&B to be up and running by Christmas.'

Linc shook her hand before she said her farewells, pulled a big pair of sunglasses down from where they'd been nested in her hair for the entire interview, and set off to enjoy the summer's day now that the sun had re-emerged from wherever it had been hiding.

Daniel was ringing up an order on the till. 'How did it go?' He looked up once he'd scribbled the details on a piece of paper and passed it to Brianna to deal with in the kitchen. 'I gave Jane extra maple syrup – her favourite – thought I'd sweeten her up a bit.'

'Well, it must've worked because she offered me the job subject to the formalities.'

'Great news!'

And what's more, he was going to accept. Funny, just a few days ago, if he'd overheard Jade and felt that disappointment in the pit of his stomach from finding out she might not be quite the girl he thought she was, he'd most probably have moved on to the next thing, left before there was a chance he'd get emotionally attached and possibly hurt all over again. But being here in the Cove had given him enough of a snapshot into permanency that he realised if he kept on running, he might never stop. And that wouldn't be the path that would make him happy forever. Already he'd begun to wonder whether he may well have jumped to conclusions about Jade and the conversation he'd heard. Or perhaps that was wishful thinking. Whatever it was, he knew that the only way to know for sure would be to talk to her.

'I might use your bathroom before I head off,' he told Daniel, who nodded before turning his attentions to the customer who came through the door. The place had cleared out after the mid-afternoon rush but Linc doubted it would be long before it filled up again.

When Linc came out of the bathroom Daniel was laughing as Brianna told him, 'You should've grabbed him as your customer first, we've got so many delicious flavours.'

'What did I miss?' Linc asked Daniel when Brianna disappeared back into the kitchen.

'My last customer was someone wanting to know where Jade's bakery was.'

'Jade's bakery?'

'He probably picked one of the two names on the posters that are still around the village following the opening. Didn't have the heart to tell him the freebies finished yesterday,' he grinned.

Linc took a bottle of Coke from the fridge and pulled some change from his pocket. 'Poor guy is going to be very disappointed.' He waved his goodbyes and left on a high. The interview had gone well and all he wanted to do now was talk to Jade, clear things up.

Swigging from the bottle of fizzy drink, he set off down across the grass area and back to The Street. He waved a hello at Lucy, who was heading into her workshop, at Zara, who was wearing an apron and writing ice-cream flavours onto a blackboard outside the ice-creamery, and then he crossed the road to head to the bakery. It wasn't like he could ask Jade about her conversation at the pub just like that but he found his legs taking him that way anyhow, as though his mood had shifted a gear now he had a job offer, now he was staying in the village.

As he drew closer and saw Jade outside giving the glass on the windows a bit of a spray and a wipe, he stopped when a tall, dark stranger who'd got to her first tapped her on the shoulder and she turned around.

Since she had her back to Linc now, he couldn't hear what she was saying – or what the man was saying, for that matter – but he didn't need to. What he did see was the man scoop Jade up into his arms and twirl her round, their bodies pressed close enough together to suggest this person was a hell of a lot more than a friend.

And then it dawned on him. He had seen this man before. In a photo. The photo that had fallen from Jade's bag. This was the Italian, the love of her life, The One, or whatever you wanted to call him. And here he was, in the village, holding Jade's hand as they made their way inside the bakery, neither of them noticing the other guy standing in disbelief, looking on.

Linc turned and walked in the opposite direction, around the bend, past the Heritage Inn and on down the road. He didn't know where he was going, he didn't care. He just wanted to walk because now, no matter what he'd hoped might happen, everything had changed.

Chapter Twelve

Jade still couldn't believe he was here. Dario. In England. In Heritage Cove. But she couldn't shut up shop and talk to him the way she needed to. Not only had they just relaunched the business after the refurbishment, but it was summer, school holidays, and there were only two members of staff at the bakery, her and Celeste.

She'd come inside with him in tow and Celeste had almost dropped the baguette she'd filled with cheese and pastrami and was trying to wiggle into a bag for the girl waiting. Celeste had come around to the customer side of the display cabinets and wrapped Dario in a hug to welcome him, her jaw practically dragging on the floor and eyes darting from him to Jade and back again as though trying to work out whether Jade had any idea this was coming. Jade was pretty sure her sister could tell from her demeanour that she'd had no idea.

And now, Celeste was busy serving, zipping from the front of the bakery to the kitchen and back again, while Jade took charge of the freshly made doughnuts that sat in rows waiting for her to push in the piping nozzle and give them their squirt of raspberry jam before they got their final roll in sugar. Dario was patiently leaning against the central benchtop watching her and every time he spoke, the velvety, thick Italian accent reminding her of what they'd once had, what she'd missed, it made her realise how much she'd dreamed of this moment until finally she'd tried to stop doing that and move on.

When Dario had turned up an hour ago, dark shades nestled in thick ebony hair that still held the colour of youth, Jade had been cleaning the windows out front. A bird had left its mark on one of the tiny criss-crossed window panes and it hardly looked appealing for a food outlet. She'd cleaned it off with warm soapy water and then gone back outside with spray and a cloth to give all the panels a bit of a once-over and a sheen. When someone tapped her on the shoulder she'd expected it to be a local, hoped perhaps it was Linc come to see her, but she'd turned around to see the man she'd once fallen head over heels in love with. It had taken her a while after he greeted her in Italian to get that rush of emotion, she was so shocked. Her mind had spun across the miles, back to Italy, back to the narrow backstreets and alleyways of Venice and the hot, dry summer days, the times they'd spent eating lunch alfresco immersed in culture and Venetian architecture, the nights they'd spent together and woken with neither of them ever wanting it to end, the long days Dario had worked at the family restaurant and she'd hung around even if all she got in those twenty-four hours were snatched moments of time to exchange a smile, a kiss or a brief "ti amo", *I love you*.

Jade turned her attention from the doughnuts to the latest bread order for six wholemeal loaves sliced thick, drowning out any possibility of conversation with Dario as she got busy and the machine chugged its way through the task. She put each loaf in turn just behind the main body of the slicer, closed the lid and watched it closely even though she didn't need to. She didn't want

Dario to distract her, to try to talk properly, not yet. She wasn't ready for this. She wasn't prepared.

The blades juddered each time a loaf was gradually pushed from behind and emerged onto the crumb tray. Jade would bag each one up, seal it with a tie and move on to the next, her mind zoning in on the task rather than anything else.

Jade thought back again to those heady nights in Venice, the night she'd met Dario. One evening she and Celeste had been from restaurant to restaurant trying to find a menu that tempted them, none of them quite being what the other was looking for. The truth was it hadn't been all that long since they'd found the best cannoli they'd tasted so far and it was too soon after these treats, with their crisp shells encasing the creamy filling, for either of them to be truly hungry. They'd stopped at a restaurant at the side of a small courtyard and although they were about to move on, the elderly woman on the door either didn't understand them saying no or she was playing dumb to get them to go and sit down at one of the tables at the side of the eatery with its arched window shapes, open to the outside. They'd found themselves jostled into their seats with menus thrust upon them before they could do much about it. It wasn't long before they'd both realised it was Nonna's job to get the customers in and everyone else's job to keep them there. A waitress had hurried over with a bottle of water for the table and wine glasses when they nodded their assent.

'I suppose it's easier than spending all evening walking around looking at menus,' Celeste had laughed.

Jade was about to reply when a waiter came to their side, the tones of Italian washing over her and casting their spell – which, along with his smile, was powerful enough for her to look so dumbstruck her sister began to laugh.

After he'd brought them their food, he wanted to know all about their travels – where they'd been, where they were going. They explained this was their last stop and he did his best to stay with them until Nonna picked up on the extra attention he'd been giving and clearly instructed him to get back to work. He'd mimed the slitting of his throat with a nod in Nonna's direction and made them both laugh.

But it wasn't the handsome waiter who'd got Jade's attention with his easy conversation, classic dark looks and ready smile, it was the man sitting on the table diagonally across from theirs, a glass of red wine between his fingers, deep-set eyes looking her way as he used a free hand to brush hair that was a bit too long at the front away from his face. It didn't stay put but he didn't seem to mind.

Celeste, meanwhile, had got the waiter's number and arranged a date on his day off later in the week and she'd been so busy flirting, she hadn't noticed her sister's attentions diverted elsewhere. The handsome stranger was eating alone and reading a book at the same time but every time Jade looked up and over at him, he seemed to sense it, lowered the book a little and surreptitiously looked her way.

When the girls paid the bill and stood to go, Celeste flirted some more with her waiter and the stranger chose that moment to pass by their table as Jade looped her small bag over a bare shoulder, her skin still tingling from the sun's rays that day. He let his hand brush hers lightly, not so much she looked straight down but enough that she knew.

'Did you enjoy our restaurant?' He leaned in close to her, his dulcet tone rendering her speechless for the first time that night. His English was good but the way he was looking at her was as though he only spoke to her this way, that he'd saved a part of himself just for her.

'Your restaurant?' She smoothed the front of her strappy linen dress she'd found at a street market in Greece.

'I'm head waiter. The restaurant belongs to my family. Has done for four generations,' he told her, large and honest eyes the shade of grey never wavering. 'You liked it?'

She was aware of her sister watching her and beneath the scrutiny of them both she needed to escape. 'I…I have to go.'

'Come back tomorrow,' he called after her. 'Si?'

All she could do was smile and walk away. He was gorgeous; maybe he did this all the time, flirted with the locals and tourists, and that was why his English was so good. He could probably speak a dozen languages to get his way every time.

But the girls had returned to the restaurant the next night because Celeste wanted to see the waiter and that time Dario had been working but he'd still cast enough glances Jade's way, his intentions obvious. The girls had gone again the night after that and on the third evening, when Celeste had gone off on a date with the handsome waiter, Jade's love affair with Dario had begun.

Celeste, true to form, had had a great time, a holiday fling that would never be anything more despite her spending a lot of time with the waiter. Jade, on the other hand, knew what she and Dario had wasn't just the buzz of a summer fling, it ran much deeper. And while Celeste worked for five weeks in a different restaurant making some cash to buy herself a new car when they returned to England, Jade spent all her time with Dario. They talked about how their lives might be together if they made the commitment. Over the weeks they planned a dreamlike future, a family. They'd both fallen head over heels and Jade had let herself believe it would last. But when it became apparent how impossible it would be with her new business in England and him a part of the family restaurant in Venice, they made the mutual decision to go their separate ways.

Saying goodbye to Dario had been painful, gut-wrenching. He'd told her, 'Non dimenticarmi', *Don't forget me*. Both of them had been devastated but they'd ripped themselves away from one another and hadn't been in touch since.

Before today, Jade had thought she had sorted her head out and was moving forwards. But she didn't know what to think now Dario was here.

The ringing phone on the wall in the kitchen took her attention from the loaves she handed to Celeste to a cake commission from a couple planning a Halloween party. They wanted a unique cake – most did when they got in touch, it was part of the excitement – and they'd run on about spiders, cobwebs, ghosts and ghouls. Jade's brain hadn't been quite able to make the leap into creativity with Dario so close by but she arranged a meeting with the couple in a few days – enough time to get her head on straight. Dario's presence was sparking a befuddled brain, not something she usually suffered from at work. Perhaps it was the shock because she'd never been anything other than comfortable in his company. Or maybe it was because she had no idea why he was here, what he wanted – and why all of a sudden?

'Where are you staying?' she asked him once she'd hung up the phone. She used a small brush to rid the bread slicer of excess crumbs, letting them fall into the plastic container she held beneath.

'I have a room at the Heritage Inn.' The words rolled off his tongue. When Jade was in Venice they'd spoken English most of the time they were together, although he'd done his best to teach her as much Italian as he could. 'I wanted to surprise you but…well, I didn't know your living arrangements, your accommodation.'

She smiled. Sometimes his sentences didn't include phrases most people would use, and sounded overly formal. 'Me and Celeste live out there.' She pointed out of the open back door, a little relieved he hadn't assumed he could stay with her.

His eyes followed the path up to the back door of the cottage. 'It's very English. And what do you say? Cute?'

'Yes, it is cute, that's another word for small, but we've got an upstairs now so it's perfect for us at the moment.'

'England is pretty.'

'It is.' She couldn't help but smile at him. He'd come all this way on a whim, no warning. His first time in England. 'What are your plans while you're here?'

'To see you.' He didn't add anything else.

Flustered, she told him, 'You'll enjoy the inn, you're in good hands there.'

'The owner, Tracy, is nice. She's a good cook, I've had an enormous breakfast. What is it called…the Full English?'

'That's right…sausages, bacon, eggs, fried bread, mushrooms…have I forgotten anything?'

'I had spinach too. I turned down the offer of a black pudding.'

'An acquired taste,' she explained before nodding to the tray of prepared doughnuts. 'I'll be back after I've taken these through.'

In the bakery Celeste was wiping down the curved glass-fronted display cabinet. 'What's he doing here?' She immediately leapt into question time. 'Did you have any idea he was planning this?'

'None at all.' Jade quickly checked Dario was still in the kitchen and he was, except he'd moved to lean against the door frame at the back and was gazing at the cottage. He looked so much like she remembered – tall, dark and outrageously handsome with a winning smile that had held her captive from the word go.

'I can handle things here if you like,' Celeste whispered as Jade unloaded the last of the doughnuts. Their shimmery sugar coating had already drawn the attentions of a woman who'd been perusing the glass-fronted cabinets, or maybe it was their doughy smell filling the air that did it.

Jade, empty tray in hand, wanted to go back to Dario and talk but at the same time she wished she could go about her normal day. 'I can't, what if we get too busy?'

'Then we get a queue out the door and people will have to wait.' Celeste popped three doughnuts into a paper bag for the lady and waved a cheery goodbye. 'Find out what he's doing here. He was the love of your life once, remember?' She winked but the doubts on her face matched Jade's own, because she had no idea what to feel. 'Find out whether this is a fleeting visit or whether he's declaring his undying love and moving in.'

'This was the last thing I expected today.'

'Me too. Give me a call if you need me.' She put a reassuring hand onto her sister's shoulder.

'I don't really want to face questions from anyone in the Cove so I'll take him into the cottage.' She knew Celeste would give her the space she needed.

Jade took a deep breath, hung her apron up on its hook at the far end of the kitchen and motioned for Dario to follow her from the bakery to the cottage.

There, she boiled the kettle without thinking, dropped tea bags into mugs before she remembered he didn't even drink it. And the only coffee he'd enjoy would be one from Etna's fancy machine, and Etna wasn't someone she wanted looking on at this conversation.

'I'm sorry, I only have instant coffee,' she said.

'I'm not here for your coffee.'

His smile and the way he was staring at her made her nervous as she took out one of the tea bags and instead added instant coffee granules. Her hand wobbled as she poured the boiling water into the mugs and she asked him about his journey to distract him from focusing on her actions. Otherwise, she was liable to pour the water everywhere and burn herself. It worked. He talked about some of the sights in London where he'd stayed for two nights until he caught a train and then a bus up here, and she managed to get the full mugs over to the table without much drama.

Sitting at the table, she watched him as he talked. It was surreal, having him here. But the moment he paused in his amusing story of trying to navigate the tube system, she said, 'I always wondered whether you'd send me an email or get in touch another way.'

The whole time he'd been here his eyes hadn't left her. When you went into a different house, someone's home, you took in the surroundings, the colour on the walls, perhaps the things dotted around that made it theirs, but Dario hadn't done any of that. His attention was on her and her alone. 'We agreed we wouldn't. I almost did, more than once.'

'Me too.'

They let the moment settle between them. And while she looked down into her mug of tea or watched the sway of the branches on the neighbouring tree beyond the kitchen window, Dario didn't waver. He watched her, made eye contact every chance he could.

'What made you come now?' she asked. She hadn't taken a sip of her tea; she suspected it would go cold before she even did.

'I wish we hadn't said goodbye at all. I regret that we did. And I'm sorry we agreed not to stay in touch. I thought it would be easier.'

'It wasn't easy, but we both decided it was the best thing at the time.'

'I thought I'd let you go and you'd move on with your life, that I would too.'

'I looked you up on the internet,' she admitted. 'You have moved on, you've done well.'

She felt skin on skin as he reached out across the table and covered her hand with his own bigger, darker hand. The hand she remembered holding more times than she could count as they explored the sights together, as he took her to popular tourist hangouts as well as the hidden gems only the locals knew about.

'I looked you up too. It's how I found you, and I remembered the name of the village.' He smiled kindly and she felt dizzy, remembering how safe she'd always felt with him. 'You've done very well too,' he added, perhaps sensing her head was all over the place and so a chance to make reference to her business might be the best thing for now.

She silently thanked him for his understanding. 'We're pleased with how quickly we settled in here and made the changes we wanted to at the bakery. The locals are friendly, supportive, but we wanted to really make the place our own, which is why we renovated.' She was babbling now, but it felt like the only release from all the tension. She recounted more details of the cottage renovation too, the way they'd added the upstairs, and he was interested enough that he asked her to show him around.

She left the mug of tea, soon to be stone-cold, and went through to the lounge. He followed after her, all the while close enough that she could feel the heat of his body unless she was mistaken and really it was the summer breeze sneaking in through any open door or window it could. They talked about paint colours on the walls, the soft furnishings, Jade going into too much detail but every exchange leaving her more relaxed and able to process the fact that he was here.

They took the stairs up to the top and she explained the conversion, how it gave them the space they needed, how it had transformed the cottage into a real home. But aware she was in her bedroom and had to move so close to him that they were almost touching when their heights meant they both needed to stand towards the tallest parts of the ceiling, she tried to head back downstairs.

He caught her hand before she could. 'I'm confused. I do not know whether you are glad I am here or not.' He was so close she could see the marks on his earlobes where once he'd worn studs and as he moved from his teens to his twenties took them out and let the holes close up.

It was good to see him but she didn't know whether she was glad he was here. All she knew was she was confused. 'It's good to see you,' she told him honestly.

'Mia cara…' *My darling*. He stepped closer and the heady feeling was back, the same way she'd reacted to him the first time he took her hand in Italy, the first time he kissed her.

She pulled back. 'How is your family?' Family was part of the reason he hadn't wanted to leave Venice; in fact, she'd say it was probably more of the deciding factor than the business and the fact he'd been born and raised there. She and Celeste were close to their parents but it wasn't determined by distance and even though they were here and their mum and dad still lived in Ireland, it didn't diminish the family relationships one bit. Their brother was still in Ireland too, as much a part of the place as a pint of Guinness, with no intention to ever live anywhere else, but Jade and Celeste had both always been keen to spread their wings. When first Celeste and then Jade had moved to London, their dad's words had been "Go live your lives, let us live ours". They'd all laughed about it because the minute Celeste and Jade left, their brother got his own place, their parents downsized and used the freed-up cash to go and do the things they hadn't been able to do before retirement – see Vienna, ride a camel in Egypt and, the last trip they'd been on, Christmas in New York, which according to her dad was not for the faint-hearted and not something he was keen to repeat with the crowds and the excitement.

'My family is good,' Dario told her. 'They all send their love.' And when she smiled, he told her, 'Nonna is still with us, still up in the early hours fussing around us all.'

When she went to ask more, he reached out and put a finger across her lips. 'Please, I don't want to talk about them, I want to talk about us, Jade. I want to know if there is – if there can be – an us.'

She froze for a moment at the contact against her lip, the familiarity, the warmth and the remembering but then she snapped out of it and headed straight back down the stairs. 'I don't know what to say, Dario. You show up like this, all of a sudden, expecting answers. And I don't have the answers. I –'

But he'd come up quickly behind her and when she turned, hands on hips to carry on telling him what she thought of this stunt, he caught her by surprise, bent his head and kissed her on the lips. Not a quick kiss to test her reaction, but a long kiss, a kiss between two lovers who'd been reunited after a long time apart.

Her head spiralled, all the way from Heritage Cove to Venice and back again.

'Why did you do that?' she mumbled into his chest when she ended the kiss and he pulled her into a hug. She felt comfortable for a split second but pulled away because she also felt more confused than ever.

'Anyone home?' a voice called out from the garden.

Jade went to the back door and saw Lois making her way towards the cottage. She'd likely come to talk about the cake again but her head couldn't grasp any of the details right now. She'd probably seen Celeste alone in the bakery and assumed Jade was here at home.

And now she'd been sprung because judging by Lois's face, she'd seen Jade and hadn't missed Dario, Jade's height and build unable to hide him as he came up behind her. And he always had an effect on people, always gave a good first impression, especially when it came to women. She'd laughed once when she'd sat at a side table in his restaurant waiting for him to finish so they could have some time together. She'd watched him work and she'd also watched the young women nudge one another whenever he went by, talk under their breath; one had very indiscreetly checked out his bottom and put her hand out to touch it until his nonna had patted the hand away and wagged her finger at the girl.

Jade had no choice but to make the introductions. 'Lois, this is Dario…a friend of mine. Dario, this is Lois, she's getting married and I'm in charge of the cake,' she blurted out.

When he uttered the Italian phrase for pleased to meet you, Lois beamed at the charismatic foreigner who'd taken her hand and kissed the top of her palm. 'Well, it's lovely to meet you too, Dario.' She looked to Jade. 'Isn't the language beautiful?'

'It certainly is. What can I do for you, Lois?' Jade knew she had to leap in and get back to it being just her and Dario. She wanted to know his reasons for showing up, his intentions. She'd been so sure of herself recently, ready to go it alone with her plan.

'I wondered whether you'd be able to make a few batches of cupcakes as well as the wedding cake.' Lois clasped her hands together hopefully. 'I know it's a big ask and late notice but I'm worried we won't have enough, what with the ball running right after the wedding and goodness knows how many guests. I want to make sure we have plenty for everybody.'

'That's a great idea and no problem at all. Better to have too much than not enough. I can get hold of some small cardboard cake boxes too if you like, that way you can make them up for the cupcakes should you need to if guests would rather take them away at the end. Let me know how many you're thinking of and we'll go from there.'

'Why don't we say four dozen? I'd say that'll be plenty. Tracy is in charge of catering this year along with Celeste and Etna, so there'll be other sweets as well as the cakes.'

'Perfect.'

'Well, it was lovely to meet you, Dario.' Jade almost caught a giggle from Lois when Dario replied in Italian that it was wonderful to meet her too.

When they were alone again Jade suggested they go for a walk. 'I could show you the cove itself, down by the water.' She'd told him about it enough times.

She picked up her keys, locked the cottage and called in through the back door of the bakery to let Celeste know she was going out. She suspected that even if Celeste was rushed off her feet, she wouldn't argue. And much as Jade didn't want to bump into any more of the locals, it was better to go somewhere other than here. Having Dario in the cottage, in her space, risked him pulling her to him in the way he'd done before and she didn't want that. It didn't help her think. But the sea air might.

They crossed the road towards the track that led down to the cove and a group of teenage girls certainly didn't miss the hot Italian in town. He had his shades pulled down and looked good in a deep-sea-blue crew-neck T-shirt and khaki shorts that showed off tanned limbs, and when he nodded a hello to them, the Italian 'Ciao!' tumbling naturally from his lips, they nudged one another. Jade suspected Dario would be the talk of the village for a while as he set hearts aflutter without even trying.

But would her heart ever beat for him again or had they had their chance and blown it?

Chapter Thirteen

Linc drove back from the clinic. He'd got used to the regularity of these appointments but he was kind of glad he was almost done. It was as though this had been a marker, a time when he helped others but also realised that he had to start thinking about himself and his own future. Finally, he was ready to move on to another phase in his life and, despite the appearance of the Italian in the Cove almost a fortnight ago, he felt good about the changes ahead.

Last week Linc had gone through a round of formal interviews with the school governors – online since it was still the school holidays – and had been observed giving a virtual music lesson to a couple of pupils from the school, and yesterday he'd been officially offered the job subject to all the relevant checks and references. Now he had also ticked one other major item off his to-do list – he'd found a place to live. Harvey was right about Melissa's cottage being perfect for his needs – he'd looked at it first thing this morning and it was plenty big enough, with a couple of reception rooms, an upstairs and some outside space front and back. It had a pretty frontage too, with flowerbeds curved around the downstairs window and a blue front door, as well as an inviting fireplace in the living room for the winter months. He was already looking forward to being in his own space, out in the countryside past the riding school yet still within walking distance to The Street, and with the school a mere thirty-five-minute walk away, he could start the day with fresh air and exercise. Plenty of his previous jobs had been at schools too far from home to go on foot and some days, when he'd been really busy, he'd felt he hadn't even seen the outside world apart from going to and from his car. Living at the cottage, he'd be able to give Etna a bit of space too because he suspected she might like to spend a little more time with Kenneth but never would with him hanging around. Linc had overheard them both talking about dinner recipes, discussing ingredients Kenneth could source from his allotment, so Linc wouldn't be surprised if there was a dinner date in the not-too-distant future.

Linc parked up in the Cove and went straight to the tea rooms. It was the day of the wedding and the Wedding Dress Ball and, along with the summer breeze, there was something in the air that he'd begun to realise was a sense of coming together, of community and friendship, that he hadn't quite found before now. People were smiling, chattering away about what was happening that day, heading here and there to make their own preparations.

When he went into the tea rooms Etna looked up from where she was pushing a fresh bunch of napkins into the holder in the centre of a table. 'Daniel is keeping you busy at the waffle shack. I didn't see you this morning.'

She didn't miss much although she'd got it wrong when it came to guessing his whereabouts. 'There's heaps to do still.'

'Is the pergola in yet?'

'Not yet. The timber has arrived so we'll get to that next.'

She paused in wiping down another table. 'It'll be a popular place to sit.'

'Don't worry, this place will still be loved by all your loyal customers.'

She swished her cloth through the air. 'I know, I'm not worried.' In the past she'd bemoaned the lack of outside space at the tea rooms but Etna and everyone else knew this place had character and stood the test of time. A couple of tables out front was an option but, so far, she'd been happy with filling the inside and flinging open the windows in the warmer months.

She looked at him more closely. 'Hang on, you look too clean to have been working with Harvey this morning.'

'I went to look at Melissa's cottage, remember?' That would be explanation enough. She didn't need to know he hadn't been there for hours but had been off somewhere else afterwards. He'd share it with her one day, just not yet.

'What did you think?'

'I've said I'll take it.'

She beamed as she headed out to the kitchen with an empty mug and a plate from one of the deserted tables. 'Your dad will be glad to hear that,' she called over her shoulder.

'I've said he can move in with me while he gets himself sorted,' he told her when she came back.

'I haven't heard him say he's definitely moving up this way, but I think we're almost there.' She crossed the fingers on both hands. 'He's agreed to get his house valued, which is a step in the right direction. I'm sure he'll be surprised how much property prices have gone up and if he's downsizing, he'll be able to choose something special here in the Cove. Both of you here with me – it'll be wonderful.' Linc didn't miss the tear in the corner of her eye. 'Mind you, I rejected his idea I sell my flat and move in with him if this plan does ahead. I think that may be a step too far and he'd hate me bossing him about all the time. Besides, I'm not past it yet, I can tackle the stairs up to my flat and they keep me fit.'

'Good for you, you keep your independence. It'll do Dad good to do the same. Independence but with plenty of people around, that's the key.' He nodded at her offer of a coffee.

Patricia bundled in through the front door. 'Cavalry's arrived,' she announced chirpily and grinning from ear to ear, no doubt thinking about the wedding later. 'Break time, Etna, I'll take over for twenty minutes.'

Etna didn't protest – which had to be a first. She merely made a coffee for Linc, a cup of tea for herself and came to sit with her nephew at the table by the window. 'I don't argue with her when she tells me to take a break but I honestly don't need one. In fact, I've told Patricia and your dad that after today I'm allowed to dictate my own break times.'

Linc savoured the bold, earthy flavour of his americano coffee and let it filter through him. 'That's good. Don't ever get rid of your machine.'

'Never,' she grinned. 'Tell me, are you looking forward to the wedding later? It's confusing this year – I don't know whether to call it a wedding or a wedding dress ball.'

'I am looking forward to it.' At least he had been before a certain Italian had shown up in the Cove. But instead of looking forward to seeing Jade – not that he'd mind seeing her, of course – he was excited about being

211

introduced to more people in the village, to really start trying to settle in with a sense of permanency rather than the constant nagging thought of where he'd move on to next.

Etna thanked Patricia for bringing over a couple of shortbread fingers for each of them. 'Do you have your outfit sorted?'

'I have a tux.'

'I shall look forward to seeing you in that, I don't think I see you smart very often.'

'And what about you, are you wearing a dress? I understand the tradition is that if you were once married, you wear the dress you wore down the aisle.'

'Indeed it is. And I did wear my wedding dress for many years but it was time for a change so I found something new…and my dress was beginning to get somewhat snug. I'm not in the best profession for staying trim and with a bakery as well as this place and the waffle shack all in the vicinity, I don't really want to,' she grinned.

'You look beautiful, you always did.'

'Luckily my job keeps me active. I'm not slowing down yet despite people trying to make me.' She'd said the latter for the benefit of Patricia, who threw Linc a glance that told him she knew it. 'But flattery will get you everywhere, young man.' She described the replacement dress she'd found at a shop by the seaside, floaty and chic, a champagne colour rather than white. 'It's much better for a woman of my age, and besides, a new dress is always a boost.'

'Who knows, if you get married again, maybe you could upgrade.'

'Drink your coffee,' she said, avoiding anything he might be hinting at, and then told him how she intended to dance this evening and keep up with the rest of them.

'Don't ever change,' he told her, setting down his empty mug.

'I'll try not to,' she laughed.

They talked some more about Melissa's cottage and Etna went into detail about the woodland walks he could access beyond there. 'In spring,' she told him, 'you can see the most gorgeous carpet of bluebells only minutes away from the cottage.'

He was about to be on his way when the bell above the door tinkled and Jade was the next customer to appear. Etna smiled her a hello but Linc was doing his best to surreptitiously look around to see if she'd brought anyone in with her. She hadn't.

Jade ordered two coffees, Etna waved Patricia away telling her she'd taken enough of a break as she headed for the coffee machine herself, and as she began on the first cup, she called out to Jade, 'I saw you with a handsome stranger earlier.' Trust Etna to get right to the point.

Jade briefly looked over at Linc, her credit card poised in her hand to make the necessary transaction and get out of here. 'An old friend,' was all she said by way of explanation. She wasn't giving much away, even when Etna brought out the coffees and hovered expectantly.

'He's not from around here,' Etna persisted, but Jade had already scooped up both coffee cups after tapping her card on the machine.

'He's visiting from Italy,' was all she said before she scarpered.

'What are you grinning at?' Etna came back to the table.

'You, being nosy.'

'I like to keep abreast of what's going on,' she said, although not defensively, before adding, 'especially where Jade's concerned.'

'Why?'

'You know why.'

'I don't.'

'Because the way you two look and act around each other tells me there's a spark there, chemistry, whatever you want to call it. Don't think I haven't noticed. I just hadn't wanted to make either of you uncomfortable by mentioning it.'

'I'd say she's already got plenty of chemistry with an Italian in her life.'

Barney and Lois came in and when Lois started running on about the Italian stallion and fed Etna more information after she'd apparently met him briefly outside the girls' cottage, Linc took it as his cue to leave. He didn't want to hear about the man whose photograph Jade had carried around with her for so long and who must surely be here in the Cove to pick up where they left off.

Instead, he headed up to the Little Waffle Shack.

*

A couple of hours later Linc felt much better. There was nothing like plunging a spade into dirt and heaving out roots or revving up a digger to battle the most stubborn brambles, weeds and stones to work out your frustrations. Harvey had been here all morning since the cottage viewing and handed over to him while he went home to take Winnie for a walk and then went back to his day job.

The buzz in the Cove preceding the wedding and the ball hadn't lessened when he left the tea rooms. He'd almost bumped into a couple of ladies rushing past with dresses in see-through plastic coverings, he'd passed Lucy and Tilly hovering outside the ice-creamery and talking up-dos, and even a few people heading away from the waffle shack had been talking about the wedding, debating whether they should even be eating waffles with the catering to come tonight. Linc had put his head down as he went to the shack and tried to forget it all, to put out of his mind the woman who'd begun to mean more to him, the fact he'd missed out on getting to know her now her past had reared it's not-ugly-at-all head.

Linc wiped the sweat from his brow when Daniel brought out a bottle of water for him. He gulped half of it in one go. 'Cheers, I needed that.'

'The water or the work?'

'Both.' He'd worked so hard that the preparation for the pergola to be put up was almost done.

'Is everything all right? Just that you seemed pretty wound up when you got here. And I called out about taking a break half an hour ago but you didn't hear me.'

Daniel put pause to the conversation when Peter hollered from the back door that his mum was here to collect him. 'I won't be a sec.'

Linc bent down and hand-picked out some of the rubble along with a few odd bits of metal or junk that had somehow found their way into the dirt he'd managed to overturn with the help of the digger. It was all going into a pile at the side and either they'd get another skip or load it into Harvey's truck to get rid of somewhere.

'Sorry about that.' Daniel was back. 'I had to find some pocket money for Peter. I like to give him extra for helping out.'

'It's nice you're still so close.'

'It is. But don't change the subject. What's on your mind? Brianna has it all in hand inside, for now, so I'm all ears.'

He was about to claim he was too busy, had too much to do if there was any hope of him finishing in time to go back to Harvey's for a shower before the event everyone in the village was so revved up about. But, somehow, he found himself admitting his feelings for Jade.

'I don't see what the problem is,' said Daniel. 'Ask her out, simple.'

'I've got competition.' He explained Dario's arrival and Daniel realised he must've been the one at the shack asking after the bakery the other day.

'Is he taking her to the wedding?'

'No idea.' Linc rested a hand on the spade he'd thrust into the ground. 'But it's not just the new man in town. It's what I overheard at the pub one night.' He explained how he'd heard the girls talking about Jade finding a baby daddy, the conversation that had prompted him to leave sharpish without even saying goodbye to her.

'You need to talk to her,' Daniel advised. 'I know you might think you know everything but believe me when I say I know a lot about misunderstandings.'

'I was going to talk to her when the Italian showed up.'

'I'd persevere if I were you. Until then, you'll never know what the truth is – and who knows, the Italian might be on his way soon.'

Linc doubted it. She hadn't looked displeased to see him and they had a history, they'd once planned a future

216

they could still be heading towards if circumstances had been different.

'Lucy and I had a few misunderstandings before we got together and if we hadn't got to the bottom of them, we might not be together now. And for what it's worth, I can't see Jade looking for a baby daddy, no matter what you overheard. She doesn't seem the type.'

Neither had Orla.

And as Linc got on with the task in hand, shoving the spade into the ground beneath the summer sunshine, sweating more and more as time wore on, he couldn't banish the thought of Jade and Dario. Were they cuddled up in bed together right now? Were they between the sheets making plans for the future?

And it was those thoughts that occupied his mind as he worked right up until it was time to go and take a shower, pull on a tux, put on a brave face and actually try to talk to her, if he could get her alone for long enough.

Chapter Fourteen

Jade, still wrapped in a thin robe, released the tongs from her hair. She'd created some loose, natural-looking waves at the front and after running her fingers through the strands to tease them into place, she chose the sparkly forget-me-not flower earrings she'd treated herself to with her last pay check from her job in London. She and Celeste had joked back then that it might be a while before they could afford to splurge again and so it had been a last hurrah, buying herself some decent jewellery.

Since Dario turned up Jade had spent the majority of her time in a daze, her sister holding the fort at the bakery as much as possible because even when Jade was there, her head was not. She'd made up a couple of customer orders wrong, she'd iced a batch of cupcakes for a christening with pale blue icing rather than pale yellow so they had to do the entire lot again, and she'd messed up a tray of jam doughnuts by dropping them all over the floor. Celeste had sent her home for an hour that day, told her to get it together before she came back.

Jade had tried to get a balance between giving herself time to think and spending time with the man who'd come all this way to see her. She and Dario had walked along the beach beyond the Cove together, somewhere they weren't likely to bump into so many people. They'd headed into Cambridge for a few hours another day so he could see the sights and she could have a chance to breathe rather than focus on him and her and where they went to from here. All the while Dario had made his feelings abundantly clear, especially on the beach one day when he'd told her in no uncertain terms that he was here to convince her to try again.

They passed a young boy that day, standing on the sands to fly his kite, its sails lapping in the wind, its strings getting in a tangle. 'You say you want me back,' Jade told Dario, trying but failing to hook her hair behind her ear – the wind had other ideas – 'but you're forgetting we're still faced with the same dilemma. My life is here, yours is there.'

He put a hand against her cheek and she let herself feel the warmth from his skin as the pad of his thumb gently moved near her bottom lip. 'Everything you say is true. But if you won't leave here, I will come to you.'

'You'd move to England? For me?'

'Si.' He kissed her on the forehead and her eyes closed. It was as though he didn't want to chance kissing her lips in case it made her say words he didn't want to hear. He murmured in Italian, 'I love you. I would do anything for you,' his face so close to hers now that she could barely breathe.

'But your restaurant, your family –'

'They know how I feel about you.'

'And I know how you feel about them and the restaurant. It was never an option for you to move here before – what's changed?'

'Maybe I've changed. Maybe I'm missing something.'

'I have to go. I need to get back to the bakery.' She couldn't do this. It was too much, and too late.

She'd headed back to the bakery then but he'd begged her to talk for longer and so they'd walked around the bend to the Heritage Inn, where he was staying.

'Please come inside,' he said. 'We can talk properly without anyone watching us.' They'd already paused their conversation when Tracy emerged from the inside to water the hanging baskets and the flowers in the huge terracotta pot by the entrance.

'We could go in the garden,' she suggested instead and he seemed happy with that.

Going through the inn and out the back, via the kitchen to pick up a jug of water, they took the table at the far end of the garden where they were unlikely to be disturbed.

Dario poured two glasses of water and wasted no time asking, 'Did you think about me much over the last few days?'

She began to laugh. 'Dario, you're all I've thought about. As well as cakes, bread, biscuits…although Celeste might well fire me from my own bakery if I don't get my act together.' At his look of confusion, she swished away the unspoken need for explanation; they weren't here for idle chitchat and she needed to remember that.

He was sitting opposite her but his legs were long enough that their knees almost touched beneath the bistro table. He reached for her hands and she set down her glass, let him hold them, as though the closer the contact now, the more it might tell her what to do. 'Remember how we said we wouldn't forget one another.' He repeated the phrase in Italian. The other language, the different time in her life he represented, only added to her confusion.

'I think we were too wrapped up in each other back then to see the practicalities. It was all so romantic.'

'And it still could be.'

'You're a wonderful man. I was so in love with you when I was in Venice, then for a long time afterwards. I wanted a future with you – you were everything I was looking for.'

'You don't want that anymore?' He looked down briefly and up again, his ebony eyelashes casting a shadow on his upper cheek-bones the same way they had when she'd watched him sleep in the morning sunshine filtering through the window of his apartment in Venice.

'Too much has happened between then and now.' She'd been debating it for days. 'It would be easy for me to say yes to being with you, but how do I know you won't long for Venice and move back?' She held up a hand before he could speak. 'You might think you won't but I know you, remember. I know your passion for the restaurant, for your home country, your little apartment with its unique position close to the Bridge of Sighs.' Even to herself it sounded like a dream. 'I would never want to be the person who took all that away from you.'

'And I know I couldn't take you away from this.' He waved a hand around, meaning the village rather than the garden at the back of the inn with its pretty blooms in an array of colours from the yellow of the sun to the blue of the sky and rich purples you might find against whitewashed houses in Greece.

She shook her head. 'You shouldn't have come.' She couldn't help but let a little bit of resentment seep into her words. He'd made everything complicated again, just when she was starting to see clearly for the first time.

'Is there someone else?'

'No, nobody else.' She shook her head. There wasn't, but there was the thought of someone else. She liked Linc, more than she should. Nothing would happen if she wanted to go ahead with having a baby, but she was strangely OK with that. What she wasn't OK with was saying yes to all of Dario's dreams because it was the easy option. And, she had a feeling, their different worlds would always keep them apart even in a small way until the one who had compromised and moved to another country began to resent what they'd given up.

'You seem settled, Jade. You have what you want. But you don't have everything. Love is important, the most important thing of all.'

There wasn't any need for him to say those words because she remembered their conversations well enough, the times they'd said I love you, the times they'd talked about how nothing else mattered when it came down to it. But that wasn't real life, and now, having him here, she was sure of that.

'I don't have everything, you're right.' There, she'd admitted it. But it was a moment of clarification too. She reached out a hand and put it to his cheek. 'We both deserve to be happy but I don't think you would be in years to come if you moved here. And I think it would ruin what was once a beautiful thing between us.'

He wasn't listening. He'd taken a deep breath and stood up, turned around and Jade hoped he wasn't crying but when he faced her once again, he was smiling. And then he did what she'd never expected at all, what she'd dreamed about so many times when they were together.

He got down on one knee just as Tracy came outside to do the plants in the back garden, the two pots, one on either side of the double doors leading onto the patio and the grass beyond, the hanging basket by the gravelled side path. And she was looking their way with shock written all over her face.

Dario snatched Jade's attention back again. 'I'm here, I want to be with you.' He'd never minded an audience. 'We're good together, we work. I love you.' And then, 'Vuoi sposarmi?' he repeated.

He might not mind an audience but she did. She waited until they were alone again and the wait told him the answer. She saw his hopes fade, realisation dawn.

'You would've said yes if I'd asked you in Venice before you left,' he said resignedly.

'Of course I would. And for a time, it would've been perfect.' She smiled, watching him with the love she'd once felt but with the common sense that overruled everything else. 'But one of us would've made sacrifices and I don't think we both would've been happy in the end – one of us would always be wanting for something else.'

After a deep breath he told her again that he loved her and pulled her in for a hug.

She let him hold her a moment longer, still alone in the garden, but when she pulled away she said, 'I think you're in love with what we once had, and so am I. I always will be. Those memories are ones I'll never forget, not ever. But it was brief, it wasn't realistic for either of us in the long term, and only now with you here in front of me can I see that.' Before today, she would've been worried she'd get carried away with the emotion, let something happen when it shouldn't, but now, after a few days apart, she knew what she wanted.

'You were right when you said I didn't have everything,' she admitted. 'I still want a family of my own and I haven't met anyone to do that with. But I don't want to be with someone just because the clock is ticking – nobody deserves that, least of all you.' With a small smile she added, 'Much as we dreamed about it and talked about it together – our part-Irish, part-Italian kids, speaking both languages and getting under our feet wherever we made our home.'

He smiled warmly at the memory too. 'We did have it all planned in those few short weeks together.'

'We really did.' Her heart went out to him. 'But I've changed since I came back, Dario. I don't think I'm that same girl who was wide-eyed and in love in Italy.' She suspected a lot of those feelings came from the buzz of travel, the freedom, the possibilities, the chance meeting with a stranger who suddenly filled her world. Yet now, every time she tried to imagine Dario being here, living the same life as her in the village, it didn't work. The only way she could picture them working was with her as a carefree traveller, him in his native surroundings. You couldn't go back – life didn't work like that – you had to keep moving forwards. And being here with him now, she knew they weren't going to do that together.

'I should've told you I was coming,' he said.

'I'm glad you showed up unexpectedly. It didn't give me the opportunity to overthink this before we had a chance to be together in the same place, face to face, have a proper conversation and time to talk.' She smiled at him tenderly. 'Could you really see yourself staying away from Italy, from Venice, for good?'

He considered his reply. 'In the short term, definitely. But in the long term…perhaps not. You are right. It wouldn't be good for us.'

'No, and imagine if there were kids involved. Kids whose parents had no idea where to live to be happy.'

He nudged her. 'I've missed you.'

But this was it and as he pulled her to her feet, she knew he felt it too. But he didn't miss the chance for one more kiss, his romantic Italian blood causing him to instigate a pause where he lingered longer than was needed, remembering this forever goodbye.

He smiled down at her, his hands still on either side of her face. 'Ciao bella.'

And she smiled before she walked away from this man for good.

Jade had kept a very low profile in the days since she and Dario said goodbye for the very last time. Celeste had worked front of shop while Jade hid away in the back baking the bread, cookies, icing buns, loading up the free-wheeling chrome trolley for Celeste to restock. She talked with Celeste, she cried on her shoulder, her grief more to do with the finality of the goodbye but also because once upon a time marrying Dario was exactly what she'd wanted.

Now, with the wedding drawing ever closer along with the ball, the event of the year for Heritage Cove, Jade took off her robe and spritzed her favourite perfume onto her décolletage and each wrist. Dario would've left the Cove this morning and Jade felt as though she had clarity once more, although seeing Linc in the tea rooms earlier had made her more confused than ever, her feelings threatening to become even stronger than those she'd once had for Dario. They felt more real, more immediate, but now she had made the decision to go ahead with her plan, how could she possibly get involved? Not that he looked as though he wanted to. Either he'd seen her with Dario or he'd decided he wasn't as interested as perhaps he once was; he certainly hadn't seemed eager to look her way or begin a conversation. And it bothered her more than she was willing to admit.

Celeste came out onto the landing when Jade emerged from her bedroom. 'You look amazing, sis.'

'Right back at you.' They went into Jade's bedroom and stood linking arms in front of the mirror. Both tall and willowy with dark hair, each of them had their own style. Celeste had gone for a sleeveless skater dress in white with a high neck and sequins that set off her emerald eyes. She looked elegant with her freshly trimmed and blow-dried pixie cut, the fringe jagged and leaving wisps on her forehead. Jade had chosen a longer dress, down to her calves, with a skirt that flowed out enough to move as she walked. In an ice blue that in some lights looked almost white, the dress was made of tulle and lace. A satin band sat high on the waist, giving her a flattering silhouette, and the sequins, beads and crystals formed tiny flowers on the bodice.

Celeste frowned. 'I know it's the Wedding Dress Ball and the whole point is that people either wear their own wedding dresses or buy something closely resembling what a bride might wear, but it feels odd this time when there really is a bride.'

Jade reminded her sister of Lois's response this morning when Celeste went round to drop off the cake and the sweet treats and had voiced her concern about the outfits. 'Lois told you she'll only have eyes for Barney. But you're right…' She picked up the satin pouch that would be her bag. Easily looped over her wrist, it was much easier to carry than anything else. She and Celeste had bought almost identical ones from Tilly's Bits 'n' Pieces. 'It does feel strange this year.'

'It's so romantic, isn't it? After all this time, they're finally getting their Happy Ever After.'

226

With a sigh, Jade agreed. 'Their feelings never went away.'

'Do you wish it had been that way for you and Dario?'

She checked her earrings were in tightly enough, paranoid about losing one. 'Honestly? No, not anymore. I'm glad he came, but I'm glad he left it so long I'd already begun to find my own way, if that makes sense.'

'And what about this plan of yours?' She hadn't mentioned it since Dario's appearance in the Cove.

'My life plan? It's still on, and even more so now. I think if I had any doubts left in my mind then Dario's appearance has cemented it for me. I could've fallen into his arms and started a family tomorrow, done it the easier way, but I know I don't want that.'

Jade linked an arm through her sister's again as both of them beamed into the mirror one more time. 'Come on, we've got a wedding to get to.'

*

A light melody came from the barn as they approached, going in the little gate at the front of Barney's cottage, following the path that turned and ran along past the front window and through the arch of juniper trees into the courtyard with a view of the barn. The barn doors, flung open to welcome everyone, were held back on their hooks and already people had gathered around chatting excitedly, glasses in hand, awaiting the nuptials and the ball. Lois's four grandchildren who'd arrived from Ireland a few days earlier were playing outside, burning off their energy by racing one another alongside the barn and back again. Jade overheard one of their parents say they were hoping they'd exhaust themselves enough that they were quiet as Lois and Barney said their vows. Then they could let loose again once the music started up and the ball began.

Jade and Celeste, who'd both worn trainers to walk here, changed into their heels and put their trainers with all the other pairs of more sensible shoes piled inside the back door out of the way. The sun was a long way off setting on what was a glorious day and when the girls went inside the barn it was a sight to behold. A long table on the far wall showcased the wedding cake as well as the extra cupcakes, all with the same pale-lemon icing and intricate flower-and-leaf detail. There was plenty of room alongside for the rest of the food, which for now was safely tucked away in the kitchen after Etna and Tracy had delivered it ready to be brought out later.

Fairy lights looped around wooden posts and ran along beams, white linen material billowed from the rafters like clouds and the stage had chairs for the musicians who were yet to arrive. A charity collection box stood on the old upturned beer barrel by the door along with the guestbook and a vase of white hydrangeas, and Jade pushed money into the box before signing in with a kind message for the happy couple. She left a pile of business cards beside the book too, as per Barney's suggestion to drum up a little extra custom.

She gave Barney a hug and a kiss, he looked so nervous. 'Is Lois getting ready for her grand entrance?'

With one hand he smoothed down grey hair that had been cut yesterday – she'd heard him chatting with Celeste in the bakery, telling her how much he was looking forward to today. 'She certainly is, and Etna is upstairs in the cottage plying her with champagne, apparently.' He held up his phone. 'She's been texting me.'

'Only forty-five minutes to go before people arrive,' Jade beamed, excited and doing her best not to make it obvious she was looking around for Linc. The butterflies that had once zipped around whenever Dario was near now lay dormant unless she thought about the Cove's newest arrival.

'Thanks for coming early and agreeing to be on the door.'

'We're not bouncers,' Celeste grinned after she'd signed in to the guestbook and slotted money into the charity collection.

'Definitely not in those dresses.' He'd been in another world but took in their outfits now. 'It must be my nerves, I apologise. You both look beautiful, exquisite. Remind me again how it can be possible that you are both single?'

'Don't you worry about us on your special day,' said Jade, 'and we're happy to help out, keep everyone in order.' Some years they had people show up to the ball without the best of intentions, namely out-of-towners, but it was easy to tell the real attendees apart from those who were only after free booze and a feed.

Jade spotted Valerie, who'd made an entrance with her husband. Thomas was in his baby carrier held against his dad's chest and Valerie had already gone over to inspect the flower arrangements. She was clearly itching to be back at work and even adjusted one or two of the stems in a tall vase at the corner of the stage before moving on to another.

The florist had well and truly delivered on the flower front, with vases dotted on every surface possible – the other barrels, tables along the far wall ready for the food, the table with the cake and cupcakes. The arrangements came in all different sizes, comprising sprays of lemon yellow, violet, shiny foliage to offset the beauty of the flowers, and the scent carried around the barn with the air of summer filtering in through the barn doors.

Barney looked relieved when the string quartet turned up in a van and parked in the gravel courtyard. He rushed to greet them and was soon busy chatting and organising, helping them set up on the stage, while the girls took their positions by the doors.

The sun high up above gave the barn a golden glow, magical and romantic at the same time. Guests who knew Barney well and people who didn't but came to support the charity event soon filled the inside although this year's tickets had made it clear the wedding would take place first, the Wedding Dress Ball an hour after that. But, it seemed, Barney's popularity had drawn most people here for the earlier time, regardless of how well they knew him. It was standing room only in front of the stage and the small space carved out for the nuptials, with a few chairs dotted around for anyone who needed a seat.

Celeste handled arrivals like a pro having been joined by Barney's best man, Harvey, and while they were manning the doors Jade slipped upstairs to check on the bride-to-be, who was getting ready in the spare room.

'Knock, knock.' She softly tapped on the closed bedroom door and Etna opened it up and told her to come in. Jade found Lois on tenterhooks just like the groom. She clasped her hands together, fingertips beneath her chin. 'You look beautiful, Lois. Barney might very well pass out when he sees you.'

In a three-quarter-sleeved champagne silk-and-lace dress, its sequins on the bodice making Lois's eyes twinkle as much as her smile as she adjusted one of the pointed sleeves to sit on her forearm, layers of material falling in pleats on the skirt section that hung from her slender waist and finished a few inches above her ankles, she asked, 'Will I do?'

'You look perfect,' Jade told her as Etna took herself off downstairs to use the bathroom before the ceremony.

When there was another knock on the door and Lois's son leaned in to see whether his mum was ready, Lois made the introductions and readied herself to walk down to the barn, towards her husband-to-be.

'I'll leave you to it,' Jade smiled and carefully made her own way downstairs again.

She paused in the hallway and sat on the carver chair for a moment. It was five o'clock. Dario would be in the air by now; he was on his way home. She'd felt terrible turning him down but she knew that in a few weeks or months he'd realise he had to let go too and she hoped he'd find someone who made him truly happy.

Etna emerged from the downstairs bathroom and checked the bouncy waves of her grey hair and her lipstick application once more in the mirror in the hallway. 'Why are you sitting out here? You should be over in the barn.'

'Just gathering myself, it's been a busy couple of days.'

Etna paused beside the carver chair. 'The Italian?'

'Dario,' Jade smiled. It was funny how people called him "The Italian" as though it was the only way to describe him. 'He'll be on his way back to Italy now.'

'Right.'

Tracy had obviously been discreet as expected – perhaps she'd seen the look on Jade's face, known it wasn't the happy event most people wanted to share.

'What happened?'

'It's a long story.'

Etna looked at the stairs but there was no sign of Lois and her son. 'We've got a bit of time, I'm a good listener you know. And when we hear Lois coming we'll scarper, but until then I'm all ears.'

Jade had thought she'd finished talking about Dario but Etna was a good sounding board. She briefly told her everything that had happened with Dario, how they'd planned a future, said goodbye, and how he'd come here wanting her back. 'He turned up here and proposed – he was offering everything I ever wanted, everything we both wanted.'

'You don't still feel the same way?'

Jade shook her head. 'I did for a long time but I was holding on to a dream that never would've worked out in the long run. I wouldn't fit over there; he said he'd come here, but I think that in the end, whatever it was that one of us had given up would drive a wedge between us. We'd end up resenting each other, and I think by the time we said goodbye he knew that too.'

'You still have your memories of him to treasure. When I married, I believed you could only ever find one true love – and the wedding today is the perfect illustration of that theory. But it doesn't always happen that way. I think if we let ourselves, we can find love again without really looking.'

Jade wondered whether Etna was referring to Kenneth or she could be talking about Linc. Either way, Jade understood where she was coming from. 'I suspect you're right.' She bit the corner of her lip, thinking. 'Can I tell you something else?' Nobody had ventured down the stairs yet and they were all alone in the hallway.

'Of course.' She was like this in the tea rooms, always willing to lend an ear. She'd let you nurse a cup of tea for hours while you talked, none of this pressure to buy something else because you were taking up a table, although you inevitably did anyway.

Jade told Etna how she longed for a family of her own, how she'd got fed up with waiting for the perfect man to turn up, and how she'd found another way by having her eggs frozen. And now she was ready to use them.

'Say something,' Jade urged as they made their way out to the barn ahead of Lois, who was by now on her way down the stairs according to one of her grandsons who had been spying and yelled the information from the back door, sending the stragglers into the barn. 'You think it's a mad idea, don't you?'

Etna stopped outside the open barn doors and kept her voice low. 'I never had children. We tried but it didn't happen for us. I think it's why I always adored Linc and his brother and still like to take them under my wing whenever I can. Back in my day, if I'd been able to find another way to have a family and I really wanted one, if I'd been on my own like you are and saw the dream slipping away,' she said, clutching Jade's wrist and giving it a little squeeze, 'nothing would've stopped me.'

Jade gave Etna a hug. 'Now, that I can believe.'

Conspiratorially, Etna whispered, 'A part of me secretly hopes you might hold off a while and see if someone may just be waiting in the wings.' She winked, and with that she left Jade to find her sister while she found Joseph and Kenneth over at the far side of the barn.

The scene inside the barn was set and the low hum of chatter swelled to murmurs of admiration as the string quartet got started with Mozart's 'Ave Verum Corpus' and Lois came into view. She walked towards Barney, and Jade wondered whether she was the only one holding her breath. They were both so nervous but the minute they were side by side they both began to grin and looked as though they couldn't imagine being anywhere else. It was exactly as love should be and they'd finally found their happy ending after all these years.

The vows were exchanged and without a dry eye in the house, the celebrant at last announced Barney could kiss his bride. Whoops, cheers and claps surrounded them and Jade turned to finally catch a glimpse of Linc, who must've come in when she was too busy to notice. He was leaning up against the side of the barn closest to the door, beyond the crowds, looking her way, gorgeous in a tux. He looked so different from the man who'd bashed about so loudly at the bakery that morning, the guy who'd teased her about carrying around an old photograph, the man who seemed to blow hot and cold when it came to her, and all she could do was stare.

Guests milled, talked amongst themselves, the bride and groom were bombarded by congratulations and the beautiful strains of the quartet continued to fill the air as Lois and Barney had their first dance as a married couple. Lois's grandchildren set off a stream of party poppers that had them leaping about in delight, and Jade only looked away for a second before Linc was swallowed up by the crowds and she lost sight of him.

A lively band replaced the string quartet as they transitioned from wedding formalities to the main event, the Wedding Dress Ball, and the happy couple surprised everyone by dancing the twist.

'Jade, come and talk to us,' Lois begged as they escaped for a breather. 'It'll stop anyone pulling us back onto the dancefloor before we've had a chance to recover.'

'You were both impressive out there,' she said, looking at the space in the barn that had been solely for them moments ago but was now filled with everyone else wanting to enjoy the ball. 'Look at Nola, my goodness!' The landlady of the pub, wearing her wedding dress – an off-the-shoulder flirty calf-length satin number – was leading the way with the dancing. People were copying her moves, even the kids. 'I was talking to Nola earlier and she said you've made firm plans to rehome the chickens when her daughter returns to work,' said Jade.

Barney nodded. 'We're looking forward to it, aren't we, Lois?'

Lois sipped from a glass of champagne, decidedly more relaxed now the official part was behind them. 'I know nothing about keeping chickens but I'm sure we'll learn fast, and they'll have plenty of space to roam.' The cottage and barn came with plenty of green space so she was right about that.

Nola had stumbled off the dancefloor, her energy levels clearly not what she'd hoped they might be, and caught the tail end of their conversation. 'They're a bugger to catch when they put their mind to it.' She reached for a sausage roll from the platter carried by Brianna from the waffle shack. 'Don't worry, I'll come over and teach you the best way to grab them, give you a few lessons.'

'I've got visions of Barney and me running all over the fields,' Lois laughed with Jade as Nola went over to find her husband.

'It'll keep us fit,' Barney declared before he and Lois were accosted by Harvey to talk with another couple of guests who'd been late arrivals.

Jade was wondering where Celeste had got to when she heard a voice behind her.

'My auntie was right, this really is the event of the year.'

She turned to smile a hello at Linc, the butterflies zipping through her insides as though they'd just been released from a net. 'I look forward to it every summer now, it's certainly a highlight. The ball, I mean, not the wedding,' she stammered.

'I guessed that was what you meant.' He seemed amused that she was at a loss for words.

He was being friendly, a lot more so than when she'd been in the tea rooms earlier, but perhaps it was a few drinks and the occasion that made him so.

'It looks like we've had the best of the day.' He nodded to beyond the barn doors where the clouds had come over and drizzle graced the courtyard.

The change of weather didn't seem to put people off milling outside though, especially not the kids, who were running around out there with another batch of party poppers. 'Barney's going to have a terrible job getting streamers out of the gravel,' she said imagining the coloured strands littering the ground for weeks to come.

'I don't think he'll mind at all.' Both of them looked to the newlyweds, who were chatting and joking with others as they did the rounds.

Jade realised it wasn't alcohol that had made Linc relax because he was sipping from a bottle of water rather than a beer or glass of champagne as favoured by the majority of the guests.

'You look beautiful tonight.'

His comment caught her off guard. 'I'm usually covered in icing sugar or flour and wearing an apron and scruffs so this is one of the few chances to dress up.

You're looking very smart yourself.' Better than smart – hot, but she wasn't going to say that.

'Come on, you two, get on the dancefloor!' Patricia urged, refixing the flower in her hair for the umpteenth time when it refused to stay put as she danced.

'Etna, take it easy,' Linc warned when he saw her dancing too. She wasn't exactly holding back and it was good to see.

'Can't hear you,' Etna trilled, 'la-la-la!' She twirled again, Joseph at her side.

'Act your age,' he called out to her, laughing.

'Never!' she hollered back as Kenneth joined her too.

Linc was still laughing when he turned to Jade and said, 'Come on, we can't be beaten by the oldies.'

'Heard that,' Patricia called out, holding the flower in her hand when it slipped yet again.

Jade had no choice but to join in with the dancing, but with a lively number it wasn't too difficult to blend in with the others. She did her best not to lock eyes with Linc too many times but as soon as the band slowed to a different tune, perhaps influenced by a few flagging older people in the crowd, she took the chance to have a breather and made to follow Etna and Kenneth as they headed in the direction of the table with the food platters.

'Not so fast.' Linc reached out and took her hand before she could leave the dancefloor. 'Unless you're waiting for someone else.'

She said nothing to that, her mouth bone-dry as he drew her in closer to him. She thought back to the way Dario had held her at the cottage that first day, again on the beach. It had been familiar, brought up memories. In Linc's arms she felt different, but, weirdly, it felt right as he led the dance, both of them moving like every other couple, the touch of his starched white shirt against her cheek, the silken edges of his bow-tie that every now and then with a subtle change of direction of his head alternated with the graze of stubble beneath his chin.

'Where is the Italian anyway?' Linc murmured as they danced, one of her hands in his, her other resting on the shoulder of his dinner jacket.

'He's gone back to Italy.'

He pulled back and looked at her, his surprise clear. Tracy really hadn't shared much with anyone about her latest guest at the inn. 'Is he coming back?'

She shook her head.

The music changed to upbeat in tempo and it was Joseph who interrupted them this time as they stood looking at each other, Linc digesting what Jade had told him.

'Etna is behaving like she's just found her legs again,' Joseph laughed. 'Would you look at her?'

'Fingers crossed her ankle doesn't play up,' said Linc, distracted and not fully paying attention to his dad. Not that Joseph noticed; he'd already darted off again as though his feet couldn't stay still.

'Are you going to move to Italy?' Linc came straight out with it.

Jade smiled. 'Are you kidding? And miss all this?'

'I'm serious.'

So was she. 'It's over, he's gone, and I'm staying here.' She noticed him swallow hard before he spoke again.

'Do you still have his photograph in your bag?'

She began to laugh. 'No, I don't. I've still got the picture but it's with all my other travel memories.'

'What made him turn up now?'

'Does it really matter?' She sensed from the way he wouldn't look at her that it did. 'He proposed.'

238

'Proposed?' She didn't miss his gaze drop to her left hand and back up again.

'I said no.'

'You said no.'

'Are you going to repeat everything I say?' He seemed to be taking it all in, but she couldn't fall harder than she already had. She'd made an appointment to talk about the IVF and it wasn't that far off. This was her plan, had been for some time, and it wasn't fair to expect someone who was more or less a stranger to be by her side while she started a family. It wasn't what it should be like at all.

He plucked a champagne flute from those grouped on a passing tray. Brianna was gripping onto it tightly in case anyone knocked into her. An overzealous dancer had already done that tonight with a tray filled with bottles of beer and if it wasn't for Lucy's quick reflex, there could've been smashed glass everywhere. 'Here, enjoy.'

'Where's yours?'

'I'll grab another water in a minute.'

'I noticed you weren't drinking. Did you have a few at the pub last night?'

'Not at all. I've got an appointment tomorrow and…er, I need a clear head.' He took a swig from the bottle of water he grabbed from a side table. 'We could have dinner at the pub tomorrow night if you like. My treat. Perhaps we could talk some more, properly.'

It sounded exactly what she wanted, but it wouldn't be right. 'There's something I should tell you.' She put out a hand, took his and led him to the front of the barn by the doors where there was a space between the revellers inside and the partygoers in the courtyard.

'You sound very serious. I'd be worried if I didn't know the Italian had gone.'

She smiled at his inability to use Dario's actual name. And with a deep breath she said, 'I am serious. I can't be with you. I can't come for dinner, I can't date you.'

He put his hand against his chest. 'Wow, that's the fastest I've ever been turned down.'

'I just want to be honest.' She looked down at a few pieces of gravel that had been kicked onto the concrete floor of the barn. 'I do like you, but it wouldn't be fair.'

'Are you still in love with him?'

'No, I'm not in love with *the Italian*.' That got a smile. 'It's complicated.'

'It always is,' he said resignedly and when the music stopped ready for the bride and groom to cut the cake, they took their places and carried on as though everything was normal.

And they didn't dance again, they didn't find each other for the rest of the night. And Jade went home wondering whether she really knew what she was doing at all.

Chapter Fifteen

Linc closed his laptop in the spare bedroom at Tumbleweed House. He'd returned from his clinic appointment earlier this morning – the reason he hadn't been drinking at the wedding last night – to find Harvey and Melissa just emerging from a lie-in so he had made them a cooked breakfast before leaving them to it and going upstairs to fire up his laptop and respond to questions from the latest blog post he'd written for the clinic. He felt a sense of finality that the appointments were done with, a feeling of freedom and a sense of accomplishment and pride too.

'We'll miss you when you've gone,' said Melissa, who was barefoot in the kitchen as she washed up the breakfast dishes when Linc came back downstairs.

'I won't be far.' He put his bag down on the floor and sat at the table. Winnie had a sniff of the bag, investigated, but finding nothing of interest, turned her attentions to him and let him fuss over her the way she loved, with a tickle behind the ears. 'Perhaps I'll stop by now and then and cook you breakfast.'

'We may hold you to that.' She pulled a face when she caught sight of the clock. 'Although it was more of a brunch than a breakfast, we did oversleep somewhat.'

'Well deserved, I'd say, after last night. Thanks again for renting the cottage to me,' he added before she had a chance to ask him why he'd been up and about way before them this morning or why he'd left the ball far earlier than they had the night before.

She pulled off her rubber gloves and set them on the side. 'Some say not to rent to friends or family but I disagree; it's easier. If I have a good feeling about someone – which I do about you, by the way – then I'm happier for them to rent my place than have someone I don't know.'

'Are you attached to the cottage?'

She sat down at the table with him while he rolled up the towel to push into his bag. 'I was once upon a time but now I'm back in the Cove, not so much. I'm making new memories right here. I did think about selling it once our tenants moved out but then you showed up. Who knows, if you love this new job at the school, perhaps I'll end up selling to you.'

'Never say never,' he smiled.

'There are all sorts of things you could do to improve it and make it yours…if you want to, that is.'

She was probing, he knew, and he wondered whether part of that was to do with Jade. He'd noticed Harvey clocking them dancing together and wouldn't have minded so much if Jade hadn't well and truly rejected him before the end of the night.

'Where are you off to anyway?' Melissa noticed the bag at his feet as she stroked Winnie's head after the dog had turned her attentions away from Linc now one of her most trusty companions was free.

'For a swim in the sea.'

Melissa laughed. 'Well, you, Linc, are far braver than I am. It's a gorgeous day out there but the water is usually freezing, no matter how much the sun is shining. And I'm only saying that as someone who dips no more than a few toes in there as I walk Winnie in the mornings.'

'You mean locals don't swim there all the time?'

She shook her head at his sarcasm. 'Enjoy yourself, it'll freshen you up if nothing else.'

He set off out of the house, sliders on his feet, a slight nip in the breeze but otherwise a beautiful day. He crossed the road, followed the track running parallel to the chapel and made his way down to the cove remembering his first visit down here with Jade. It was certainly far easier in the daylight. And when he jumped down onto the sands and found it deserted apart from a lone dog walker about to head back up to the village and a scattering of people too far away for him to call out to, he was happy he'd come.

He stripped off his T-shirt and already felt the cool air against his chest. He wondered briefly whether a wetsuit would've been a wiser choice than board shorts, but it was summer – what kind of man would he be in that kind of get-up in England's warmest months of the year?

But already he sensed this was going to be harder than he'd anticipated. And so he did the only thing he could do under the circumstances – he ran as fast as he could across the sand, down to the water, and didn't stop until he was almost thigh-deep, when he dived head first into an oncoming wave.

He emerged somewhat refreshed the other side, gave a shiver and swam around to let his body get used to the temperature. It wasn't long before he relaxed and lay on his back floating like a starfish, squinting when the sun peeked out from behind a cloud and took its time to creep behind another. He swam almost the width of the curved cove three times, back and forth, his limbs cutting through the water, the salty tang leaving him refreshed, until he began to tire and headed back for shore.

With a towel draped around his shoulders, he wiped the droplets from his face and rubbed his hair at the sides to stop the water snaking its way across his face. The sand felt warm beneath his feet, the cry of a gull up above had him watching it soar the same way he'd swum but at twice the speed, and he shook off a piece of seaweed that had attached itself to his left calf. It was beautiful down here, its relative seclusion likely what made it so, and swimming this morning after his final clinic appointment and with just a few weeks to go until his move to the cottage and the new job awaiting him, it felt as though he'd marked out his fresh start. His breathing settled but he felt more alive and clear-headed than he had in a long time.

He stood enjoying the feel of the sun as he looked out to the cove but didn't miss something in his peripheral vision. Or rather, someone. And when he turned to look more closely, he realised it was Jade. But she hadn't spotted him. She must've been down this way walking and was finally coming into view from behind the slippery rocks covered in seaweed that led away from the cove to a small patch of sand unseen from here, the part people rarely ventured to, according to Etna, as there wasn't much sand there at all with the way the tide curved around the cove itself and trickled into any inlet it could find.

He raised a hand to get her attention but she wasn't looking. And it wasn't until she got even closer that he saw she was upset.

He jogged over to her. 'What happened?'

She clearly hadn't seen him approach and startled a moment before she said, 'I'm fine, honestly.'

'I've got enough experience of kids lying to me that I know the signs,' he said, bending his knees a little in an attempt to have her meet his gaze. It didn't work.

'And what might those be?' She was trying to be nonchalant and failing miserably.

'Mumbling, turning your head in the hope of shifting focus to something or someone else. Not maintaining eye contact,' he added when she still wouldn't do that. 'I've got a can of Coke in my bag. I'll give it to you if you come and sit down with me for a bit.'

She seemed about to turn him down flat and reiterate what she'd told him at the ball last night but instead she at last looked at him and began to walk over to where he'd left his things.

As promised, he found the can of Coke, flipped the ring pull and handed it to her. 'You need sunscreen?' She had the palest of skin, it suited her, he'd hate to see it turn pink.

'Already done,' she said but then relented. 'I've been here a while so if you've got some?'

His skin tanned easily but he still had factor 30 when he was stripping down, swimming and drying off beneath the midday sun. He found the bottle and after she'd pushed the can of drink down into the sand so it would stand up by itself, he squirted enough onto each of her forearms for her to rub in, more in her hands for her legs and then some more again for her to do her face, although she did have a straw hat that she'd been carrying and she pulled it on now as they sat with no shade, the water lapping gently, and him patiently waiting. He put some sunscreen on his chest as she looked out to sea sipping from the still-cold can of drink and when he was done, sat down beside her.

'Any idea what they raised for White Clover this year with the Wedding Dress Ball?' he asked after they'd sat in silence for a few minutes – anything to break the ice.

'I don't know but if it's anything like last year it'll be in the thousands.'

'It goes to show what a village can do when everyone pulls together.'

It fell quiet between them once again. He was about to start up conversation, talk about the cottage he was soon to move into, perhaps talk about anything other than what was bothering her, when she suggested they walk.

He looked back at the rocks. 'Let me put my bag out of sight. If anyone nicks it, good luck to them – there'll just be a soggy towel inside and sloppy sunscreen, and a squashed empty can of what was once a fizzy drink,' he added, taking the finished Coke can from her and crushing it down.

'I'm sorry, I didn't save any for you.'

'It's fine, honestly.'

His bag out of the way, they walked the length of the sands up to the breakwaters, stepped over those and made conversation about the different sections of beach, how they attracted different people. On this part of the beach there were a couple of families, one playing beach cricket, the other putting up their windbreak and opening up deck chairs. They talked about the wedding again, the ball, but avoided any mention of their dancing or the abrupt end to their time together. It seemed easier that way and he was happy to be spending time with her. He and Orla had never done this. They'd met in a pub, got together that night, and had never taken the time to get to know each other before they leapt into bed and went full steam ahead into a relationship. Perhaps that was where they'd gone wrong.

'Are you looking forward to starting the school term?' she asked him when they eventually turned back. Whatever had been on Jade's mind still seemed to be causing a frown above those beautiful green eyes, but at least it had lessened, and Linc liked to think he had something to do with that.

'I am. It's taken a while to be interested in a permanent role, but I've got a good feeling about this one.'

'And things are falling into place with the cottage.'

'They certainly are. Melissa floated the idea of selling it at some point and it did get me thinking I might well be interested.'

'That's great.' But her enthusiasm had a sadness behind it, perhaps the same sadness he'd seen in her eyes last night when she turned down his offer of dinner at the pub, told him she couldn't get involved. 'You think you could make a home here in the Cove?'

'I think a change is exactly what I needed and I already feel a part of things here, especially after last night – not that I can remember everyone's name, I was introduced to that many people.'

'You'll get there. And it's nice you feel as though you belong already.'

'Is that why you didn't want to go to Venice? Because you belong here?' He shook his head at his own stupidity because he'd vowed not to pry but, instead, to be there for her to talk to when she was ready. 'I apologise, you don't have to answer that.'

'It's part of the reason,' she volunteered and then clammed up again.

'Talking might help.'

'I know.'

It was at least a couple of minutes before she took a deep breath and stopped walking. They were opposite the cove once again and he followed suit when she sat down.

She looked at him and her expression left him in no doubt she was about to be entirely honest. She recapped on her time in Venice, how she'd left there and said goodbye to Dario but had returned to England devastated. 'I felt that what we'd had was it, my chance to settle down and have the future I wanted. I took a while to pick myself up once we got back to England and I took a big step after that. Celeste was fully supportive but I'm not sure she ever thought I'd take the step that followed, which I'm now ready to do.'

He smiled at her. 'I'm OK at doing a crossword, not bad at Sudoku, but riddles are something I've never been able to get to grips with.'

She puffed out her cheeks. 'I froze my eggs.'

It took a moment for his mind to compute what she meant. 'That's a big step.'

'I know. Huge. But by the time I did it, I was thinking clearly and it made me feel I was in control, that I no longer had to panic that I wouldn't be able to have a family, that I'd never find the right person to settle down with. Does that make sense?'

He raked a hand through his damp hair. 'You took control. That part does make sense. But what do you mean about the next step?'

'I've made an appointment at a clinic to talk about using them.'

'That's a huge step.' He stopped her jumping to conclusions. 'I'm not saying it's bad – it's a lot to take in, that's all. I had no idea you were thinking that way.'

'I don't exactly broadcast it.'

'No, I don't suppose you would.'

He wanted to blurt out what he'd been doing, the reasons why, the stories he'd read before he decided to go ahead with the process, the conversations he'd heard, the blog entries that had sparked thanks, gratitude and the sharing of sad scenarios that had progressed to joyful outcomes for the lucky ones.

'I've made an appointment in a few weeks,' she added. 'I have the money saved up, the business is at a point where we can manage it between us should I be lucky enough to fall pregnant. I'd made the decision to do this before Dario turned up…' She hesitated and he wondered was she also thinking she'd made this decision before he turned up in the Cove too? 'Him being here made it all the more difficult. It had me questioning whether I was crazy to do this alone when he was offering me the world. But I couldn't be with him for the wrong reasons.'

It took Linc a minute to realise that what he'd overheard in the pub definitely wasn't what it had sounded like and all he felt was relief. She was exactly the person he thought she was – and more so with her determination to go it alone. He felt terrible that he'd assumed otherwise, left the pub that night without a word of goodbye. 'Wait here.' He ran over to the rocks to grab his bag and came back over to her.

'Tell me honestly, Linc, am I crazy?' she asked the second he came to her side.

'Crazy to want everything you've ever dreamed of?' He shook his head. 'Not at all.'

'It's expensive too. I've got enough money to do it a couple of times, three if I'm lucky. Celeste says she's behind me. I think it took her a few days to process that my actions after Venice, the freezing of my eggs, had led to this, to actually taking it further. She worries about me – the feeling is mutual – but she's on my side.'

'You're having doubts.' It was an observation rather than a question.

'Of course I am.' She briefly put her face in her hands but she had at least stopped frowning. 'Is anyone ever ready for this?'

'I know couples who are hopelessly in love and still not ready.'

'See, that doesn't help me, does it?' When he grinned, she asked, 'What if I'm a terrible mother? What if the business is what I should be focusing on and I can't share my attentions?'

'Something tells me you'll take it in your stride and multitask.'

'You do know we're talking about a baby and not a loaf of bread to be made alongside a batch of cupcakes, don't you?' She began to smile back at him, finally. 'You've really cheered me up, you know. Thank you.'

'Hey, happy to help.' He took his time with his next question, dug his toes into the sand to pluck up the courage. 'Have you chosen the lucky father-to-be yet?'

'Not yet. But I've talked to my sister and Tilly and their support brings me one step closer. I told Etna too.'

'You did? Did she think you were crazy?' He had a vested interest in his auntie's reaction given what he'd been involved in.

'Well, apart from dropping an almighty hint that I might like to look around me at certain men in the Cove, she thought it was a great idea.'

'She's progressive, I'll give her that.' And he couldn't be happier with Etna's response. 'So, who are these men she's been hinting at?' Her look gave him an answer.

'Ah, I see. I'm surprised she hasn't meddled some more.'

'Perhaps she knows I've got enough going on in my head at the moment. She might never have been a mum but she treats you like a son, you know.'

'She does and I love every second. When I was younger, I could always rely on her to be on my side. She was a fun auntie but never let me take advantage – I think I needed that. And after Mum died, she was there for me again. We didn't always talk about it at home but she let me vent, she let me talk, when I think Dad needed to process his grief in his own way. Not that he wasn't there for me too, but grief is one hell of a journey.'

They let his words settle and when the time was right, he nudged her gently and dipped his head towards hers. 'I saw you at the pub with your friend when she had her baby in a carrier and I could tell you were smitten.'

'Valerie is a good mum.'

'And you will be too. You will,' he repeated when he registered doubt.

She began to laugh. 'I saw Tracy the other day with her head in her hands at the reception desk at the Heritage Inn – she looked done in. When I asked her what was wrong, she told me she thought she was finished with kid dramas but she'd have her toddlers back any day over girls who were grown-up enough that they now came with attitude.'

'The fun of parenting.'

'What about you? Do you want that someday?'

'Yes,' he said definitively. 'One day I really do.'

'You don't think it's weird I'm on the verge of choosing the father of my baby from a database and basing my decision on his vital statistics?'

His laughter carried out to sea but he assured her that wasn't because of her. 'It's not weird at all. And what's funny isn't what you intend to do, but my part in something so incredibly close to what you're talking about.' At her confusion, he knew it was time to open up, time to admit what he'd been up to.

'I haven't told anyone about this,' he said, 'not my dad, not Etna, nobody.' He briefly looked at her and then back out at the waves, churning and rolling towards the shore. 'The reason I wasn't drinking last night is because I had an appointment today.'

'Sorry, I've been so wrapped up in myself I didn't ask you anything more. There's nothing wrong, is there?'

'No, there's nothing wrong.' He remembered how it had gone when he told his last girlfriend what he was doing, her reaction that it was weird, something to be ashamed of, and even though he knew Jade wouldn't react that way it was still hard to tell someone new. 'I went to a clinic but not because I have a health condition. I mean, I've had screening tests and blood tests…' He was rambling. He needed to get to the point. 'I was at the clinic to donate.' He put his head in his hand. 'Honestly, I don't know why I can't say it. When I'm there we all talk openly, candidly, there's no embarrassment. I've written blog posts on the subject, answered questions; this is the first time I've been so tongue-tied.'

'So, out with it,' she urged. 'What were you donating? A kidney, some plasma, your time?'

'You're enjoying this.'

'Kind of,' she admitted with a grin.

'I need to start at the beginning, a bit like you did with the story of you and Dario.' She waited patiently as he scooped grains of sand into his palm and let them filter through his fingers.

He told her all about Orla, he told her how she'd fallen pregnant on purpose, how she'd been so desperate for a baby she was with him for the wrong reasons. He explained how his brother had contracted mumps when he was in the Army and how it left him infertile. 'He and his wife, Tammy, were devastated. They'd been trying for a family for a while with no success, went for routine tests to check everything was in working order and found out it wasn't. Zach took it worse than Tammy. He saw it as failing her, he felt guilty for a long while after that and there were times when Dad and I weren't sure they'd make it.'

'I can't imagine the stress.'

'One day they came to see Dad and me. I remember, it was in the depths of winter, Zach was on leave and they showed up when it was hailing but I knew, watching Tammy come down the front path, I knew it was good news. She was pregnant. They'd kept it to themselves but they'd been through IVF using a sperm donor and for them it had worked on the second attempt. They were ecstatic. And so were we. I thought my brother had too much pride to use another man's sperm the way he talked about it when they found out the problem lay with him, and it did take him a while to get his head around the idea, but he'd have done anything for Tammy. And now they have two beautiful little girls who are their whole world.'

'You were donating sperm,' she said, finally understanding.

It felt oddly liberating telling someone who wasn't a member of staff at the clinic or someone looking for advice or sharing an experience. 'After what my brother

253

and Tammy went through and then Orla falling apart when she lost the baby, I went online and did some reading – actually, a lot of reading. One day I saw a Facebook post with a link to a story about a black market for sperm – I assume the algorithms or whatever they are had interpreted what I'd been searching for online and so filled my newsfeed with more of the same or similar. It was as creepy and distressing to read as it sounds, by the way, but it also went on to say how desperate some couples or single women become that they end up using these places. There's a real shortage of medically screened sperm in the UK and I thought about Zach and Tammy, knew they'd gone down the right route but wondered what would've happened if they hadn't been able to. Before I could think too much about it, I was on the phone and had arranged an appointment at a clinic to go and discuss it. I wanted to do something to help.'

'And that's where you were this morning.'

'Yes. For the last time. I've made all the donations; today was the final one. All that's required of me now is to return to the clinic in six months for a follow-up. I'll have a couple of tests and if the doctors are happy with the results of those, they'll use the samples that were frozen along the way.'

She took a moment to digest everything he'd told her. 'You know what you've done is incredible, don't you?'

'Not the way my last girlfriend reacted,' he said. 'She acted as though it was a little perverted, what I was doing. I mean, the process of donating is something we don't need to go into detail about, but at the end of the day, it's all pretty clinical when you're there.'

'She's the one with the problem, Linc. You know that, right?'

'Of course.' He raised his eyebrows and made her laugh.

'You're a good man.'

Her eyes had filled with tears and he reached out to stop one that almost overflowed. 'Again, I know.'

This had her laughing until she asked him seriously, 'How you feel about maybe having biological children running around out there someday?'

Her choice of words felt good to his ears – biological children, because they wouldn't be his, he was doing this for others. 'I'm fine with it. And I've already given my family and medical information as well as writing a bit about myself so that if the donor-conceived child wants to know more information, they can find out once they've reached the age of eighteen.'

'It's such a selfless thing to do.' She looked out to the water. 'You've been surprising me ever since you arrived in the Cove.'

'No more so than that first morning, eh?'

When her phone pinged and she glanced at it, she gasped. 'I have to go! That was Celeste.'

He grabbed his bag as she started to walk away.

'She has a spa appointment and I promised I'd be back at the bakery in time,' she called over her shoulder.

They walked as quickly as they could across the uneven sand and towards the steps that would lead up to the track.

'Celeste has picked up a lot of slack for me lately…' The words came out staccato as she broke into a jog, then walked when it got steep, then tried to jog again as they reached the final piece of track. 'I've booked her a spa appointment this afternoon as a thank you,' she puffed.

255

When they finally reached the end, ready to cross the road to the bakery, he stopped her. 'Jade –'

'Don't say anything.' She reached a hand up to his face, touching his cheek tenderly.

She had a habit of cutting him off when he ventured towards asking her out. Should he be done with it and take the hint?

'We've shared a lot today.' She took her hand away and smiled although turned her head towards the bakery more than once, eager to go and relieve Celeste of her duties. 'Could we leave it there, let things settle down?'

'I know how I feel.'

The way she looked at him told him she knew it too. 'Give me some time.'

How long? he wanted to ask. 'I can do that.'

'I'll see you soon then.'

'Yeah,' he sighed. 'See you soon.'

He couldn't believe the parallels in the stories they'd shared down there on the sands of the cove, his admission and hers. He wasn't sure where this left them – if it left them anywhere at all. All he could do now was head back to Tumbleweed House and then up to the waffle shack to help with putting up the pergola, and do as she'd asked by giving her the time and space she needed.

Chapter Sixteen

It had been over two weeks since Jade bumped into Linc down at the cove. He'd come into the bakery twice since then and she'd seen him in the tea rooms once, but although they'd had a brief exchange each time, there'd been no mention of their candid talk on the sand that day.

The sisters had been busy with their beautifully renovated bakery and Jade had taken on another two cake commissions, both for weddings in the early part of next year and both as a result of the cake on display at Barney and Lois's wedding. Celeste had briefly tried to get Jade to talk about the IVF plans but she'd put a stop to it quickly, asking her sister to please give her time to process her decision for herself, because Dario's arrival and departure had thrown so much up into the air, and, whether Celeste knew it or not, the newcomer in the Cove had a lot to do with it too.

Carly stopped at the bakery just before closing on her way home from a job interview and had already told Celeste all about it by the time Jade came through from the kitchen after washing the last of the cake tins. They were on to talking about the welcome-home bash to be held for Barney and Lois on the beach tonight. It was somewhere totally different to the usual venues for village functions – which were either the barn for the ball or the pub. Tilly had been the instigator, according to Celeste, and had come up with the novel idea to welcome the newlyweds back from their honeymoon in Italy.

Barney and Lois had chosen Venice for their honeymoon and while once the big reveal of their destination might have left Jade's head spinning, she'd farewelled them from the Cove with a smile and even given them the name and location of Dario's restaurant. She'd assured them they wouldn't be sorry if they went along for a meal because the food was some of the best she and Celeste had tasted during their stay.

'Are you looking forward to rehoming the chickens?' Jade asked Carly as she took the bread rolls and apple danish round, which Celeste bagged up for her.

Carly found the exact amount in cash and placed it onto the top of the counter in exchange for the bag. 'The kids still aren't happy about it but I've told them they can go to the barn any time.'

'Talk to Melissa and Harvey later on,' said Celeste as she shut the till with a clunk. 'Both of them practically grew up with Barney for company, roaming the fields around there – it's a kids' haven, according to Melissa.'

'I've heard their stories,' smiled Carly. 'So, I'll do that and perhaps get the kids over there the moment the chickens go, then they'll know it's not the worst thing in the world,' she added with an eye roll.

Carly waved goodbye to the girls and once they'd served Mrs Filligree with two cheesy-topped baps and a cream doughnut, and then Kenneth, who came in at the last minute for a simple wholemeal bloomer, Celeste turned the sign hanging on the inside of the door to *Closed*.

'Summer holidays are almost over.' Jade took the float out of the till ready to put in the safe at the very back of the larder cupboard in the kitchen. 'I love being busy but this summer feels crazier than ever.'

'We've had a lot going on.' Celeste followed her out into the kitchen. 'Renovations, weddings, ex-boyfriends, hot locals…' She leaned against the benchtop watching her sister.

'I'm impressed.'

'Impressed?'

'You've been itching to say something since the ball and you haven't said a word.'

'I know…it's absolutely killing me.'

Jade began to laugh. 'Come on, let's clear up in here and perhaps over a glass of wine we can talk.'

'Hallelujah!' Celeste threw both arms into the air.

They went through the well-oiled routine of finishing a day at the bakery – leftovers were put into bags ready for Celeste to hand to Patricia, who would take them, along with any leftovers from the tea rooms, to a homeless shelter where she volunteered; every surface was cleaned, the floors swept and mopped. They marked off the procedures they followed on the grid pinned to the side of a cupboard – it helped them and everyone else know they observed protocol and didn't skip steps.

Over the couple of weeks since Jade had seen Linc on the beach and they'd talked, her emotions had stopped swinging like an out-of-control pendulum and she felt ready to see him tonight at the do. In fact, she'd been discreetly watching the clock all day, the time dragging despite the busyness.

Celeste let out a sudden squeal when she saw two familiar faces peering in the window of the bakery and raced from the kitchen to the front to undo the door. Jade followed on and sentences overlapped as they all tried to talk at once.

After they'd hugged, Lois declared, 'Venice was an absolute dream.' She clasped her hands against her chest. 'From the architecture to the alleyways zigzagging everywhere and plagues of tourists, of course – it was everything we imagined it to be.'

'And we found Dario's restaurant,' Barney put in, stopping Jade from having to ask. 'He sends his love.'

'Thanks, Barney.' Jade was glad there were no hard feelings and that Dario had welcomed her friends. She hoped he'd find whatever it took to make him happy. 'We had a lovely meal,' Barney went on. 'His nonna talked non-stop.'

Jade was confused. 'She doesn't speak a lot of English.'

'No, she doesn't, but that didn't stop her.' He pretended to be exasperated but Jade knew he would've loved every second. The man thrived on company and it's likely he would've been enthralled with the Italian dialogue plus the odd English word or gesture thrown in.

'We're both exhausted now,' said Lois, 'so we've got one hour to put our feet up before we head down to the cove.'

'You don't mind the welcome-home party?' Celeste worried.

'Never, I've missed everyone,' cried Barney and with that he waved a goodbye and set off down The Street with Lois.

Celeste locked up again and turned off the lights in the bakery as Jade went around doing the same in the kitchen and then locked the back door behind them. Back in the cottage Jade headed for the shower first and when she was dressed and it was her sister's turn, she poured a couple of glasses of wine.

By the time Celeste came downstairs Jade had positioned the deck chairs outside as sunset approached.

'Imagine if we didn't have this garden space.' Jade had chosen jeans and a pale blue shirt that tied at the waist this evening and an open-weave cardigan that was just enough with the light early-September breeze.

'Plus a business and a home of our own, and so close to each other, no commute – that's the best part.' Celeste relaxed into her deck chair.

'Remember your commute in London?'

'I would rather forget. I was knackered before my working day even started.'

'Lois and Barney looked well, didn't they?'

'They did. But I'm not interested in talking about them.' Celeste checked her watch. 'We don't have long before we have to leave so you need to tell me everything you've been holding in. I've done well not to ask,' she said, congratulating herself before admitting, 'I saw you with Linc the day of my spa appointment.'

'Why didn't you ask me about it?'

'Because I'm learning that while we share a lot, we can't always expect each other to disclose every detail, sometimes we might need to keep things to ourselves to process.'

'Thank you.' She enjoyed another sip of the crisp white wine. 'I was walking on my own down at the cove and we bumped into each other. He'd been swimming and caught me a bit upset.'

'Because of Dario leaving?'

'No. Him leaving was for the best, it was a final goodbye.'

'So why were you upset?'

261

'You really don't know?' The way Celeste waited patiently told Jade that her sister had a pretty good idea even before the admission that was to come.

'I was so sure of my decision to go it alone and have a baby. But when Linc turned up in the Cove I liked him right from the start and it's been difficult to push away those feelings. I was determined because I didn't want anything or anyone clouding my judgement. Then when Dario turned up it was even worse. If he'd proposed in Venice I would've said yes and a tiny part of me thought about it, only for a second, because he was offering me everything. But it never would've worked, we both saw that in the end.'

'So where does this leave Linc?'

'I told him at the ball that I couldn't get involved.'

'Why not? It's obvious how he feels.'

She leaned back in her chair. 'The problem is that I do want a family but I don't want to trap any man into my plans.'

'But you wouldn't be. You like him, he likes you, it's simple.'

'It's not.'

'Jade, it might well be, if you let it. I know you've always been very good at making decisions and following them through, but sometimes you may just need to go with the flow.' She downed the rest of her wine, stood up and held out a hand.

Jade almost didn't want to move she was so relaxed, but knowing Linc would be there tonight, perhaps it was time to pick up their conversation from where they'd left off on the beach that day.

*

The sun crept lower towards the horizon as they made their way down the track to the cove, watching their

262

footing, soaking up the pleasant evening temperature that wouldn't last much longer now another summer was preparing to draw to a close. They could make out people congregating on the sands as light faded, the flames from a campfire flickered to illuminate part of the way and plenty of laughter and chatter greeted them as the guests of honour regaled the crowd with tales of their honeymoon to the background tones of music playing softly from a stereo Jade couldn't even see.

Harvey's dog Winnie was doing the rounds for a fuss and had settled at dog walker Gracie's feet. Benjamin helped Tilly hand out beers and if Jade wasn't mistaken, those two looked as though they were getting friendlier by the day. A few nights ago she'd seen them talking outside the chapel so perhaps it wouldn't be long before another romance was announced in the Cove. Patricia was standing gossiping with Etna as though they didn't get to talk every single day at the tea rooms, and Valerie and her husband had come alone having found a last-minute babysitter. Celeste quizzed Daniel about the latest changes at the waffle shack, and others who had brought chairs down here were busy having chitchat over drinks.

Jade accepted a glass of fizz from Patricia, who'd suddenly taken over distribution of the good stuff when nobody else seemed to be doing it and the bottles lay forlorn, poking their necks out of the ice in the cool box. Lottie, who ran the convenience store in the Cove, was next to appear and you couldn't miss the big crate of packets of marshmallows in her arms as she assured the younger members of the crowd who were very interested in her offering that yes, of course, she'd brought skewers.

'He's good, isn't he?' Etna had somehow come to Jade's side without her realising.

Confused, she looked around. 'Who is?'

'Linc.'

So, the music was him rather than a stereo. Jade should've known. 'He's very good, yes.' Was she gulping her fizz too fast? With any luck, she could excuse herself in a second and go off to find another glass.

'Top up!' Patricia cried out from a couple of metres away, sixth sense alerting her to an almost drained glass.

'You know,' Patricia confided in them both after she'd filled Jade's glass, 'tonight reminds me of when I was a girl and I'd sneak down here with my boyfriend to be alone…if you know what I mean.'

'I think we all know what you mean,' said Etna before nudging her friend. 'There's Joseph, let's go and join him.'

'How can you see in the dark?' But Patricia followed on, leaving Jade to enjoy her champagne once again.

She was about to go and mingle but when she turned, she bumped into the solidity of a man's chest. And all of her senses heightened as she looked up at Linc. But how could the music still be playing?

'You thought it was me?' he grinned, seeing her reaction. 'I'll be playing later on. This is a CD I recorded, and I wanted to be a part of the gathering tonight, even if only at the start.'

She gulped back more champagne. He looked gorgeous with a cheeky smile that hid how sensitive and kind he really was, which did little to tell you this was a man who was on your side and who listened. 'Don't tell people you're taking requests,' she advised. 'You'll be playing all night if you do and they'll be dancing until dawn.' They both looked over at a group of girls dancing away already.

'It's not a school night so I'm happy with that.'

'Speak for yourself,' she laughed, 'I'll be up at 4:30 a.m.'

'Go from the party to work.'

She burst out laughing. 'Maybe ten or fifteen years ago I might have done just that.'

Lucy came over proffering skewers with marshmallows pushed onto them. She was doing the rounds and urged them to get in there quick with a turn at the campfire.

As they plunged their skewers towards the flames – not too much, not too little, just enough that the marshmallows wobbling on the ends took on a charcoal tinge on the outside – Jade asked whether he'd settled in at the cottage.

'Yup. Moved in three days ago. I have to be honest, it's good to have my own place.'

She inspected her marshmallow one more time and decided it was done. 'I'll bet.'

Deeming his marshmallow done too, he stepped away and let someone else have a turn. But he'd only just bitten into his gooey treat when he pulled a face.

'Not a fan?'

He lowered his voice so as not to offend Lottie, who'd brought the marshmallows in a valiant effort to supply everyone here. 'They're a bit overrated.' But he demolished the rest before stowing the spent stick and Jade's into the rubbish box someone had thoughtfully brought down here.

When Linc inclined his head towards the water's edge, Jade walked that way with him and as soon as she was on the wet sand she took off her sandals and looped them over her fingers. With her other hand she pulled her hair away from her face again as they walked, leaving the revellers behind, the darkness not alerting anyone else to their departure.

'How have you been?' Linc braved.

'I've been good.' She wasn't sure what to say. 'I've been doing a lot of thinking.'

'Me too.' He seemed a bit stuck for words, like she was. 'I've mainly been considering how surprising life can be. Sometimes in bad ways that push us to the edge, but sometimes in a good way.' He took his time, considered his words. 'If my life hadn't been in such a rut, I never would've come this way. Heritage Cove was just a village where my auntie lived; I never thought it could be a place I might settle down, or where I could be happy.'

He was happy? She turned to look at him but as they walked with the sea on the right, the beach on their left, he kept his gaze fixed ahead.

He continued. 'I wasn't in the best place when I first came to the Cove and I think that's why I didn't ask you out before. I needed to get my own head sorted first.'

'I can understand that.' And she did, more than most.

'If you'd told me a few months ago that I'd take a job helping refit a bakery or shifting rubble outside a waffle shack and helping to build an outdoor area, I never would've believed you.'

'Are you trying to say that things happen for a reason?'

'No, I hate that saying.' He moved ahead of her and turned so they were facing each other as they came to a stop. 'I prefer the word serendipity.'

'Serendipity,' she smiled. 'So, it was serendipity when you woke me up by banging that morning and

266

making all kinds of noise when it was my only chance to catch up on sleep before I went back to early mornings?'

His laughter competed with the whoosh of waves against the shore, the fizz as they fell back ready to go all over again. 'Saying it was serendipity sounds better than saying it your way. I suppose what I'm trying to say is that I came here to get away, do something different and as Etna dramatically puts it sometimes, Find Myself.' He put the final bit in inverted commas with his fingers but she could tell he meant it. 'I always assumed I'd have my summer here and then go back home, pick up the supply teaching and carry on. But then things kept falling into place – the job, the cottage.' He looked down at the sand just for a second. 'What I didn't expect to find was you.'

She felt the same way but how could it be the right time? 'I'm too complicated for you.'

'Complicated is someone who doesn't know how they feel, someone who will change their mind all the time. But I don't think that's you. You know what you want, you're willing to head in a direction that's scary and I kind of admire that.'

He looked up to the night sky, took a deep breath and with a smile as he looked down again and into her eyes, he told her, 'I gave you time and space because I know you've got a lot to think about, but I'm not ready to give up on you.'

'Some might say that what I intend to do is a little unhinged.'

'I wouldn't,' he said matter-of-factly. 'And perhaps some people think that's what I am, after what I've been up to over the last few months.'

'Don't do that.' She put a hand out and touched his arm briefly. 'Don't joke about what you did. The method

267

might be awkward to talk about but what you did is amazing for whoever gets to realise their dreams of having a family because of it.'

'I tell you what. I won't think I'm unhinged, as long as you don't imply you are either.' He took a deep breath. 'I wondered how you were feeling about the clinic appointment now. Am I allowed to ask that?'

She found it easy to be honest with Linc. 'You are allowed to ask. This is what I mean when I say I'm too complicated. How can I think about getting involved when I'm set on a path to go it alone?'

'But the path isn't set in stone.' The CD came to an end and Linc heard his name being called. 'Looks like I'm up.'

When he didn't move, she told him she'd hang around.

'You promise?' He took both of her hands in his and bit down on his bottom lip, reluctant to go.

'Promise.'

'Good, because I'm not quite finished with you yet.'

Her heart did a little leap as he headed back to the crowds as if appearing from nowhere. Celeste hadn't missed their interlude, however, and came to her sister's side the minute Jade was closer to the party again. 'What were you two up to?'

'Talking, nothing sordid.' The music started up and she caught Linc's eyes through the crowds. His face was aglow from the nearby campfire, golden like the surface of his guitar. He looked back at her and she felt a connection she didn't want to ignore.

'I saw him, you know,' said Celeste, registering the way Jade was looking at the handsome guitar player like everyone else was, yet with something more. 'I don't mean the day you two talked at the cove, I'm talking about the day after my spa. I came back to the village and saw him loitering outside the bakery. I'd been to make a delivery to Aubrey House and even after I'd parked up, he was still standing there. I tapped him on the shoulder and asked him why he was lurking.'

'And what did he say?'

'He said he didn't want to go into the bakery but he was a bit worried about you. He told me to keep an eye on you.' She sighed. 'The way he said it told me all I needed to know. He cares – I mean *really* cares. His concern was part of the reason I didn't quiz you too much. I guessed that you and he must've talked and I didn't want to get in the way of that. I knew you'd need to process whatever was going on in your own head.' Celeste squeezed her shoulder and whispered, 'Remember what I said…sometimes you need to go with the flow.' And with a kiss on her cheek, she was off to have a dance with Lucy and Tilly.

*

Jade managed a bit of dancing, a lot of talking about Venice with Lois, and eventually the campfire died down and crowds dispersed as the evening inched towards the time when most people were ready for their beds.

After Jade had yawned for about the hundredth time she mouthed the word Goodnight to Linc, who was still taking requests, and turned to go.

'And that's all we've got time for, folks,' came Linc's voice and she turned back to see him slot his guitar into its case. She heard him ask his dad to take it back to the cottage for him and settled it beside Joseph's deck chair. Neither he nor Kenneth looked like they had any intention of moving for a while and with Etna, Barney and Lois happily ensconced nearby, Jade suspected it would be well after midnight before any of them left the beach behind.

Linc came over to her, took her hand without hesitation and led her to the rocks at the far side of the beach where he'd seen her emerge from that day. 'We didn't finish what we were talking about earlier,' he said once they were past the rocks.

He pulled her close urgently, as though this was his last chance, and her heart thudded at the closeness.

'As I told you, I've done a lot of thinking – and I carried on thinking while I was playing the guitar. It's been rather distracting, in fact, but everyone is so inebriated I doubt they noticed any of my mistakes.'

'I didn't,' she grinned.

'When I teach, I tell some of my students not to overthink things, to go with it and let the music happen. Sometimes they've got something stuck in their head that stops them from letting go and getting better. That's what I'm trying to do here, with you.' He gulped. 'So here goes. I'm going to come right out with it and ask you, where do we go from here?' He stopped her from saying anything just yet by adding, 'I'm not asking about fitting me into a big picture of how you want your life to be, I'm asking how you feel in the now, in this moment.'

The way it all gushed out had her trying to honour his request. 'You're right, I am decisive and I know what I want when it comes to so many things; the bigger picture is always at the back of my mind.' She chose her words carefully. 'But right now, I know I've fallen for you. I think I did the day you ate my cake.'

'The day I ate your masterpiece? You looked like you'd throttle me,' he laughed, a low rumbling sound she could feel as he clasped her hands in his against his chest.

270

'I wanted to at first but then I heard from Etna that you'd been working for Harvey as well as stepping in to save the day at the tea rooms.'

'I am kind of a legend.'

'I cancelled my appointment with the clinic,' she blurted out as he moved closer, their bodies touching, their hands squeezed between his chest and hers.

'You did?'

'I'm not saying I won't go through with the plan, but I will take pause, I'll put a pin in it and go with the flow.' She echoed her sister's wise words. 'I'll give us a chance to find out where we're going. If that's what you want.'

'What I want?' But he wasn't expecting an answer. 'I think we both know what I want.'

He bent his head and kissed her, he moved his hands to her neck, up through her hair, nothing separating their bodies now. And after he'd kissed her, he lifted her off her feet and swung her around.

He lowered her and looked deep into her eyes but the moment was broken when instead of crashing waves or the sounds of distant partygoers heading home for the night, they heard wolf whistles. And when they looked round, Etna was one of the most raucous, standing on her tiptoes so she could see them.

They got a round of applause too but Jade didn't mind. She knew now that this was a man who saw her for who she was. And what they didn't know about each another they could take their time to learn. Her life plan was on hold and she was fine with that, for now. She was going to have to let each chapter unfold along the way.

They sneaked back around the rocks to the sand of the cove as anyone left on the beach turned their attentions back to one another and they managed to get to the steps that would lead them away without being seen. Jade spotted Celeste still dancing away now the stereo music had been switched up to something a lot livelier.

And when Linc stopped to kiss her again she reminded him she had an early start in the morning.

'Then we'd better not waste any more time,' he grinned. 'Your place or mine?'

'Mine...I've got to be up in five hours.'

Her face in his hands, he kissed her once more. 'Suits me...and I promise to find a gentler way to wake you up in the morning than on the day we met.'

She put her hand in his as they headed for the cottage and the start of a new beginning for the both of them.

THE END

For more books by Helen J Rolfe, visit
www.helenjrolfe.com/books

If you would like all of Helen's latest book news direct
to your inbox you can also sign up for her monthly
newsletter at www.helenjrolfe.com/newsletter

The New York Ever After Series

If you enjoyed the Heritage Cove books you might like to try the New York Ever After series… there are six books in total and each can be read as standalone, but if you'd like to start at the beginning, this is book one…

Christmas at the Little Knitting Box
(New York Ever After series, Book One)

Christmas is coming and New York is in full swing for the snowy season. But at The Little Knitting Box in the West Village, things are about to change …

The Little Knitting Box has been in Cleo's family for nearly four decades, and since she arrived fresh off the plane from the Cotswolds four years ago, Cleo has been doing a stellar job of running the store. But instead of an early Christmas card in the mail this year, she gets a letter that tips her world on its axis.

Dylan has had a tumultuous few years. His marriage broke down, his mother passed away and he's been trying to pick up the pieces as a stay-at-home dad. All he wants this Christmas is to give his kids the home and stability they need. But when he meets Cleo at a party one night, he begins to see it's not always so easy to move on and pick up the pieces, especially when his ex seems determined to win him back.

When the snow starts to fall in New York City, both Cleo and Dylan realise life is rarely so black and white and both

274

of them have choices to make. Will Dylan follow his heart or his head? And will Cleo ever allow herself to be a part of another family when her own fell apart at the seams?

Full of snow, love and the true meaning of Christmas, this novel will have you hooked until the final page.

Praise for the New York Ever After series

'Beautiful, magical and incredibly moving; Christmas at The Little Knitting Box is a book that keeps on giving. Easily one of my favourite books, ever.' - **The Writing Garnet - Christmas at the Little Knitting Box**

'feel good, heartwarming reading. It's a book version of a Hallmark movie. I'm not gonna lie, I teared up at the end!' **Amazon Reviewer - Snowflakes and Mistletoe at the Inglenook Inn**

'Truly fabulous read … I feel as if these characters are my old buddies... can't wait for book 4 in the series' **Jeanie - Amazon Customer - Wedding Bells on Madison Avenue**

'a charming, festive, cosy and enchanting feel... a story that has a heart and just ticks all the boxes...' **Yvonne B - Top 1000 Amazon Reviewer - Christmas Miracles at the Little Log Cabin**

Acknowledgements

Many thanks to Katharine Walkden for her thorough editing and proofreading skills which help to polish every story before it goes out into the big wide world.

Thank you to Berni Stevens for designing such outstandingly beautiful covers. I'm so pleased this one is orange! We were aiming for bright and summery and I think we delivered.

To my husband and children for their support and encouragement with this and every other novel I have written. Summer Serendipity at the Twist and Turn Bakery is my 22nd published book and it's lovely to have you all cheering me on every step of the way.

And once again thank you to all my readers who picked up this book and many others. Thank you for the kind posts on social media, the support via email, and the wonderful reviews you write and share. It really does mean the world to me. I do hope Summer Serendipity at the Twist and Turn Bakery gave you some much-needed escapism and left you smiling long after you finished the story.

Helen J Rolfe x

Printed in Great Britain
by Amazon